Forest Dark

Also by Nicole Krauss

GREAT HOUSE

THE HISTORY OF LOVE

MAN WALKS INTO A ROOM

Forest Dark

Nicole Krauss

B L O O M S B U R Y
LONDON · OXFORD · NEW YORK · NEW DELHI · SYDNEY

Bloomsbury Publishing
An imprint of Bloomsbury Publishing Plc

50 Bedford Square   1385 Broadway
London   New York
WC1B 3DP   NY 10018
UK   USA

www.bloomsbury.com

BLOOMSBURY and the Diana logo are trademarks of Bloomsbury Publishing Plc

First published in Great Britain 2017

© Nicole Krauss, 2017

Nicole Krauss has asserted her right under the Copyright, Designs and Patents Act, 1988, to be identified as Author of this work.

British Library Cataloguing-in-Publication Data
A catalogue record for this book is available from the British Library.

ISBN: HB: 978-1-4088-7178-2
TPB: 978-1-4088-7179-9
EPUB: 978-1-4088-7180-5

2 4 6 8 10 9 7 5 3 1

Printed and bound in Great Britain by CPI Group (UK) Ltd, Croydon CR0 4YY

MIX
Paper from
responsible sources
FSC® C020471

To find out more about our authors and books visit www.bloomsbury.com. Here you will find extracts, author interviews, details of forthcoming events and the option to sign up for our newsletters.

To my father

ולגב״א

The expulsion from Paradise is in its main significance eternal. Consequently the expulsion from Paradise is final, and life in this world irrevocable, but the eternal nature of the process makes it nevertheless possible that not only could we remain forever in Paradise, but that we are currently there in actual fact, no matter whether we know it here or not.

—KAFKA

Contents

I

Ayeka

At the time of his disappearance, Epstein had been living in Tel Aviv for three months. No one had seen his apartment. His daughter Lucie had come to visit with her children, but Epstein installed them in the Hilton, where he met them for lavish breakfasts at which he only sipped tea. When Lucie asked to come over, he'd begged off, explaining that the place was small and modest, not fit for receiving guests. Still reeling from her parents' late divorce, she'd looked at him through narrow eyes—nothing about Epstein had previously been small or modest—but despite her suspicion she'd had to accept it, along with all the other changes that had come over her father. In the end, it was the police detectives who showed Lucie, Jonah, and Maya into their father's apartment, which turned out to be in a crumbling building near the ancient port of Jaffa. The paint was peeling, and the shower let down directly above the toilet. A cockroach strutted majestically across the stone floor. Only after the police detective stomped on it with his shoe did it occur to Maya, Epstein's youngest and most intelligent child, that it may have been the last to see her father. If Epstein had ever really lived there at all—the only things that suggested he had inhabited the place were some books warped by the humid air that came through an open window and a bottle of the Coumadin pills he'd taken since the discovery of an atrial fibrillation five years earlier. It could not have been called squalid, and yet the place had more in common with the slums of Calcutta than it did with the rooms in which his children had stayed with their father on the Amalfi coast and Cap d'Antibes. Though, like those other rooms, this one also had a view of the sea.

IN THOSE FINAL months Epstein had become difficult to reach. No longer did his answers come hurtling back regardless of the time of day or night. If before he'd always had the last word, it was because he'd never not replied. But slowly, his messages had become more and more scarce. Time expanded between them because it had expanded in him: the twenty-four hours he'd once filled with everything under the sun was replaced by a scale of thousands of years. His family and friends became accustomed to his irregular silences, and so when he failed to answer anything at all during the first week of February, no one became instantly alarmed. In the end, it was Maya who woke in the night feeling a tremor along the invisible line that still connected her to her father, and asked his cousin to check on him. Moti, who had been the beneficiary of many thousands of dollars from Epstein, caressed the ass of the sleeping lover in his bed, then lit a cigarette and stuffed his bare feet into his shoes, for though it was the middle of the night, he was glad to have a reason to talk to Epstein about a new investment. But when Moti arrived at the Jaffa address scrawled on his palm, he rang Maya back. There must be a mistake, he told her, there was no way her father would live in such a dump. Maya phoned Epstein's lawyer, Schloss, the only one who still knew anything, but he confirmed that the address was correct. When Moti finally roused the young tenant on the second floor by holding down the buzzer with a stubby finger, she confirmed that Epstein had in fact been living above her for the last few months, but that it had been many days since she'd last seen him, or heard him, really, for she had gotten used to the sound of him pacing on her ceiling during the night. Though she couldn't know it as she stood sleepily at the door addressing the balding cousin of her upstairs neighbor, in the rapid escalation of events that followed, the young woman would become accustomed to the sound of many people coming and going above her head, tracing and retracing the footsteps of a man she hardly knew and yet had come to feel oddly close to.

The police only had the case for half a day before it was taken over by the Shin Bet. Shimon Peres called the family personally to say that mountains would be moved. The taxi driver who'd picked Epstein up six days earlier was tracked down and taken in for questioning. Scared out of his wits, he smiled the whole time, showing his gold tooth. Later he led the Shin Bet detectives to the road along the Dead Sea and, following some confusion as a result of nerves, managed to locate the spot where he had let Epstein off, an intersection near the barren hills halfway between the caves of Qumran and Ein Gedi. The search parties fanned out across the desert, but all they turned up was Epstein's empty monogrammed briefcase, which, as Maya put it, only made the possibility of his transubstantiation seem more real.

During those days and nights, gathered together in the rooms of the Hilton suite, his children tossed back and forth between hope and grief. A phone was always ringing—Schloss alone was manning three—and each time it did, they attached themselves to the latest information that came through. Jonah, Lucie, and Maya learned things about their father that they hadn't known.

But in the end, they got no closer to finding out what he had meant by it all, or what had become of him. As the days passed, the calls had come less often, and brought no miracles. Slowly they adjusted themselves to a new reality in which their father, so firm and decisive in life, had left them with a final act that was utterly ambiguous.

A rabbi was brought in who explained to them in heavily accented English that Jewish law required absolute certainty about the death before the mourning rituals could be observed. In cases where there was no corpse, a witness to the death was considered enough. And even with no corpse and no witness, a report that the person had been killed by thieves, or drowned, or dragged off by a wild animal was enough. But in this case there was no corpse, no witness, and no report. No thieves, or wild animals, as far as anyone knew. Only an inscrutable absence where once their father had been.

NO ONE COULD have imagined it, and yet it came to seem like a fitting end. Death was too small for Epstein. In retrospect, not even a real possibility. In life he had taken up the whole room. He wasn't large, only uncontainable. There was too much of him; he constantly overspilled himself. It all came pouring out: the passion, the anger, the enthusiasm, the contempt for people and the love for all mankind. Argument was the medium in which he was raised, and he needed it to know he was alive. He fell out with three-quarters of everyone he had fallen in with; those that remained could do no wrong, and were loved by Epstein forever. To know him was either to be crushed by him or madly inflated. One hardly recognized oneself in his descriptions. He had a long line of protégés. Epstein breathed himself into them, they became larger and larger, as did everyone he chose to love. At last they flew like a Macy's parade balloon. But then one day they would snag themselves on Epstein's high moral branches and burst. From then on, their names were anathema. In his inflationary habits Epstein was deeply American, but in his lack of respect for boundaries and his tribalism he was not. He was something else, and this something else led to misunderstanding again and again.

And yet he'd had a way of drawing people in, bringing them over to his side, under the expansive umbrella of his policies. He was lit brightly from within, and this light came spilling out of him in the careless fashion of one who hasn't any need to scrimp or save. To be with him was never dull. His spirits swelled and sank and swelled again, his temper flared, he was unforgiving, but he was never less than completely absorbing. He was endlessly curious, and when he became interested in something or someone, his investigations were exhaustive. He never doubted that everyone else would be as interested in these subjects as he was. But few could match his stamina. In the end, it was always his dinner companions who insisted on retiring first, and still Epstein would follow them out of the restaurant, finger stabbing the air, eager to drive home his point.

He had always been at the top of everything. Where he lacked natural facilities, by sheer force of will he drove himself beyond his limits. As a young man he had not been a natural orator, for example; a lisp had gotten in the way. Nor was he innately athletic. But in time he came to excel in these, especially. The lisp was overcome—only if one listened microscopically could a slur be detected where he had performed the necessary operation— and many hours in the gym, and the honing of a wily, cutthroat instinct, turned him into a champion lightweight wrestler. Where he encountered a wall, he threw himself against it over and over, picking himself up again until one day he went right through it. This enormous pressure and exertion were perceptible in everything he did, and yet what might have come off as striving in anyone else, in him seemed a form of grace. Even as a boy, his aspirations were gargantuan. On the block where he grew up on Long Beach, Long Island, Epstein had charged ten houses a monthly retainer fee, for which he was available twenty-four hours a day, with a cap of ten hours a month, to deliver his services, outlined in an ever-expanding menu he sent out with the invoice (mowing, dog walking, car washing, even unclogging toilets, for he did not have the switch in him that seemed to turn others off). He was going to have endless money because that was his fate; long before he married into it, he already knew exactly what to do with it. At thirteen, he bought with his savings a blue silk scarf that he wore as casually as his friends wore their gym sneakers. How many people know what to do with money? His wife, Lianne, had been allergic to her family fortune; it stiffened her and made her quiet. She spent her early years trying to erase her footsteps in the formal gardens. But Epstein taught her what to do with it. He bought a Rubens, a Sargent, a Mortlake tapestry. He hung a small Matisse in his closet. Under a ballerina by Degas, he sat without pants. It wasn't a question of being crude or out of his element. No, Epstein was very polished. He was not refined—he had no wish to lose his impurities—but he had been brought to a high shine. In pleasure he saw nothing to be ashamed of; his was large and true, and so he could make himself at home among even the most exquisite things. Every summer he rented the same "shabby" castle in Granada where the newspaper could be thrown down and the feet put up. He chose a spot on the plaster wall to pencil in the children's growth. In later years he grew misty-eyed at the mention of the place—he had gotten so much wrong, he had made a mess of it, and yet there, where his children had played freely under the orange trees, he had gotten something right.

But at the end there had been a kind of drift. Later on, when his children looked back and tried to make sense of what had happened, they could pinpoint the beginning of his transformation to the loss of his interest in pleasure. Something opened up between Epstein and his great appetite—it receded beyond the horizon a man carries within himself. Then he lived separately from his purchase of exquisite beauty. He lacked what it took to bring it all into harmony, or got tired of the ambition to do so. For a while the paintings still hung on the walls, but he no longer had much to do with them. They carried on their own lives, dreaming in their frames. Something had changed in him. The strong weather of being Epstein no longer gusted outward. A great, unnatural stillness settled over everything, as happens before radical events of meteorology. Then the wind shifted and turned inward.

It was then that Epstein began to give things away. It started with a small maquette by Henry Moore handed off to his doctor, who had admired it during a home visit. From his bed, laid up with the flu, Epstein instructed Dr. Silverblatt on which closet he could find the bubble wrap in. A few days later, he twisted the signet ring off his pinkie and dropped it in the palm of his surprised doorman, Haaroon, in place of a tip; flexing his naked fist in the autumn sunlight, he smiled to himself. Soon afterward he gave away his Patek Philippe. "I like your watch, Uncle Jules," his nephew had said, and Epstein unbuckled the crocodile strap and handed it to him. "I like your Mercedes, too," said his nephew, at which Epstein only smiled and patted the boy's cheek. But quickly he redoubled his efforts. Giving farther, giving faster, he began to bestow with the same ferocity with which he had once acquired. The paintings went one by one to museums; he had the crating service on automatic dial, and knew which of the men liked turkey on rye and which baloney, and had the deli delivery waiting when they arrived. When his son Jonah, trying not to appear driven by self-interest, tried to dissuade him from further philanthropy, Epstein told him he was clearing a space to think. If Jonah had pointed out that his father had been a rigorous thinker all his life, Epstein might have explained that this was thought of an entirely different nature: a thinking that didn't already know its own point. A thinking without hope of achievement. But Jonah—who had so many chips on his shoulder that one evening, on a private tour of the new Greek and Roman galleries at the Met, Epstein had stood before a second-century bust and seen his firstborn in it—had only answered him with injured silence. As with everything Epstein did, Jonah took his father's deliberate draining of assets as an affront, and yet another reason to feel aggrieved.

Beyond this, Epstein made no effort to explain himself to anyone, except once to Maya. Having arrived thirteen years after Jonah, and ten after Lucie, at a less turbulent and agitated epoch in Epstein's life, Maya saw her father in a different light. There was a natural ease between them. On a walk through the northern reaches of Central Park, where icicles hung from the great outcrops of schist, he told his youngest daughter that he had begun to feel choked by all the things around him. That he felt an irresistible longing for lightness—it was a quality, he realized only now, that had been alien to him all his life. They stopped at the upper lake, thinly sheeted with greenish ice. When a snowflake landed on Maya's black eyelashes, Epstein gently brushed it away with his thumb, and Maya saw her father in fingerless gloves pushing an empty shopping cart down Upper Broadway.

He sent friends' children through college, had refrigerators delivered, paid for a pair of new hips for the wife of the longtime janitor of his law office. He even made the down payment on a house for the daughter of an old friend; not any house, but a large Greek Revival with old trees and more lawn than the surprised new owner knew what to do with. His lawyer, Schloss—the executor of his estate, and his longtime confidant—was not allowed to interfere. Schloss had once had another client who'd caught the disease of radical charity, a billionaire who gave away his houses one by one, followed by the ground under his feet. It was a kind of addiction, he told Epstein, and later he might come to regret it. After all, he was not yet seventy; he could still live thirty more years. But Epstein had barely seemed to listen, just as he hadn't listened when the lawyer strenuously argued against letting Lianne walk away with the entirety of her fortune, and just as he didn't listen a few months later when Schloss again tried to dissuade him, this time from retiring from the firm where he'd been a partner for twenty-five years. Across the table, Epstein had only smiled and changed the subject to his reading, which had recently taken a mystical turn.

It had begun with a book Maya had given to him for his birthday, he told Schloss. She was always giving him strange books, some of which he read, and many of which he didn't, a practice that never seemed to bother her—naturally free-spirited, she was the opposite of her brother, Jonah, and rarely took offense at anything. Epstein had opened the cover one evening with no intention of reading it, but it had pulled him in with an almost magnetic force. It was by an Israeli poet, Polish-born, who had died at sixty-six, two years younger than the age Epstein had just turned. But the little autobiographical book, the testament of a man alone facing God, had been written when the poet was only twenty-seven. It had overwhelmed him, Epstein told Schloss. At twenty-seven, he himself had been blinded by his ambition and appetite—for success, for money, for sex, for beauty, for love, for the magnitudes but also the nitty-gritty, for everything visible, smellable, palpable. What might his life have been if he had applied himself with the same intensity to the spiritual realm? Why had he closed himself off from it so completely?

As he spoke, Schloss had taken him in: his darting eyes, the silver hair that came down over his collar, striking because of how meticulous he had always been about his appearance. "What do you have to say about the steak versus its competitors?" Epstein was known to demand of the waiter. But now the plate of Dover sole remained untouched, belying his usual appetite. Only when the waiter came by to ask if anything was wrong did Epstein look down and remember the food, but all he did then was push it around with his fork. It was Schloss's sense that what had happened to Epstein—the divorce, the retirement, everything coming loose, coming away—had begun not with a book but rather with the death of his parents. But afterward, when Schloss put Epstein into the back of the dark sedan waiting outside the restaurant, the lawyer paused for a moment with his hand on the car's roof. Looking in at the strangely vague Epstein in the dark interior, he wondered briefly whether there was something more grave going on with his longtime client—a kind of neurological turbulence, perhaps, that might develop toward the extreme before it was diagnosed as medical. At the time, Schloss had brushed the thought off, but later it came back to him as prescient.

AND INDEED AT LAST, after nearly a year of chipping away at the accumulations of a lifetime, Epstein arrived at the bottommost layer. There, he hit on the memory of his parents, who had washed up on the shores of Palestine after the war and conceived him under a burned-out bulb that they had not had enough money to replace. At the age of sixty-eight, having cleared a space to think, he found himself consumed by that darkness, deeply moved by it. His parents had brought him, their only son, to America, and once they'd learned English, resumed the screaming match that they'd begun in other languages. Later his sister Joanie came along, but she, a dreamy, unresponsive child, refused to take the bait, and so the battle remained triangulated. His parents screamed at each other, and they screamed at him, and he screamed back at them, together and separately. His wife, Lianne, had never been able to accustom herself to such violent love, though at the beginning, having come from a family that suppressed even its sneezes, she had been attracted to its heat. Early on in their courtship, Epstein had told her that from his father's brutality and tenderness he'd learned that a person can't be reduced, a lesson that had guided him all his life, and for a long time Lianne thought of this—of Epstein's own complexity, his resistance to easy categorization—as something to love. But in the end it had exhausted her just as it had exhausted so many others, though never his parents, who remained his tireless sparring partners, and who, Epstein sometimes felt, had lived on with such tenacity only to torment him. He'd taken care of them until the end, which they'd lived out in a penthouse he bought for them in Miami, with deep-pile carpets that came up to their ankles. But he had never found peace with them, and only after their deaths—his mother following his father within three months—and after he'd given nearly everything away did Epstein feel the sharp stab of regret. The naked bulb sputtered on and off behind his inflamed lids when he tried to sleep. He couldn't sleep. Had he accidentally given sleep away, along with everything else?

He wanted to do something in his parents' names. But what? His mother, while still alive, had proposed a memorial bench in the little park where she used to sit, while upstairs his father was giving up his mind in the presence of Conchita, the live-in nurse. Always a big reader, his mother would bring a book with her to the park. In her last years, she had taken up Shakespeare. Once Epstein overheard her telling Conchita that she had to read *King Lear*. "They probably have it in Spanish," she'd told the nurse. Every afternoon, when the sun was no longer at its peak, his mother rode down in the elevator with a large-print edition of one of the Bard's plays in the knockoff Prada bag she had bought— over Epstein's protests that he would buy her a real one—from an African selling them at the beach. (What did she need with real?) The park was run-down, the play equipment caked with the shit of seagulls, but there was no one in the neighborhood under the age of sixty-five to climb on it, anyway. Had his mother been serious about the bench, or had she suggested it with the usual sarcasm? Epstein couldn't say, and so, to be sure, a bench of ipe that could withstand the tropical weather was ordered for the grimy Florida park, bolted with a brass plate that read,

In Memory of Edith "Edie" Epstein. "I am not bound to please thee with my answer."—William Shakespeare. He left the Colombian doorman of his parents' building $200 to shine it twice a month at the same time that he polished the brass in the lobby. But when the doorman texted him a photo of the pristine bench, it seemed to Epstein that it was worse than if he had done nothing. He remembered how his mother used to call him when too much time had gone by since he'd last phoned, and in a voice hoarse from sixty years of smoking, would quote God who called out to the fallen Adam: "Ayeka?" *Where are you?* But God knew where Adam was physically.

On the eve of the first anniversary of his parents' deaths, Epstein decided two things: to take out a $2 million line of credit on his Fifth Avenue apartment, and to go on a trip to Israel. The borrowing was new, but Israel was a place he'd returned to often over the years, drawn back by a tangle of allegiances. Ritually installing himself in the fifteenth-floor executive lounge of the Hilton, he had always taken visits from a long line of friends, family, and business associates, getting into everything, dispensing money, opinions, advice, resolving old arguments and igniting new ones. But this time his assistant was instructed not to fill his schedule as usual. Instead, she was asked to set up appointments with the development offices of Hadassah, the Weizmann Institute, and Ben-Gurion University, to explore the possibilities of a donation in his parents' names. The remaining time should be kept free, Epstein told her; perhaps he would finally hire a car to tour parts of the country he had not been to for many years, as he had often spoken of doing but hadn't, because he'd been too busy having it out, getting overly involved, and going on and on. He wanted to see the Kinneret again, the Negev, the rocky hills of Judea. The mineral blue of the Dead Sea.

As he spoke, his assistant, Sharon, glanced up, and in the familiar face of her employer she saw something she didn't recognize. If this worried her a little, it was only because knowing what Epstein wanted, and exactly the way he liked things, was what made her good at her job, and it mattered to her to be good at it. Having survived his explosions, she'd become aware of the generosity that lived alongside Epstein's temper, and over the years he'd won her loyalty with his.

THE DAY BEFORE leaving for Israel, Epstein attended a small event with Mahmoud Abbas, hosted by the Center for Middle East Peace at the Plaza Hotel. Some fifty people representing the American Jewish leadership had been invited to sit down with the president of the Palestinian Authority, who was in town to address the UN Security Council, and had agreed to quell their Jewish fears over a three-course meal. Once Epstein would have leaped at the invitation. Would have gone barreling in and thrown around his weight. But where could it get him now? What could the square-hewn man from Safed tell him that he didn't know already? He was tired of it all—tired of the hot air and lip service, his own and other people's. He, too, wanted peace. Only at the last minute did Epstein change his mind, firing off a text to Sharon, who had to scramble to snatch back his place from a late-joining delegation from the State Department. He had given up much, but he had not yet lost his curiosity. Anyway, he was going to be around the corner at the office of the bank's lawyers beforehand, signing documents—despite Schloss's pleas—for the loan against his apartment.

And yet as soon as Epstein was seated at the long table shoulder to shoulder with the banner carriers of his people busily loading chive butter onto their rolls while the soft-spoken Palestinian spoke of the end of conflict and the end of claims, he regretted his change of heart. The room was tiny; there was no way out. Once he would have done it. At a state dinner honoring Shimon Peres at the White House only last year, he'd gotten up to take a piss halfway through Itzhak Perlman's rendition of *Tempo di Minuetto*—how many hours total of his life had he spent listening to Perlman? A solid week? The Secret Service had convulsed toward him; after the president was seated, no one was allowed to leave the room. But when the call of nature comes, all men are equal. "It's an emergency, gentlemen," he'd said, pushing past the dark suits. Something gave, as it had always given for Epstein; he was escorted past the brass-buttoned military guards to the restroom. But the need to assert himself had gone out of Epstein.

The Caesar salad was served, the floor opened, and Dershowitz's sonorous voice—"My old friend, Abu Mazen"—was carrying. To Epstein's right, the ambassador of Saudi Arabia was fiddling with the cordless microphone, at a loss for how it worked. Across the table, Madeleine Albright sat heavy-lidded like a lizard in the sun, radiating an inward intelligence; she too was no longer really there, having moved on to matters of a metaphysical nature, or so it seemed to Epstein, who was struck by the desire to take her aside and discuss these deeper concerns. He patted his inside pocket for the small book bound in worn green cloth that Maya had given him for his birthday, and which he had carried with him everywhere for the last month. But it wasn't there; he must have left it in his coat.

It was then, removing his hand from his pocket, that Epstein first noticed, out of the corner of his eye, the tall, bearded man in a dark suit and large black skullcap standing at the edge of the group, not distinguished enough to have been granted a seat at the table. The little smile on his lips brought out the crinkles around his eyes, and his arms were folded across his chest as if he were bracing a restless energy. But Epstein sensed it was not self-control in the service of humility at work in him, but something else.

The American Jewish leadership went on unspooling their questionless questions; the salad dishes were removed by the Indian waiters and replaced with poached salmon. At last it came Epstein's turn to speak. He leaned forward and flipped the switch on the mic. There was a loud pop of static that made the Saudi Arabian ambassador jump. In the silence that followed, Epstein looked around at the faces turned expectantly toward him. He had not given any thought to what he wanted to say, and now his mind, which had always honed in on its target like a drone, drifted leisurely. He looked slowly around the table. The faces of the others, at a loss for how to respond to his silence, suddenly fascinated him. Their discomfort fascinated him. Had he once been immune to the discomfort of others? No, immune was too strong a word. But he had not paid it much attention. Now he watched them look down at their plates and shift uncomfortably in their seats until finally the moderator broke in. "If Jules—Mr. Epstein—has nothing to add, we'll move on to—" but the moderator was forced to swivel around just then, being interrupted by a voice behind her.

"If he doesn't want his turn, I'll take it."

Searching for where the intrusion had come from, Epstein met the keen eyes of the large man in the black knitted skullcap. He was about to answer when the man cut in again.

"President Abbas, thank you for coming today. Forgive me:

like my colleagues, I don't have a question for you; just something to say."

A ripple of relieved laughter rolled through the room. His voice carried easily, making the use of the microphones seem fussy.

"My name is Rabbi Menachem Klausner. I've lived in Israel twenty-five years. I'm the founder of Gilgul, a program that brings Americans to Safed to study Jewish mysticism. I invite all of you to look us up, perhaps even to join us on one of our retreats—we're up to fifteen a year now, and growing. President Abbas, it would be an honor to welcome you, though of course you know the elevations of Safed better than most of us."

The rabbi paused and rubbed his glossy beard.

"As I stand here listening to my friends, I'm reminded of a story. A lesson, actually, that the rabbi once taught us in school. A real *tzadik*, one of the best teachers I had—had it not been for him, my life would have turned out differently. He used to read aloud to us from the Torah. That day it was Genesis, and when he got to the line, 'On the seventh day God finished his work,' he stopped and looked up. Did we notice anything strange? he wants to know. We scratch our heads. Everyone knows that the seventh day is the Sabbath, so what was so strange?

"'Aha!' the rabbi says, leaping up from his seat, as he does whenever he's excited. But it doesn't say that God rested on the seventh day! It says that he *finished his work*. How many days did it take to create the heavens and the earth? he asks us. Six, we say. So why doesn't it say God finished *then*? Finished on the *sixth*, and on the seventh rested?"

Epstein glanced around, and wondered where all of this was going.

"Well, the rabbi tells us that when the ancient sages convened to puzzle over this problem, they concluded that there must have been an act of creation on the seventh day, too. But what? The sea and the land already existed. The sun and the moon. Plants and trees, animals, and birds. Even Man. What could it be that the universe still lacked? the ancient sages asked. At last a grizzled old scholar who always sat alone in the corner of the room opened his mouth. '*Menucha*,' he said. 'What?' the others asked. 'Speak up, we can't hear you.' 'With the Sabbath, God created *menucha*,' the old scholar said, 'and then the world was complete.'"

Madeleine Albright pushed back her chair and made her way out of the room, the material of her pantsuit making a soft scuffing noise. The speaker seemed unfazed. For a moment Epstein thought he might even seize her empty chair, just as he had seized the turn Epstein had forfeited. But he remained standing, the better to command the room. Those nearby had edged back to open a space around him.

"'So what is the meaning of *menucha*?' the rabbi asks us. A bunch of restless kids staring out the window, whose only interest in the world is to be out playing ball. No one speaks. The rabbi waits, and when it becomes clear that he's not going to give us the answer, a kid at the back of the room, the only one with polished shoes, who always goes straight home to his mother, the many-generations-removed progeny of the grizzled old scholar who carried within him the ancient wisdom of sitting in corners, opens his mouth. 'Rest,' he says. 'Rest!' the rabbi exclaims, spit spraying from his mouth as it does when he's excited. 'But not only! Because *menucha* doesn't simply mean a pause from work. A break from exertion. It isn't just the opposite of toil and labor. If it took a special act of creation to bring it into being, surely it must be something extraordinary. Not the negative of something that already existed, but a unique positive, without which the universe would be incomplete. No, not just rest,' the rabbi says. 'Tranquillity! Serenity! Repose! *Peace*. A state in which there is no strife, and no fighting. No fear and distrust. *Menucha*. The state in which man lies still.'

"Abu Mazen, if I may"—Klausner dropped his voice and adjusted the *kippah* that had slipped to the back of his head— "in that classroom of twelve-year-olds, not a single one of us understood what the rabbi meant. But I ask you: Do any of us in this room understand it any better? Understand that act of creation that stands alone among the others, the only one that didn't establish something eternal? On the seventh day God created *menucha*. But He made it to be fragile. Unable to last. Why? Why, when everything else he made is impervious to time?"

Klausner paused, sweeping his gaze across the room. His enormous forehead glistened with sweat, though otherwise he gave no sign of exerting himself. Epstein leaned forward, waiting.

"So that it falls to Man to re-create it over and over again," Klausner said at last. "To re-create *menucha*, so that he should know that he is not a bystander to the universe, but a participant. That without his actions, the universe God intended for us will remain incomplete."

A lone, lazy clap rang out from the far reaches of the room. When, unaccompanied, it drifted into silence, the leader of the Palestinians began to speak, pausing for his translator to convey his message about his eight grandchildren who had all attended the Seeds of Peace camp, about living side by side, encouraging dialogue, building relationships. His comments were followed by a few last speakers and then the event came to an end, with everyone rising to their feet, and Abbas pumping a row of extended hands as he made his way down the table and out of the room, followed by his entourage.

Epstein, also eager to be on his way, headed toward the coat check. But while standing in line, he felt a tap on his shoulder. When he turned, he came face-to-face with the rabbi who had delivered the sermon on stolen time. A head and a half taller than Epstein, he radiated the wiry, sun-beaten strength of someone who has lived a long time in the Levant. Close up, his blue eyes shone with stored-up sunlight. "Menachem Klausner," he repeated, in case Epstein had missed it earlier. "I hope I didn't step on your toes back there?"

"No," Epstein said, smacking the chip for his coat down on the table. "You spoke well. I couldn't have said it better myself." He meant it, but had no desire to get into it now. The woman working the coat check had a limp, and Epstein watched her head off to fulfill her task.

"Thanks, but I can't take much credit. Most of it is from Heschel."

"I thought you said it was your old rabbi."

"Makes for a more captivating story," Klausner said, raising his eyebrows. Above them, the pattern of deep lines on his forehead changed with each exaggerated expression.

Epstein had never read Heschel, and anyway the room was warm and what he wanted above all was to be outdoors, refreshed by the cold. But when the coat clerk returned from the revolving rack, it was with someone else's coat slung over her arm.

"This isn't mine," Epstein said, pushing the coat back across the table.

The woman looked at him with contempt. But when he returned her hard stare with a harder one of his own, she capitulated and limped back to the rack. One leg was shorter than the other, but it would take a saint not to hold it against her.

"Actually, we've met before," Menachem Klausner said behind him.

"Have we," said Epstein, barely turning.

"In Jerusalem, at the wedding of the Schulmans' daughter."

Epstein nodded but could not recall the encounter.

"I never forget an Epstein."

"Why's that?"

"Not an Epstein, or an Abravanel, or a Dayan, or anyone with lineage that can be traced back to the dynastic line of David."

"Epstein? Unless you're referring to the royalty of some backwater shtetl, you're wrong about Epstein."

"Oh, you're one of us, all right."

Now Epstein had to laugh.

"Us?"

"Naturally; Klausner is a big name in Davidic genealogy. Not quite the same clout as Epstein, mind you. Unless one of your ancestors pulled the name out of thin air, which seems unlikely, then the chain of begetting that led to you backs right up to the King of Israel."

Epstein had the competing urges to pull a fifty out of his wallet in order to get rid of Klausner and to ask him more. There was something compelling about the rabbi, or there would be at another time.

The coat clerk continued to spin the rack lazily, stopping it now and then to inspect the numbers on the hooks. She took down a khaki trench coat. "Not it," Epstein called out before she could try to pass it off to him. She shot him a disapproving look and went back to her spinning.

Unable to stand it any longer, Epstein maneuvered his way behind the table. The clerk leaped back with exaggerated surprise, as if she expected him to club her over the head. But her expression was replaced by one more smug as Epstein began to look through the coats himself without luck. When she limped off to try to take Menachem Klausner's chip, the sermon-maker with a three-thousand-year-old bloodline protested—"No, no. I don't mind waiting. What does the coat look like, Jules?"

"It's navy," Epstein muttered, slapping the tweed and woolen sleeves as they swung past. But the coat, which he could not say was rather like the one on the table, only far softer and more expensive, was nowhere to be found. "This is ridiculous," he sputtered. "Someone must have taken it."

Epstein could have sworn that he heard the clerk laugh. But when he spun around to look, her stooped, squarish back was turned and she was already helping the person in line behind Klausner. Epstein felt the heat rise to his face and his throat constrict. It was one thing to give away millions of his own volition, but to have the coat taken off his back was something else. All he wanted was to be away from there, to walk alone through the park in his own coat.

There was a ring as the elevator arrived and its doors rolled open. Without another word, Epstein snatched the coat lying on the table and hurried toward it. Klausner called after him, but the doors closed just in time and the elevator carried Epstein down alone through the floors.

At the hotel's side exit Abu Mazen's men were piling into the limousine. On the last of them Epstein spotted his coat. "Hey!"

he shouted, waving the rough garment in his arm. "HEY! You're wearing my coat!" But the man didn't hear or chose not to, and as he slammed the door behind him, the limo pulled away from the curb and floated down Fifty-Eighth Street.

Epstein looked after it in disbelief. The hotel doorman eyed him nervously, concerned, perhaps, that he might make a scene. Glancing morosely at the coat in his hands, Epstein sighed instead and dipped one arm and then the other into the sleeves and shrugged it onto his shoulders. The cuffs hung over his knuckles. As he crossed Central Park South, a cold gust blew through the thin material, and Epstein reached instinctively into his pockets for his leather gloves. But all he came up with was a little tin box of mints printed with Arabic script. He popped one into his mouth and began to suck; it was so spicy it made his eyes tear. So that was how they grew the hair on their chests. He descended the stairs and, entering the park, made his way along the path that edged the pond filled with reeds.

The sky was a dusty rose now, failing orange to the west. Soon the lamps would come on. The wind picked up, and overhead a white plastic bag billowed past, slowly changing shape.

The soul is a sea that we swim in. It has no shore on this side, and only far away, on the other side, is there a shore, and that is God.

It was a line from the little green book Maya had given him for his birthday almost two months ago, parts of which he had read so many times that he knew them by heart. Passing a bench, Epstein doubled back and sat down, reaching into the inside pocket of his suit jacket. Recalling that it was empty, he jumped

25

up in alarm. The book! He'd left it in his coat! His coat, which at the moment was making its way east on the back of one of Abbas's henchmen. He fumbled around for his phone to text his assistant, Sharon. But the phone was also nowhere to be found. "Fuck!" Epstein shouted. A mother pushing a double stroller along the path gave him a wary look and increased her speed.

"Hey!" Epstein shouted, "Excuse me!" The woman glanced back, but continued moving briskly. Epstein ran after her. "Listen," he said falling breathlessly in step beside her, "I just realized I misplaced my phone. Can I borrow yours a second?"

The woman glanced at her children—twins, it seemed, bundled into fur-lined sleeping bags, noses wet and dark eyes alert. With a clenched jaw, she reached into her pocket and pulled out her phone. Epstein plucked it out of her palm, turned his back on her, and dialed his own number. It rang through to his voice mail. Had he turned his phone off earlier, at the closing for the loan, or was it Abbas's man who'd done it? The thought of his calls going through to the Palestinian filled him with anxiety. He dialed Sharon's number, but there was no answer there, either.

"Just a quick text," Epstein explained, and with numb fingers tapped out the message: *Contact UN Security Council ASAP. Coat mix-up at Plaza. One of Abbas's cronies made off with mine: Loro Piana, navy cashmere.* He pressed send, then typed another line: *Phone and other valuables in coat pocket.* But just as he was about to shoot that one off, too, he thought better of it and erased it, lest he tip Abbas's man off to what he unknowingly had in his possession. But, no: that was ridiculous. What could he possibly want with a stranger's phone and an obscure book by a dead Israeli poet?

The twins started to sneeze and snuffle, while the mother

shifted impatiently from foot to foot. Epstein, who had no experience with the receiving side of charity, retyped the text, sent it, and went on holding the phone, waiting for it to buzz to life with the assistant's response. But it remained inert in his hands. Where the hell was she? *Not my phone, obviously*, he typed. *Will try you again soon.* He turned to the woman, who grabbed back the phone with a grunt of exasperation and marched off, not bothering to say good-bye.

He was supposed to meet Maura at Avery Fisher Hall in forty-five minutes. They had known each other since they were children, and after his divorce Maura had become his frequent companion at concerts. Epstein began to angle west and northward, cutting across the grass, frantically composing texts in his head. But as he passed a bush, a flock of brown sparrows shot up from it and scattered into the dusky sky. At their sudden burst of freedom, Epstein felt a wave of consolation. It was only an old book, wasn't it? Surely he could track down another copy. He would put Sharon on the case. Or better yet, why not just let the book go as easily as it had come? Hadn't he already taken what he needed from it?

Lost in thought, he entered a tunnel under a pedestrian overpass. As he shivered in the dank air, a homeless man stepped out of the dark and into Epstein's path. His hair was long and matted, and he reeked of urine and something festering. Epstein removed a twenty-dollar bill from his wallet and stuffed it into the man's callused palm. As an afterthought, he fished out the box of mints and offered those as well. But it was the wrong decision because now the man moved jerkily, and in the darkness Epstein saw the flash of a knife.

"Gimme the wallet," he grunted.

Epstein was surprised—Really? Could the afternoon strip him any further? Had he given so much that, stinking of benefaction, the world now felt free to take from him? Or, just the opposite, was it trying to tell him that he hadn't yet given enough, that it wouldn't be enough until there was nothing left? And was it really possible that there was still a mugger left standing in Central Park?

Surprised, yes, but not frightened. He'd dealt with plenty of lunatics in his life. It might even be said that, as an attorney, he possessed a certain gift with them. He assessed the situation: the knife wasn't large. It could hurt but not kill.

"All right, then," he began calmly. "How about if I give you the cash? There must be at least three hundred dollars in here, maybe more. You take it all, and I'll just keep the cards. You don't have any use for those—they'll be canceled in two minutes, and anyway you'll probably just toss them in the trash. This way we both go away happy." As Epstein spoke, he held the wallet in front of him, away from his body, and slowly removed the wad of bills. The man snatched it. But he wasn't through with Epstein apparently, for now he was barking something else. Epstein failed to understand.

"What?"

The man raked the blade quickly across Epstein's breast. "What's in there?"

Epstein stepped back, clamping his hand over his heart.

"Where?" he gasped.

"On the inside!"

"Nothing," he said quietly.

"Show me," the homeless man said, or so Epstein thought; it was almost impossible to make out his slurred speech. The thought of his father, whose own speech had become permanently slurred after a stroke, flashed through Epstein's mind, while the man continued to breathe heavily, weapon poised.

Slowly, Epstein unbuttoned the coat that wasn't his, and then the gray flannel suit jacket that was. He opened the silk-lined pocket that usually held the little green book, and tipped forward on his toes to show the man that it was empty. It was all so absurd that he might have laughed, had there not been a knife so near his throat. Perhaps it could kill after all. Glancing down, Epstein saw himself lying underfoot in a pool of blood, unable to call for help. A question came into focus in his mind, one that had lingered vaguely for some weeks, and now he tried it, as if to test its fit: Had the hand of God reached down and pointed at him? But why him? When he looked up again, the knife was gone, and the man had turned and was hurrying away. Epstein stood frozen for a moment, until the man disappeared into the circle of light at the other end, and he was left alone in the tunnel. Only when he lifted his hand to touch his throat did he realize that his fingers were shaking.

Ten minutes later, having safely arrived in the lobby of the Dakota, Epstein was borrowing another phone. "I'm a friend of the Rosenblatts'," he'd told the doorman. "I was just robbed. My phone, too." The doorman lifted the house phone to call up to 14B. "Don't bother," Epstein said quickly. "I'll just make a call and be on my way." He reached behind the desk and dialed himself once more. It went through to his voice again, recorded long ago but still arriving. He cut the line and called Sharon. She picked up, full of apologies for having missed his earlier call. She'd already put in calls to the UN. Abbas was speaking in fifteen minutes, and at the moment no one in his party could be reached, but she was getting in a cab now and would make sure to intercept them before they left the building. Epstein told her to call Maura to say that she should go ahead to the concert without him.

"Tell her I was mugged," he said.

"OK, you were mugged," said Sharon.

"I really was," Epstein said, more softly than he had meant to, for once again he saw himself sprawled on the ground, the dark blood slowly spreading. Glancing up, he caught eyes with the doorman, who he saw didn't believe him either.

"Seriously?" his assistant asked.

Epstein cut her off: "I'll be home in half an hour. Call me then."

"Listen," he said to the doorman, "I'm in a pinch. Can you lend me a twenty? I'll remember you at Christmas. In the meantime, the Rosenblatts are good for it."

Having handed over the bills, the doorman hailed a cab going south on Central Park West. Having nothing left to tip him with, neither cash nor rings, Epstein offered only a humble nod and gave the address of his building, across the park and fifteen blocks north. The taxi driver shook his head in annoyance, rolled down the window, and spat thickly. It was always the same: if you diverted them from their natural course and asked them to reverse direction, they always took it badly. It was a nearly universal aspect of the psychology of New York City taxi drivers, Epstein had often lectured to anyone who was with him in the backseat. Once they were in motion, having been stymied by traffic jams and red lights, everything in them longed to continue the motion. That money was to be made by turning around and going in the opposite direction hardly mattered at the moment the news was delivered: they felt it as a defeat and resented it.

The atmosphere in the cab only darkened when the traffic going uptown on Madison turned out to be at a dead standstill, and the streets going west were blocked off. Epstein rolled down the window and called to a policeman, fat and muscular like a ballplayer, stationed by a sawhorse.

"What's going on here?"

"They're filming a movie," the officer reported dully, scanning the sky for fly balls.

"You're kidding me, right? That's the second time this month! Who told Bloomberg he could sell the city to Hollywood? Some of us still happen to live here!"

RELEASED FROM THE smelly cab, Epstein marched down Eighty-Fifth Street, which was lined with humming trailers powered by a giant, roaring generator. Passing the catering table, he lifted a doughnut without slowing down and bit into it, the jelly spurting.

But when he turned onto Fifth Avenue, he halted, for there he found that snow had fallen. The trees, lit by huge lights, were cloaked in white, and along the sidewalk great drifts sparkled like mica. All was silent and sedated; even the team of black horses hitched to a hearse stood unmoving with bowed heads, the snow swirling down around them. Through the carriage's glass windows, Epstein saw the long shadow of an ebony coffin. A flood of grave respect coursed through him—not just the reflexive awe one feels at the passing of life, but something else, too: a sense of what the world, with its unfathomable pockets, was capable of. But it was fleeting. A moment later the camera crane came rolling down the street, and the magic was broken.

As at last he came in sight of the warmly lit lobby of his building, a wave of exhaustion broke over Epstein. All he wanted now was to be home, where he could ease himself into the giant bathtub and let the day drain away. But as he began to walk toward the entrance, he was thwarted once more, this time by a woman in a puffy anorak wielding a clipboard.

"They're shooting!" she hissed. "You have to wait at the corner."

"I live here," Epstein snapped back.

"So do plenty of others, and they're all waiting. Have some patience."

But Epstein was all out of patience, and when the woman glanced back at the creaking hearse now starting up behind the horses, he sidestepped her and, with a last burst of strength, began to sprint toward the building. He could see Haaroon, the doorman, peering out at the action on the street. He was always there, face to the glass. When there was no excitement, he liked to scan the sky for a sighting of the red-tailed hawk that nested on a ledge down the block. At the last moment Haaroon caught sight of Epstein barreling toward him, and with a look of surprise pulled open the door just before the tenant of Penthouse B could smack into it. Epstein sailed smoothly in, and the doorman bolted the door shut again, spun around, and flattened his back against it.

"It's a movie, Haaroon, not a revolution," Epstein said, breathing hard.

Ever amazed at the new ways of his adopted country, the

32

doorman nodded and straightened the heavy green cape with golden buttons that was his uniform in the cold months. Even confined indoors, he had refused to remove it.

"You know what's wrong with this city?" Epstein said.

"What, sir?" Haaroon asked.

But, catching the doorman's earnest eyes, still filled with wonder after five years of watching Fifth Avenue go past, Epstein thought better of it and let it go. The doorman's hands were bare, and suddenly Epstein wished to ask him what he had done with the signet ring. But here, too, he swallowed his words.

When the wood-paneled elevator opened to the familiar colored rug from Isfahan in his foyer, Epstein sighed with relief. Once inside, he turned on the lamp, hung the wrong coat in the closet, and put on his slippers. He had lived here for ten months since he and Lianne had divorced, and there were still nights when he missed his wife's body in the bed beside him. He had slept next to her for thirty-six years, and the mattress felt different without her weight, however slight, and without the rhythm of her breath the dark had no measure. There were times he woke feeling cold from the lack of the heat that once came from between her thighs and behind her knees. He might have even called her, if he could have momentarily forgotten that he already knew everything she could possibly say. In truth, if he was touched by longing, it was not for what he'd had and given up.

The apartment wasn't large, but its main rooms overlooked Central Park and the Metropolitan Museum to the south, where the Temple of Dendur was housed under glass. This nearness to the ancient world meant something to him; though the Roman copy of an Egyptian temple had itself never impressed him, catching sight of it at night, he sometimes felt his lungs inflate, as if his body were remembering what it had forgotten about the vastness of time. What it had been necessary to forget, in order to believe in the grandness and the uniqueness of the things that happened to one, which could mark life the way a new combination of letters could be impressed on the ribbon of a typewriter. But he was no longer young. He was made of matter more ancient than any temple, and lately something was returning to him. Was coming back into him, as water comes back into a dry riverbed it formed long ago.

Now that the walls of the apartment were rid of paintings, and he had given away the expensive furniture, he needed only stand in the middle of the empty living room, looking out at the darkly moving treetops, to feel goose bumps rise on his arms. For what? Simply the fact that he was still there. That he had been alive long enough to arrive at a point where the circle was drawing to a close, that it had almost been too late, he had very nearly missed it, but in the nick of time he had become aware of it. Of what? Of time as a shaft of light moving across the floor, and how at the end of its long tail was the light falling across the parquet in the house where he had been a child, in Long Beach. Or the sky over his head, which was the same sky he had walked under since he was a boy. No, it was more than that. He had rarely lifted his head above the powerful currents of his life, being too busy plunging through them. But there were moments now when he saw the whole view, all the way to the horizon. And it filled him equally with joy and with yearning.

Still here. Stripped of furnishings, of cash, of phone, of the coat on his back, but not yet, after all, ethereal, Epstein felt a gnawing in the pit of his stomach. He'd barely eaten at the

Plaza, and the doughnut had whetted his appetite. Poking in the refrigerator, he discovered a chicken leg that the chef who cooked for him three times a week had left, and ate it standing at the window. A great-great-great-great-great-grandrelative of David. The boy shepherd who slung a stone at the head of Goliath, of whom the women used to say "Saul has slain his thousands, and David his ten thousands," but whom, so that he should not remain a cold and calculating brute, so that he be given Jewish softness, Jewish intelligence, Jewish depth, they later made author of the most beautiful poetry ever written. Epstein smiled. What else was there still to learn about himself? The chicken was good, but before he got to the bone he tossed the rest in the trash. Reaching up to open the cabinet for a glass, he thought better of it, ducked his head under the tap, and drank thirstily.

In the living room Epstein touched a switch, and the lights, wired to an automatic dimmer, came to life, illuminating the burnished gold of two halos on a small panel that hung alone on the east wall. Though he had seen it happen countless times before, he could not watch this effect without feeling a tingle in his scalp. It was the only masterpiece he'd kept, a panel of an altarpiece painted nearly six hundred years ago in Florence. He had not been able to bring himself to give it away. He wished to live with it a little more.

Epstein moved toward them: Mary bent and nearly bodiless in the pale pink folds that fell from her dress, and the angel Gabriel, who might himself be taken for a woman were it not for his colored wings. From the little wooden stool wedged beneath Mary one gathered that she was kneeling, or would be kneeling, if under the dress there were still anything physical left of her—if what was Mary had not already been erased so that she could be filled up with the son of God. Her curved shape was an exact echo of the white arches overhead: already she was something no longer herself. Her long-fingered hands were folded over her flat breast, and on her face was the grave expression of a mature child meeting her difficult, exalted destiny. A few feet away, the angel Gabriel looked lovingly down on her, hand over his heart, as if he, too, felt there the pain of her necessary future. The paint was shot through with cracks, but that only added to the sense of breathlessness, of a great and violent force that strained below the still surface. Only the flat golden discs around their heads were strangely static. Why did they insist on painting halos like that? Why, when they had already discovered how to create the illusion of depth, did they always revert, in this instance alone, to a stubborn flatness? And not just any instance, but the very symbol of what, drawn close to God, becomes suffused with the infinite?

Epstein took the frame down off the wall and carried it under his arm to his bedroom. Last month, a nude by Bonnard had been carried out on her back, and since then the wall opposite his bed had been empty. Now he had the sudden desire to see the small annunciation hang there: to wake to it in the morning, and to look on it last as he drifted off to sleep. But before he could manage to catch the wire on the hook, the phone rang, disturbing the silence. Epstein strode toward the bed, propped the frame against the pillows, and picked up the receiver.

"Jules? It's Sharon. I'm sorry, but apparently the guy with your coat was feeling ill and went back to his hotel."

Outside, across the expansive dark, the lights of the West Side glimmered. Epstein sank down on the bed next to the Virgin. He pictured the Palestinian in his coat, kneeling over a toilet.

"I left a message but haven't gotten through yet," Sharon continued. "Would it be all right if I waited until tomorrow to go over? Your flight isn't until nine at night, which leaves plenty of time for me to go first thing in the morning. It's my sister's birthday tonight, and there's a party."

"Go." Epstein sighed. "Never mind about this. It can wait."

"Are you sure? I'll keep trying by phone."

But Epstein was not sure; such had been the slow unfurling of self-knowledge these last months, but only now, when his assistant posed the question, did he feel the wing beat of clarity pass overhead. He did not wish to be sure. Had lost his trust in it.

Out in the Blue

THE IDEA OF being in two places at once goes back a long way with me. Goes back for as long as I can remember, I should say, since one of my earliest memories is of watching a children's show on TV, and suddenly spotting myself in the small studio audience. Even now I can call up the sensation of the brown carpet in my parents' bedroom under my legs, and of craning my neck to see the TV, which seemed to be mounted very high above me, and then the sickening feeling that spread through my stomach as the excitement of seeing myself in that other world gave way to the certain knowledge that I'd never been there. One could say that the sense of self is still porous in young children. That the oceanic feeling persists for some time until the scaffolding is at last removed from the walls we labor to build around ourselves under the command of an innate instinct, however touched by the sadness that comes of knowing we'll spend the rest of our lives searching for an escape. And yet even today, I have absolutely no doubt about what I saw then. The little girl on the TV had my face exactly, and she wore my red sneakers and striped shirt, but even those could be chalked up to coincidence. What could not is that in her eyes, for the few seconds that the camera came to rest on them, I recognized the feeling of what it was to be me.

It may have been one of the earliest things my brain preserved, but as the years passed, I didn't think much about it. There was no reason to; I never encountered myself anywhere again. And yet the surprise of what I'd seen must have settled down through me, and as my sense of the world was built up on top of it, it must have alchemized into belief: not that there were two of me, which is the stuff of nightmares, but that I, in my uniqueness, might possibly be inhabiting two separate planes of existence. Or maybe it would be more accurate to look at it from the opposite angle, and call what began to crystalize in me then a sense of doubt—a skepticism toward the reality foisted on me, as it is foisted onto all children, which slowly displaces the other, more supple realities that naturally occur to them. In either case, the possibility of being both *here* and *there* was stored substrata along with all my other childish notions, until one autumn afternoon when I came through the door of the house I shared with my husband and our two children, and sensed that I was already there.

Simply that: already there. Moving through the rooms upstairs, or asleep in the bed; it hardly mattered where I was or what I was doing, what mattered was the certainty with which I knew that I was in the house already. I was myself, I felt utterly normal in my own skin, and yet at the same time I also had the sudden sense that I was no longer confined to my body, not to the hands, arms, and legs that I had been looking at all my life, and that these extremities, which were always moving or lying still in my field of vision, and which I had observed minute by minute for thirty-nine years, were not in fact my extremities after all, were not the furthest limit of myself, but that I existed beyond and separately from them. And not in an abstract sense, either. Not as a soul or a frequency. But full-bodied, exactly as

I was there on the threshold of the kitchen, but, somehow—elsewhere, upstairs—*again*.

Outside the window the clouds seemed to be passing swiftly, but otherwise nothing seemed strange or out of place. Just the opposite: everything in the house, every last cup, table, chair, and vase, seemed in its right place. Or even, in *exactly* the right place in a way they rarely do, because life has a way of enacting itself on the inanimate, forever shifting objects a little to the left or right. Over time this shifting accumulates to something noticeable—the frame on the wall is suddenly crooked, the books have receded to the back of the shelf—and so a great deal of our time is spent idly, often unconsciously, moving these things back to where they belong. We, too, wish to enact ourselves on the inanimate, which we want to believe we're sovereign over. But really, it's the unstoppable force and momentum of life that we want to control, and with which we're locked in a struggle of wills that we can never win.

But on that day, it was as if a magnet had been passed under the house, snapping each thing back to its proper position. Everything was touched by stillness, while only the clouds hurried by, as if the world had begun to turn a little more quickly. And as I stood halted in the kitchen doorway, that was my first thought: that time had sped up, and somehow I, on my way home, had fallen behind.

The skin down my back prickled as I stood frozen, afraid of moving. Some sort of error had occurred, neurological or metaphysical, and while it might have been as benign as déjà vu, it also might not have been. Something had become misaligned, and I felt that if I moved, I might destroy the chance of it naturally correcting itself.

Seconds passed, and then the telephone rang on the wall.

Instinctively, I turned to look at it. Somehow that broke the spell, because when I looked back again, the clouds were no longer racing, and the feeling that I was at once here and there—upstairs—was gone. The house was empty again but for me standing there in the kitchen, returned to the familiar limits of myself.

I had been sleeping badly for weeks. My work wasn't going well, and this left me feeling constantly anxious. But if my writing was a kind of sinking ship, the larger landscape—the sea in which I had begun to sense that every boat I tried to sail would eventually go under—was my failing marriage. My husband and I had drifted far apart. We were so devoted to our children that our growing distance could first be excused, then masked, by all the love and attentiveness that were regularly present in our house. But at a certain point the helpfulness of our shared love for the children had reached a kind of apex, and then began to decline until it was no longer helpful to our relationship at all, because it only shone a light on how alone each of us was, and, compared to our children, how unloved. The love we had once felt for and expressed toward each other had either dried up or been withheld—it was too confusing to know which—and yet day in and day out we each witnessed and were moved by the other's spectacular powers of love, evoked by the children. It was against my husband's nature to talk about difficult feelings. These he had learned long ago to hide not only from me but also from himself, and after many years of trying unsuccessfully to bring him into conversation about them, I'd slowly given up. Conflict was not allowed between us, let alone fury; everything had to go unspoken, while the surface remained passive. In this way, I'd found myself returned to a boundless loneliness that, while unhappy, was at least not foreign to me. "I am essentially a buoyant person," my husband once told me, "while you are a person who ponders everything." But over time the conditions both within and without had proved too much for his buoyancy, and he, too, was sinking in his separate sea. In our own ways, we had each come to understand that we had lost faith in our marriage. And yet we didn't know how to act on this understanding, as one does not know how to act on the understanding, for example, that the afterlife does not exist.

THAT IS WHERE things stood in my life. And now I also couldn't write, and, increasingly, couldn't sleep. It might have been easy to pass off the strange sensation I'd experienced that afternoon as the slip of a stressed and addled brain. But on the contrary, I couldn't remember my mind ever feeling as clear as it had during the moments that I'd stood in the kitchen, convinced that I was also somewhere else close by. As if my mind had been not just touched by clarity, but poised at its very pinnacle, and all my thoughts and perceptions had arrived etched in glass. And yet it wasn't the usual sort of clarity that results from understanding. It was as if foreground and background had shifted, and what I had been able to see was all that the mind normally blocks out: the endless expanse of not-understanding that surrounds the tiny island of what we can grasp.

Ten minutes later the doorbell rang. It was UPS, and I signed for the package. The deliveryman took back his little electronic device and handed me the large box. I saw the beads of sweat on his forehead, at odds with the chill in the air, and inhaled the smell of damp cardboard. From the street, my neighbor, an elderly actor, called out hello. A dog lifted its leg and relieved itself on the wheel of a car. But all of this did nothing to dim the intensity and strangeness of the sensation I'd just experienced. It didn't begin to dissolve, the way a dream does on contact with waking life. It remained incredibly vivid as I went about opening the cabinets and taking out the ingredients for dinner. The sensation was still so powerful that I had to sit down to try to absorb it.

Half an hour later, when the babysitter came home with the children, I was still sitting at the counter. My sons danced around me, full of the news of their days. Then they sprang loose from their orbit and went racing around the house. My husband arrived soon afterward. He came into the kitchen still wearing the reflector vest that he had biked home in. For a moment, he shone. I felt the sudden urge to describe to him what had happened, but when I was finished he gave me a strained half-smile, glanced at the unmade dinner ingredients, removed the folder of takeout menus, and asked if I felt like Indian. Then he went to go find the children upstairs. I immediately regretted having said anything. The incident touched a fault line between us. My husband prized facts above the impalpable, which he'd begun to collect and assemble around himself like a bulwark. At night he stayed up watching documentaries, and at social gatherings, when someone expressed surprise that he knew what percentage of the bills printed in the US were $100s, or that Scarlett Johansson was half Jewish, he liked to say that he made it his business to know everything.

THE DAYS PASSED, and the sensation didn't come again. I'd just gotten over the flu, which kept me in bed shivering and sweating and looking out at the sky with the slightly altered consciousness that illness always brings on me, and I started

44

to wonder if maybe that had something to do with it. When I'm sick, it's as if the walls between myself and the outside become more permeable—in fact they have, since whatever has made me ill has found a way to slip in, breaching the usual protective mechanisms the body employs, and as if mirroring the body, my mind too becomes more absorbent, and the things I normally keep at bay because they are too difficult or intense to think about begin to pour in. This state of openness, of extreme sensitivity in which I become susceptible to everything around me, is heightened by the loneliness of lying in bed while everyone else is busily going about their activities. And so it was easy to attribute the unusual sensation I'd experienced to my illness, even though by then I was already on the mend.

Then one evening a month later, I was listening to the radio while doing the dishes, and a program came on about the multiverse—the possibility that the universe actually contains many universes, perhaps even an infinite set of them. That as a result of the gravitational waves that occurred in the first fraction of a second after the Big Bang—or a series of Big Bang repulsions, as evidence now suggests—the early universe experienced an inflation that caused an exponential expansion of the dimensions of space to many times the size of our own cosmos, creating completely different universes with unknown physical properties, without stars, perhaps, or atoms, or light, and that, taken all together, these comprise the entirety of space, time, matter, and energy.

I had no more than a layman's understanding of current theories of cosmology, but whenever I came across an article about string theory, or branes, or the work being done at the Large Hadron Collider in Geneva, my interest was always piqued, and so by now I knew a little bit. The physicist being interviewed had a mesmerizing voice, at once patient and intimate, full of deep, underground intelligence, and at some point, at the host's inevitable prodding, he began to touch on the theological ramifications of multiverse theories, or at least the way they confirmed the role of chance in the creation of life, since if there is not one but an infinite or nearly infinite set of worlds, each with its own physical laws, then no condition can any longer be considered the result of extraordinary mathematical improbabilities.

When the program came to an end, I switched the radio off and heard the low, rising hum of cars approaching as the traffic lights turned a few blocks away, and the clear, bright sound of children's voices in the nursery school run out of the basement of the neighboring apartment building, and then the deep, mournful horn of a ship in the harbor some three miles away, like a finger left down on the harmonium. I'd never allowed myself to believe in God, but I could see why theories of a multiverse could get under a certain kind of person's skin—if nothing else, to say that everything might be true somewhere not only carried the whiff of evasion but also rendered any searching useless, since all conclusions become equally valid. Doesn't part of the awe that fills us when we confront the unknown come from understanding that, should it at last flood into us and become known, we would be altered? In our view of the stars, we find a measure of our own incompleteness, our still-yet unfinishedness, which is to say, our potential for change, even transformation. That our species is distinguished from others by our hunger and capacity for change has everything to do with our ability to recognize the limits of our understanding, and to contemplate the unfathomable. But in a multiverse, the concepts of known and unknown are rendered useless, for everything is equally known and unknown. If there are infinite worlds and infinite sets of laws, then nothing is essential, and we are relieved from straining past the limits of our immediate reality and comprehension, since not only does what lies beyond not apply to us, there is also no hope of gaining anything more than infinitesimally small understanding. In that sense, the multiverse theory only encourages us to turn our backs even further on the unknowable, which we're more than happy to do, having become drunk on our powers of knowing—having made a *holiness* out of knowing, and busying ourselves all day and night in our pursuit of it. Just as religion evolved as a way to contemplate and live before the unknowable, so now have we converted to the opposite practice, to which we are no less devoted: the practice of knowing everything, and believing that knowledge is concrete, and always arrived at through the faculties of the intellect. Since Descartes, knowledge has been empowered to a nearly unimaginable degree. But in the end it didn't lead to the mastery and possession of nature he imagined, only to the illusion of its mastery and possession. In the end, we have made ourselves ill with knowledge. I frankly hate Descartes, and have never understood why his axiom should be trusted as an unshakable foundation for anything. The more he talks about following a straight line out of the forest, the more appealing it sounds to me to get lost in that forest, where once we lived in wonder, and understood it to be a prerequisite for an authentic awareness of being and the world. Now we have little choice but to live in the arid fields of reason, and as for the unknown, which once lay glittering at the farthest edge of our gaze, channeling our fear but also our hope and longing, we can only regard it with aversion.

To all of that, the idea that began to take shape in my mind after I turned off the radio came as a form of relief. What if, I thought, rather than existing in a universal space, each of us is actually born alone into a luminous blankness, and it's we who snip it into pieces, assembling staircases and gardens and train stations in our own peculiar fashion, until we have pared our space into a world? In other words, what if it's human perception and creativity that are responsible for creating the multiverse? Or maybe—

What if life, which appears to take place down countless long hallways, in waiting rooms and foreign cities, on terraces, in hospitals and gardens, rented rooms and crowded trains, in truth occurs in only one place, a single location from which one dreams of those other places?

Was it really so far-flung? Just as plants need us to be drawn to their flowers so they can thrive and multiply, might not space also depend on us? We think we've conquered it with our houses and roads and cities, but what if we're the ones who have unwittingly been made subordinate to space, to its elegant design to propagate itself infinitely through the dreams of finite beings? What if it isn't we who move through space, but space that moves through us, spun on the loom of our minds? And if all of that is so, then where is this place from which we lie and dream? A holding tank in nonspace? Some dimension we're unconscious of? Or is it somewhere in the one finite world from which billions of worlds have been, and will be, born, a single location different for each of us, equally banal as any other?

In that moment, I knew unequivocally that if I was dreaming my life from anywhere, it was the Tel Aviv Hilton.

TO BEGIN WITH, I was conceived there. In the wake of the Yom Kippur War, three years after my parents were married in high winds on the Hilton's terrace, they were occupying a room on the hotel's sixteenth floor when the unique conditions that were the prerequisites for my existence suddenly aligned. With only the foggiest sense of the consequences, my mother and father instinctively acted on them. I was born in Beth Israel Hospital in New York City. But less than a year later, swimming upstream, my parents brought me back to the Tel Aviv Hilton, and from then on, almost every year, I've returned to that hotel perched on a hill between Hayarkon Street and the Mediterranean Sea. (Every year, that is, if one is operating under the belief that I ever left it at all.) But if the place has a kind of mystical aura for me, it isn't only because life began for me there, or that later I spent so many vacations at the hotel. It's also the spine-tingling nature of something that once happened to me there, an experience that only increased my awareness of an opening—a small tear in the fabric of reality.

It occurred in the hotel's swimming pool when I was seven. I spent a lot of time in that pool, which was set on a large terrace overlooking the sea, and fed by its salt water. The year before, our visit had overlapped with Itzhak Perlman's, and one morning after breakfast we came out and found him parked by the deep end, throwing a ball to his children, who took turns leaping into the pool, trying to catch it. The sight of the great violinist in his glinting wheelchair, along with a murky awareness that the polio that had crippled him had something to do with swimming pools, terrified me. The next day I refused to go down to the pool altogether, and the day after that we left Israel and flew back to New York. The following year I returned to the hotel with a feeling of unease, but Perlman didn't reappear. Furthermore, on the first day back my brother and I discovered that the pool was full of money—shekels everywhere, shimmering mutely on the floor of the pool, as if the drain were hooked up to Bank Hapoalim. Whatever lingering fears I had about swimming were shunted aside by the steady flow of cash we could turn up. As in any well-run operation, we soon divided and specialized: my brother, two years older, became the diver, and I, with a smaller lung capacity and keener eyes, became the spotter. At my direction, he would plunge down and grope around at the blurry bottom. If I had been right, as I was about sixty-five percent of the time, he would burst excitedly to the surface, clutching the coin.

One afternoon after a string of false calls I began to feel desperate. The day was wearing on, and our time in the pool was almost up. My brother was wading morosely along the wall of the shallow end. I couldn't help myself, and from the middle of the pool shouted: "There!" I was lying—I'd seen nothing—but I couldn't resist the chance to make my brother happy again. He came splashing toward me. "Right there!" I yelled.

He went below. I knew there was nothing at the bottom, and now, treading water at the top, I waited miserably for my brother to find out, too. The crushing guilt I felt in those few moments comes vividly back even more than thirty years later. It was one thing to lie to my parents, but to so blatantly betray my brother was something else again.

As for what happened next, I have no explanation for it. Or

none beyond the possibility that the laws we cling to in order to assure ourselves that all is as it seems have occluded a more complex view of the universe, one that forgoes the comfort of squeezing the world to fit the limited reach of our comprehension. Otherwise, how else to explain that when my brother surfaced and uncurled his fingers, lying in his palm was an earring with three diamonds and, beneath them, hanging from a gold loop at the bottom, a ruby heart?

In dripping bathing suits, we followed our mother through the frigid, air-conditioned hallways of the hotel to the H.Stern's in the lobby. She explained the situation to the balding jeweler, who looked at us dubiously as he pushed a tray lined with blue velvet across the glass countertop. My mother laid the earring down, and the jeweler fit the loupe to his eye. He studied our treasure. When he lifted his head at last, his giant, magnified eye swiveled over us. "Real," he pronounced. "The gold is eighteen-karat."

Real. The word catches in the throat and won't go down. It never occurred to me then that the earring might be fake in the way my mother had suspected it was. And yet only I knew just how *unreal* it really was, how against the odds was my brother's discovery of it. How it had materialized in answer to a need. No young child naturally believes that reality is firm. To her its springs are loose; it is open to her special pleading. But slowly she is taught to believe otherwise, and by then I was seven, old enough to have mostly come around to accepting that reality was fixed and utterly indifferent to my longings. Now, at the last minute, a foot was put in the way of a door closing.

Back in New York, my mother had the earring made into a pendant, which she strung for me on a chain to wear around my neck. I wore it for years, and though my mother couldn't have known it, the necklace served to remind me of some unknown will, of the accordion folds tucked beneath the surface of all that appears to be flat. Only last year, my brother and I learned that it was our father who'd thrown all those coins into the pool— our father, who back then could turn to us with either love or terrifying fury, neither of which we were ever prepared for. I'd thought the necklace lost, but it had turned up when my parents emptied a safe-deposit box where they had stored some of my mother's jewelry. It was returned to me in a tiny bag, which also contained one of my father's ubiquitous labels, tapped out long ago on his trusty Brother P-touch: *Nicole's necklace, found in Hilton pool.* The necklace provoked some reminiscing, and it was then that my father casually mentioned that it was he who had filled the pool with coins. He was surprised that we'd never guessed. But no, he'd had nothing to do with the earring with the ruby heart.

WHEN THE IDEA came to me of dreaming my life from the Hilton, I was, as I've said, in a difficult place in my life and my work. The things I'd allowed myself to believe in—the unassailability of love, the power of narrative, which could carry people through their lives together without divergence, the essential health of domestic life—I no longer believed in. I had lost my way. And so the theory of having always been solidly somewhere, only dreaming of being lost, was especially appealing. I was between books, and knew it could take me years to find my way into a new one. During those exhausting and incoherent periods, I sometimes think I can feel my mind itself disintegrating. My thoughts become agitated and restless, and my imagination darts around, picking things up before judging them useless and dropping them again.

But now something different began to happen. The Hilton became lodged in my mind like a kind of blockage, and for months little else presented itself to me when I sat down to write. Day after day, I dutifully reported to my desk—reported, as it were, to the Tel Aviv Hilton. At first it was interesting: Maybe there was something in it? And then, when there seemed not to be, it became exhausting. Finally, it was only maddening. The hotel wouldn't go away, but neither could I squeeze anything from it.

And not just any hotel: a massive concrete rectangle on stilts that dominates the Tel Aviv coast, built in the Brutalist style. The long sides of the rectangle are lined with terraces, fourteen rows down and twenty-three across. On the south side the grid is unbroken, but on the north side it's interrupted two-thirds of the way across by a giant concrete column that appears to have been wedged in as an afterthought to make certain the building could pass muster with even the most extreme Brutalists. The top of this concrete column rises above the roof and is emblazoned on the south side with the Hilton logo. Above it stretches a tall antenna whose tip glows red at night, so that light aircraft headed for Sde Dov airport don't crash into it. The longer one considers this monstrosity cantilevered out over the shore, the more one begins to sense that some larger purpose is being served that can only be guessed at, geological or mystical—something to do not with us but with far greater entities. When viewed from the south, the hotel stands alone against the blue sky, and encoded in the unrelenting grid there seems to be a message nearly as mysterious as the one we've yet to unlock at Stonehenge.

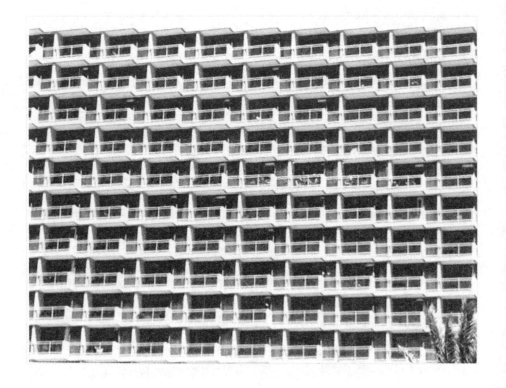

It was to this monolith that I was mentally confined for half a year. What began as a whimsical idea of dreaming all of life from a fixed point now became a disquieting sense of being tethered to that point, shut up inside it, without access to the dream of other spaces. Day in and day out, month after month, the needle of my imagination scratched a deeper groove. I could hardly explain my preoccupation to myself, let alone to anyone else. Slowly, the hotel passed into unrealness. The more I remained stuck on it, locked in a futile attempt to wrestle something from it, the further removed the hotel became from being real, and the more it seemed to be a metaphor to which I couldn't find the key. The more it seemed to be my mind itself. Desperate for relief, I imagined a flood in which the Hilton would break loose from the shore.

Then one morning in early March my father's cousin Effie called from Israel. Retired from his work in the Foreign Service, Effie still kept the habit of reading three or four newspapers a day. Occasionally coming across a mention of me, he would phone me up. Now we discussed his wife Naama's colitis, the results of the recent elections, and whether or not he would get arthroscopic surgery on his knee. When the conversation came around to me, and Effie asked how my work was going, I found myself telling him about my struggle with the Hilton and the way I'd become haunted by it. I don't often speak about my work while I'm in the middle of it, but over the course of four decades, ever since the hotel opened in 1965 and my grandparents began staying there, Effie had sat with my family in the lobby, by the pool, or in the King Solomon restaurant more times than anyone could remember, and I thought that he of all people might understand the Hilton's strange grip on me. But he was distracted just then by a call from his granddaughter coming through on his cell phone, and after he'd briefly answered her and switched back to me, the subject shifted to her budding career as a cabaret singer.

Our conversation drew to an end. Effie asked me to send his love to my parents. We were on the verge of hanging up when, as casually as if he'd remembered some bit of family news he'd almost forgotten to mention, he said, "Did you hear that a man fell to his death there last week?"

"Where?"

"You were talking about the Hilton, no?"

I assumed it was a suicide, though in the days that followed, without knowing the first thing about the dead man, not even his name, I came to wonder whether it hadn't been an accident. Though the long sides of the rectangular building face north and south, the windows and terraces protrude at a diagonal, in a sawtooth pattern, to allow for a better view of the Mediterranean to the west. This makes it possible to take in part of the sea, but when you look out, whether northwest toward the port of Tel Aviv or southwest toward Jaffa, a feeling of irritation arises of not being able to see enough of it—of being kept from seeing it properly. Rare must be the guest who doesn't curse the hotel's architects. How many times had I, in frustration, opened the sliding door in my room and stepped out onto the terrace for a better view? But even there the dissatisfaction persists, because it's still impossible to face the sea and the horizon head-on, as every atom in your body cries out to do. All that's left is to lean out over the terrace's railing, craning your head. In this way, desirous of a better view of the waves that brought the cedars from Lebanon and carried Jonah to Tarshish, you could easily go too far—far enough that you might go over.

Effie promised to try to find the clipping, but was dubious about turning it up: Naama always took out the trash on Sunday, and he had read the story at least a week earlier. I could find no mention of the death anywhere in *Haaretz* or Ynet, or any other English source of Israeli news online. That afternoon I wrote to my friend Matti Friedman, a journalist from Jerusalem via Toronto, asking if he would search the Israeli press for the report of a death at the Hilton. Because of the time difference, I didn't receive his reply until the following morning. He'd been unable to find anything, he wrote. Was I sure it had been the Hilton?

IF I'D ALREADY suspected Effie's reliability, I had my reasons. Throughout my childhood, he'd been the Israeli consul to a series of countries, each smaller than the last—first Costa Rica, then Swaziland, and finally Liechtenstein, after which he had no choice but to retire. He was twelve years older than my father, and rationing during World War II had stunted his growth, leaving him stalled at five foot. When I was a little girl, I'd developed the impression not only that his bodily size was relevant to his diplomatic appointments but that everything about these small nations was scaled down in size like my father's cousin: the cars, the doors and chairs, the minuscule fruit, and the house slippers ordered in child's sizes from the factories of larger countries. In other words, Effie seemed to me to live in a slightly fanciful world, an impression that, like so many formed in childhood, never fully left me. If anything, it was only further confirmed when Effie phoned me back a few days later. Having risen at dawn all his life—the night, like everything else, was too large for him—he had no qualms about calling early, but on that day, at seven in the morning, I happened to be already at my desk.

A roar came through the phone, and I couldn't understand what was being said on the other end.

"What was that?" I interrupted. "I didn't hear the first part."

"Fighter jets. Hold a second." There was a muffled noise of a hand being placed over the phone. Then Effie came back on. "Must be training exercises. Can you hear me now?"

The article hadn't turned up, Effie said, but something else had, something he thought would be far more interesting to me. He'd received a phone call the day before, he told me. "Out in the blue," he added. He took a special joy in English idioms but rarely got them right.

"It was Eliezer Friedman. We used to work for Abba Eban together. I left, but Eliezer stayed on when Eban became foreign minister. He became involved in intelligence. Later he went back to university, and became a professor of literature at the university in Tel Aviv. But you know how these things go—he never gave up his ties to the Mossad."

While Effie spoke, I looked out the window. There'd been a storm all that morning, but the rain had let up and the sky had opened to let down a soft light. I worked on the top floor, in a room that overlooked the roofs of the neighboring houses. While Effie carried on talking, telling me about how his friend wanted to get in touch, the hatch on the roof across the way suddenly popped open, and my neighbor climbed out onto the wet, silvery skin of his pristine roof. He was wearing a dark suit, as if dressed for his job on Wall Street. Without any signs of caution, this tall, skinny man from the northern flatlands of Holland approached the edge of the roof in polished black dress shoes. With the meticulousness of a surgeon, he pulled on a pair of blue rubber gloves. Then he turned his back to me, reached into his pocket as if to answer a call on a ringing phone, and removed a plastic bag. Standing at the very edge of the slick roof, he peered over. For a moment, it seemed he meant to jump. If he didn't, surely he would slip in the smooth leather dress shoes. But in the end all that happened was that he kneeled down and began to fish wet leaves out of the gutter. This operation, which seemed full of obscure meaning, took three or four minutes. When he'd finished, he knotted the bag, briskly retreated to the open hatch, lowered himself down backward, and pulled it closed behind him.

"So what do you think?" Effie was saying.

"About what?"

"You'll talk to him?"

"Who? Your Mossad friend?"

"I told you, he has something he wants to discuss."

"With me?" I laughed. "You're not serious."

"I couldn't be more serious," he said gravely.

"What does he want?"

"He won't tell me. Only wants to talk to you."

It occurred to me that Effie might be starting to lose his grip—he was already seventy-nine; the mind doesn't last forever. But, no, probably he was just exaggerating in his usual fashion. When the time came, I would find out that it wasn't actually his friend who was a former Mossad agent, but a friend of his friend. Or that his friend only delivered the mail in the Mossad offices, or performed at their holiday parties.

"All right, so give him my number."

"He wants to know if you have plans to come to Israel anytime soon."

But I had no such plans, I told Effie, and as I said it I realized that I lacked plans in general, and had not managed to make them for some time. When I brought the calendar up onto my computer screen, it was largely empty except for the children's activities. To plan things, one must be able to imagine oneself into a future that is an extension of the present, and it seemed to me that I had ceased to imagine that, whether out of inability or lack of desire, I couldn't say. But of course Effie couldn't know as much. He knew only that I still traveled to Israel often—my brother now lived in Tel Aviv with his family, and my sister also had an apartment there where she spent part of the year. Along with them, I had many close friends in Tel Aviv, and my children had already spent enough time there that they, too, had incorporated the place into the landscape of their childhoods.

"I might come soon," I said, without attaching much meaning to the words. Effie said he would talk to Friedman and get back to me, and I did not attach much meaning to his words, either.

A moment of silence passed between us, and there was a sudden brightening outside, as if the light had been rinsed clear. Then Effie reminded me to tell my father to call him.

A MONTH LATER I said good-bye to my husband and children and flew from New York to Tel Aviv. The idea to go had come to me in the middle of the night during one of the long passages outside of time, in which I found myself wide awake even as I became increasingly exhausted. Or rather, I'd dragged a suitcase out of the downstairs closet at three in the morning and filled it with an assortment of clothes, without having spoken to my husband about the idea of going, and without having called the airlines about a flight. Then I finally fell asleep and forgot about the suitcase entirely, so that when I awoke its squat, hopeful presence by the door came as a surprise not only to my husband but to me as well. In this way, I seemed to have gotten around the impossibility of planning. I was already going, as it were, having skipped the planning stage altogether, which would have required a sense of conviction and powers of projection currently unavailable to me.

When my sons asked the reason for my trip, I said that I needed to conduct research for my book. What is it about? the younger one asked. He was constantly writing stories, as many as three a day, and would not have been troubled by such a question concerning his own writing. For a long time he'd spelled the words as he thought they might be spelled, without any spaces between them, which, like the Torah's unbroken string of letters, opened his writing to infinite interpretations. He had only begun to ask us how things were spelled once he'd started to use the electric typewriter he was given for his birthday, as if it were the machine that had demanded it of him—the machine, with its air of professionalism and the reproach of its giant space bar, that required that what was written on it be understood. But my son himself remained ambivalent about the matter. When he wrote by hand, he returned to his old habits.

I told him that the book had to do with the Hilton in Tel Aviv, and asked if he remembered the hotel, where we had sometimes stayed with my parents. He shook his head. Unlike my older son, whose memory was like a steel trap, the younger one seemed to recall little of his experience. I chose to think of this not as a native lack, but rather the result of being too absorbed in the invention of other worlds to pay very much attention to what happened in the one world he had so little say in. My older son wanted to know why I needed to research a hotel I had been to so many times, and the younger one wanted to know the meaning of "research." Naturally they are both artists, my children. After all, the world population of artists has exploded, almost no one is not an artist now; in turning our attention inward, so have we turned all of our hope inward, believing that meaning can be found or made there. Having cut ourselves off from all that is unknowable and that might truly fill us with awe, we can only find wonderment in our own powers of creativity. My children's progressive, highly creative private school was primarily engaged with teaching every child enrolled there to believe that he or she was, and could only be, an artist. One day, speaking about my father on the walk to school, my younger son suddenly stopped short and looked up at me in wonder. "Isn't it *amazing*?" he asked. "Just *think* of it. Grandpa is a doctor. A *doctor*!"

After they went to sleep, I called the Hilton to see whether a room was available. If I was going to write a novel about the Hilton, or modeled on the Hilton, or even razing the Hilton to the ground, then it made sense, I reasoned, that the obvious place to finally begin writing was at the actual Hilton itself.

THE EL AL FLIGHT was oversold as usual, ensuring that even before takeoff the atmosphere was tense and hostile; the mixing of the orthodox and the secular in such cramped quarters only aggravated things, as did the mounting tension of the situation. In recent weeks, the shooting of a young Palestinian by the IDF had been followed by brutal killings of both Israeli and Palestinian youth, lengthening the long chain of savage revenge. Houses were demolished in the West Bank, and rockets were fired from Gaza, a few reaching as far as the sky above Tel Aviv, where they were exploded by Israel's interceptor missiles. I heard no one around me speak of this; it was an all too familiar script. But less than an hour into the flight, the edginess erupted in an argument between a woman in a drab headscarf and a college student who had reclined her seat. "Get out of my lap!" the Orthodox woman shrieked, pounding the back of the girl's chair with both fists. An American passenger in his forties put his hand on the woman's arm in an effort to calm her, but this new affront—an Orthodox woman may not be touched by any man other than her husband—nearly sent her into an apoplectic fit. In the end, only the purser, trained to deal with sociological friction just as he is trained to deal with a loss of cabin pressure or a hijacking, was able to calm the woman by finding someone willing to switch seats with her. While all of this was happening, an elderly couple seated across the aisle from me went steadily at each other's throats, as they must have been doing for the last half century ("Why the hell would I know? Leave me alone. Don't talk to me," the man spat, but the wife, immune to his insults, went on talking to him all the same). Some of us are touched too much, and some too little: it is the balance that seems impossible to get right, and the lack of which unravels most relationships in the end. In front of the married couple, a woman balanced a wig on her fist, calmly brushing out the coppery tresses while gazing transfixed at the small screen on the seatback in front of her where Russell Crowe was traipsing around in his metal gladiator skirt. When she'd finished with the hair, the woman retrieved a Styrofoam head mold from under her feet, popped the *sheitel* onto it, and, with a carelessness that belied all the brushing, tossed the whole thing into the overhead compartment next to the bulging carry-on of the loquacious wife, which had been squeezed into its tight spot only thanks to the strength of three teenage boys from Birthright.

TWELVE HOURS LATER, Meir, the taxi driver who'd been retrieving my family from Ben Gurion Airport for thirty years, met me outside of the baggage claim. After I spent a summer during college living with a family in Barcelona, Meir had gotten into the habit of addressing me in Spanish, since he had spoken Ladino to his parents growing up, and his Spanish was better than both his English and my Hebrew. Over the years I had forgotten what little Spanish I'd once had, so that where once I understood him somewhat, now I understood him hardly at all. As soon as we pulled away from the curb, he began to speak excitedly and at great length about the missiles and the success of the Iron Dome, and I pretended to understand what he was saying because it was far too late to explain that I didn't.

It was winter in Tel Aviv, and as such the city didn't make sense, being based around the sun and the sea, a Mediterranean city up at all hours that got more frenetic the later it became. Dirty leaves and pages of old newspapers blew down the streets, and sometimes people plucked them out of the air and put them over their heads to protect themselves from the occasional rain. The apartments were all cold because they had stone floors, and during the hot months, which felt interminable, it seemed absurd to imagine it could ever be cold again, so no one bothered to install central heating. I opened the window of Meir's taxi, and in the sea air mixed with the rain I could almost smell the metallic scent of electric heaters, their brilliant orange coils aglow in people's apartments like artificial hearts, forever threatening to explode or, at the very least, to short-circuit the city.

As we made our way through the streets, I saw again the familiar set of everything Israeli—jaws, postures, buildings, trees—as if the strange conditions of enduring in that small corner of the Levant produced a uniform shape; the hard, determined form of that which lives and grows in opposition.

Why had I really come to Tel Aviv? In a story, a person always needs a reason for the things she does. Even where there appears to be no motivation, later on it is always revealed by the subtle architecture of plot and resonance that there was one. Narrative cannot sustain formlessness any more than light can sustain darkness—it is the antithesis of formlessness, and so it can never truly communicate it. Chaos is the one truth that narrative must always betray, for in the creation of its delicate structures that reveal many truths about life, the portion of truth that has to do with incoherence and disorder must be obscured. More and more, it had felt to me that in the things I wrote, the degree of artifice was greater than the degree of truth, that the cost of administering a form to what was essentially formless was akin to the cost of breaking the spirit of an animal that is too dangerous to otherwise live with. One could observe the truth of the animal at closer range, without the risk of violence, but it was a truth whose spirit had been altered. The more I wrote, the more suspect the good sense and studied beauty achieved by the mechanisms of narrative seemed to me. I didn't want to give them up—didn't want to live without their consolation. I wanted to employ them in a form that could contain the formless, so that it might be held close, as meaning is held close, and grappled with. It should have felt impossible, but instead it felt merely elusive, so I couldn't give up the aspiration. The Hilton had seemed to promise itself as such a form—the house of the mind that conjures the world—but in the end I failed to fill it with any meaning.

Lost in these thoughts, the burble of Meir's Spanish passing over me in rising and falling syllables, I hardly noticed as we drove up the driveway of the actual Hilton. Only when we pulled up under the concrete canopy that overhangs the entrance to the lobby, and my eyes fell on the giant revolving door encased in a steel cylinder with the words HILTON TEL AVIV above it, was I suddenly hit with the strangeness of arriving there. I'd been inhabiting the hotel psychically for so many months that now its real, physical manifestation was jarring; and yet, at the same time, the place was—and could only be—profoundly familiar. Freud called this confluence of sensations the *unheimlich*, a word that captures the creeping horror at the heart of the feeling far better than the English *uncanny*. I'd read his paper on the subject in college but only vaguely remembered it, and when I got to my room, I was too exhausted to do anything but take a nap. On top of which, now that I was finally there at the hotel, it struck me—the carpeted hallways, sterile furniture, and plastic card keys—as all so mundane that I couldn't help feeling foolish about the absurdity of my last few months' obsession.

All the same, the following morning, after calling home and speaking to my children, I tracked down Freud's paper, which now struck me as critical reading for my Hilton novel, without which I couldn't possibly begin. Laid out across the hotel bed, I began to read about the etymology of the German word, which derives from *Heim*, "home," so that *heimlich* means "familiar, native, or belonging to the home." Freud wrote his essay in response to the work of Ernst Jentsch, who'd described the *unheimlich* as the opposite of *heimlich*: as the result of an encounter with the new and unfamiliar, which causes a feeling of uncertainty, of not knowing "where one is." But while *heimlich* may mean "familiar" and "homelike," its secondary meaning, Freud points out, encompasses both "concealed" and "kept from sight," as well as "to discover or disclose what is secret," and even "withdrawn from conscious" (Grimm's dictionary), so that as *heimlich* progresses through its shades of meaning, it eventually coincides with its opposite, *unheimlich*, which the German writer Schelling defined as "the name for everything that ought to have remained . . . hidden and secret, and has become visible."

Of the circumstances likely to cause an uncanny feeling, the first Freud mentions is the idea of the double. Like a slap to the forehead, I recalled what had happened half a year earlier, when I'd arrived home and felt certain that I was already there, an experience that had begun the chain of thoughts that brought me here, to the Hilton. Other examples Freud gives are an involuntary return to the same situation, and the repetition of something random that creates a sense of the fateful or inescapable. What all of these share is the centrality of recurrence, and, arriving at the heart of his study, Freud finally proposes the *unheimlich* as a special class of anxiety that arises from something repressed that recurs. In the annals of etymology, where *heimlich* and *unheimlich* reveal themselves as one and the same, we find the secret to this very particular kind of anxiety, Freud tells us, which arises from the encounter not after all with something new and foreign but rather with something familiar and old from which the mind has been estranged by the process of repression. *Something that ought to have been kept concealed, but that has nevertheless come to light.*

I shut my laptop and went out onto the balcony. But a sudden wave of nausea hit me as I glanced down at the stone walkway twelve floors below, and remembered the man who may have snapped his spine or smashed his skull there. The day before, on my way out for an evening walk in the thin rain, I'd spotted the hotel's general manager in the lobby and had almost chased him down to question him about the incident. But he'd stopped to shake the hand of a guest, and I saw how he radiated a smooth confidence that came, so it seemed to me, of knowing his guests' minds even better than they knew themselves, of understanding their desires and even their weaknesses, while at the same time pretending *not* to know, for the secret to his job must lie in making the guest feel that it is *he* who was in control, *he* who asks and receives, *he* whose commands send everyone scurrying. Watching the general manager in action, glowing with hidden intelligence, light glinting off the gold pin on his lapel that signaled some obscure order of excellence, I lost all hope of getting anything out of him. If one of his guests had fallen or jumped to his death, surely this general manager would have done everything in his power to keep the news under wraps in order not to unsettle the other guests, just as now he had done everything possible to enable them to ignore the fact that the occasional missile might be lobbed over from Gaza: after all, in a matter of seconds it would be converted from real into unreal overhead, with nothing but a sonic boom as evidence.

Now the sun had come out again, the world sharpened again by its intelligence. There was no sign of any disturbance. Light sparkled on the blue-green surface of the water. How many times had I looked out at this view? Many more times than I could remember, that much was certain. If Freud were right about the uncanny stemming from something repressed that comes to light, what could be more *unheimlich* than returning to a place that one realizes one may never have left?

Heim—home. Yes, the place one has always been, however hidden from one's awareness, could only be called that, couldn't it? And yet, in another way, doesn't home only become home if one goes away from it, since it's only with distance, only in the return, that we are able to recognize it as the place that shelters our true self?

Or maybe I was turning to the wrong language for the answer. In Hebrew, the world is *olam*, and now I remembered that my father had once told me that the word comes from the root *alam*, which means "to hide," or "to conceal." In Freud's examination of where *heimlich* and *unheimlich* dissolve into one another and illuminate an anxiety (something that ought to have been kept concealed, but that has nevertheless come to light), he nearly touched the wisdom of his Jewish ancestors. But in the end, stuck with German and the anxieties of the modern mind, he fell short of their radicalism. For the ancient Jews, the world was always both hidden and revealed.

WHEN I FINALLY met Eliezer Friedman two days later, I was more than half an hour late. A plan had been made to meet for breakfast at Fortuna del Mare, a few minutes' walk from the Hilton. But having finally fallen asleep at three in the morning, I slept through the alarm I'd set and only woke up when Friedman rang the room. It was the first time we'd spoken—all the arrangements had been made through Effie—and yet his accent, Israeli but inflected with a childhood German, was deeply familiar to me from my grandmother and her friends, the women she took me to visit as a child whose apartment doors opened in Tel Aviv but whose hallways led to lost corners of Nuremberg and Berlin.

I sputtered an apology, threw on some clothes, and raced down to the beach through the hotel's back exit. I'd been to the restaurant before, a little Italian place with a handful of tables in view of the masts of the sailboats in the marina. Seated at the farthest table in the corner was a little man with a crown of gauzy white hair; all of the color had been sucked down into his dark, bushy eyebrows. Two deep furrows extended from just above his nostrils to either side of his lips, which turned sharply downward at the corners. Altogether the effect was of a gravity that looked to be irreversible until it reached the chin, which tilted upward in proud defiance. He was dressed in an old khaki field vest with bulging pockets, though, judging by the cane hooked neatly on the table edge next to his right leg, any kind of fieldwork had long become impossible. I hurried over to the table and spilled out more apologies.

"Sit," Friedman said. "I won't get up, if you don't mind," he added. I shook the thick-fingered hand he extended and sat down across from him, still trying to catch my breath. Fumbling with the buttons of my jean jacket, I felt him studying me with a steady gaze.

"You're younger than I thought."

I stopped myself from saying that he was more or less as old as I'd thought, and that I was no longer as young as I looked.

Friedman called the waitress over and insisted I order some breakfast even though I wasn't hungry. I assumed he'd ordered for himself already, and chose something so he wouldn't have to eat alone. But when she returned, it was with a plate of food for me and only a cup of coffee for him. Despite his shortness—it was no wonder he and Effie had sought each other out—there was something commanding about him. And yet when he lifted the spoon to wring out the tea bag, I thought I saw his hand shake. But his gray eyes, magnified behind the smoky lenses, seemed to miss nothing.

He wasted no time with small talk, and right away started in with questions. I hadn't expected to be interviewed. But it wasn't only his authoritative presence that made me prone to revealing myself; it was also something about the attentiveness with which he listened to my answers. It was a windy day, and the sailboats gently rocked and clinked in the marina while whitecaps rammed the breakwater. I found myself speaking freely about my many memories of Israel, of stories my father had told me of his childhood in Tel Aviv, and of my own relationship with the city, which often felt to me more like my true home than anywhere else. When he asked me what I meant, I tried to explain how I felt comfortable with people here in a way I never did in America, because everything could be touched, so little was hidden or held back, people were hungry to engage with whatever the other had to offer, however messy and intense, and this openness and immediacy made me feel more alive and less alone; made me feel, I suppose, that an authentic life was more possible. Many things that were possible in America were impossible in Israel, but in Israel it was also impossible to feel nothing, to provoke nothing, to walk down the street and not exist. But my love for Tel Aviv went further than that, I told him. The shameless dilapidation of the buildings, sweetened by the bright fuchsia bougainvillea that grew over the rust and the cracks, asserting the importance of accidental beauty over that of keeping up appearances. The way the city seemed to refuse constriction; how everywhere, always, suddenly, one ran into pockets of surreality where reason was exploded like an unclaimed suitcase at Ben Gurion.

To all this, Friedman nodded and said that he wasn't surprised, he had always sensed an affinity with this place in my work. Only then did he at last begin to guide the conversation toward my writing, and the reason he'd asked to meet.

"I've read your novels. We all have," he said, gesturing toward the other tables in the restaurant. "You're adding to the Jewish story. For this, we're very proud of you."

It was unclear who the "we" in question was, since the restaurant was empty but for an old dog with a dusty coat of curly hair, lying on its side in the sunlight. Regardless, the compliment touched a nerve in me, as it has been touching a nerve in Jewish progeny for millennia. On the one hand, I was flattered. I *wanted* to please. From the time I was a child, I'd understood the necessity of being good and doing whatever possible to make my parents proud. I don't know that I ever fully explored what was behind the necessity, beyond that it plugged a hole through which darkness could otherwise spill, a darkness that always threatened to pull my parents under. But even as I brought home accolades by the armful and stuffed my parents with pride, I resented the burden and the contortions it required, and knew all too well how it hemmed me in. The very first Jewish child was bound and nearly sacrificed for something more important than him, and ever since Abraham came down from Mount Moriah, a terrible father but a good Jew, the question of how to go on binding has hung in

74

the air. If a loophole was found out of Abraham's violence, it was this: Let the ropes be invisible, let there be no proof that they exist, except that the more the child grows, the more painful they get, until one day he looks down and sees that it's his own hand doing the tightening. In other words, teach Jewish children to bind themselves. And for what? Not for beauty, like the Chinese, and not even for God, or the dream of a miracle. We bind and are bound because the binding binds us to those who were bound before us, and those bound before them, and those before them, in a chain of ropes and knots that goes back three thousand years, which is how long we've been dreaming of cutting ourselves loose, of falling out of this world, and into another where we aren't stunted and deformed to fit the past, but left to grow wild, toward the future.

But now there was more. The need to make one's parents proud is deforming enough; the pressure to make one's whole people proud is something else again. Writing had begun so differently for me. At the age of fourteen or fifteen, I'd grasped it as a way to organize myself—not just to explore and discover, but to consciously grow myself. But if it had been a serious occupation, it had also been playful and full of pleasure. And yet as time passed, and bit by bit what had been only an obscure, idiosyncratic process became a profession, my relationship to it had changed. It was no longer enough for it to be the answer to an inner need; it also had to be many other things, to rise to other occasions. And as it rose, what had begun as an act of freedom had become another form of binding.

I wanted to write what I wanted to write, however much it offended, bored, challenged, or disappointed people, and disliked the part of myself that wished to please. I'd tried to rid myself of it, and on a certain level had succeeded: my previous novel had bored, challenged, and disappointed an impressive number of readers. But because the book, like the ones before it, was still undeniably Jewish, filled with Jewish characters and the echoes of two thousand years of Jewish history, I'd avoided sloughing off the pride of my landsmen. If anything, I'd managed to increase it, as part of me must have secretly hoped to do. In Sweden or Japan they didn't care much about what I wrote, but in Israel I was stopped in the street. On my last trip, an elderly woman in a sun hat secured with a strap under her chubby chin had cornered me at the supermarket. Gripping my wrist between her meaty fingers, she'd backed me into the dairy section to tell me that reading my books was, for her, as good as spitting on Hitler's grave (never mind that he doesn't have one), and that she would read every page I wrote until she herself was in the ground. Pinned against the kosher yogurt display, I smiled politely and thanked her, and only after she held up my wrist in the air like a heavyweight champion's and shouted out my name to the disinterested checkout girl did she finally leave off, though not before flashing the faded green numbers tattooed on her forearm like the badge of an undercover police.

A few months before that, my brother had gotten married at the King David Hotel in Jerusalem. The toasts had gone on for a long time, and when they were finally finished I'd made a beeline for the ladies' room. I'd made it halfway across the lobby when a woman in a headscarf had pushed a stroller into my path. I tried to move around her, but she wouldn't let me pass, and, looking me in the eyes, she'd spoken my name. Frazzled and confused, I was also on the verge of wetting myself. But I wasn't getting away so easily. With a flick of the wrist, she tore back the hood of the stroller to reveal a tiny red-faced infant. In a hoarse voice, she whispered the name of a girl in one of my books. The baby swiveled its tiny head, and when its myopic gray eyes passed over me, both seeing and not seeing, her hands jerked out in front of her like a monkey trying and failing to grasp the branch, and she let out an earsplitting scream. I looked up at the mother's swollen face and saw tears welling in her own eyes. "Because of you," she whispered.

But worst of all was the previous year, when I had come to attend the International Writers Festival in Jerusalem, been taken on a special tour of Yad Vashem, and afterward was separated out from the other (non-Jewish) festival writers and escorted to the museum's back offices. There, under a brooding oil painting of Wallenberg dark enough to look like it had been rescued from a house on fire, I was presented with photocopied papers concerning my murdered great-grandparents, along with a bag from the museum gift shop. "Go on, open it," the director encouraged, pushing the bag into my hands. "Oh, I'll open it later," I suggested. "Open it *now*," she commanded through a smile of gritted teeth. Three or four of the staff hovered around me, watching feverishly. I opened the bag and peered in, then closed it again, but the director grabbed it away, dug into it, and lifted out a blank notebook commemorating the sixty-fifth anniversary of the liberation of Auschwitz. Could the message have been any clearer if the endpapers had been printed with piles of dead children's shoes? Back at home in New York, I tossed the notebook in the trash, but an hour later, overcome with guilt, plucked it out again. Sitting down at my desk, I desperately tried to write something on the first page to strip it of its power, but after sweating it out for a quarter of an hour, all I'd managed was to scribble down a list of things to do—*(1) Call plumber, (2) Gyn apt, (3) Fluoride-free toothpaste*. Then I'd shut the cover and buried it at the back of a drawer.

"So? You're writing a new novel?" Friedman asked me now.

I felt a trickle of sweat roll down my chest despite the cool air.

"Trying," I said, though I had not been trying, had in fact avoided trying these last three days, as no sooner had I checked in than I understood that beginning a novel about the Hilton while actually at the Hilton would be even more impossible than beginning a novel about the Hilton while at home in Brooklyn.

"And what is the subject?"

"I haven't gotten that far," I said, shifting my eyes to the hotel looming on the cliff above the beach.

"Why? What's wrong?"

When I didn't reply, Friedman gently folded the napkin on his lap and returned it in a neat rectangle to the table. "You must be wondering why I asked to meet you."

"Beginning to, yes."

"Let's walk."

I glanced at the cane by his arm.

"Don't let it fool you." Friedman unhooked the stick and deftly hoisted himself to his feet. The old dog lying prostrate on the floor jerked up her head and, when she saw that Friedman really meant to go, pushed herself back on her haunches, splaying her front paws to leverage her weight against the floor, and creakily rose from the thighs. Then she cast off her inertia with a spasmodic shake, sending thousands of motes of dust exploding into the light.

We made our way past a small shop with sun-faded surfboards in the window and up to that promenade that runs along the sea. The dog followed discreetly after us, occasionally sniffing halfheartedly at a boulder or pole.

"What kind of dog is she?"

"Shepherd," Friedman replied.

But the dog bore no resemblance whatsoever to a shepherd, German or otherwise. If anything she was more sheep, only one lifted from pasture and put away in storage for a very long time, where its woolly and colorless coat had begun to disintegrate.

A motorcycle shot past and the driver shouted something to Friedman, who shouted back in return. Whether I'd witnessed a brief skirmish or a greeting of acquaintances, I couldn't say.

"I don't need to tell you that this is a difficult country," he said, leading us toward Hayarkon Street. "There's no end to our problems, and every day we have new ones. They multiply. We deal with them poorly or not at all. Slowly they're burying us."

Friedman stopped and looked back at the sea, perhaps for some sign of the missiles. More had been exploded yesterday, preceded by the deafening whine of the sirens. The first time it happened, I'd left my café table and gone down into the basement shelter. The seven or eight people gathered in the concrete room had about them the air of people waiting in line at the grocery store, except that when the boom sounded, there was a smattering of low "wows," as if someone in the line had tried to purchase something extraordinary. The second time the siren sounded, I was with my friend, Hana, who merely stopped what she was saying and tilted her face toward the sky. Almost everyone around us had remained in place, too, either because they believed in the impenetrable dome above or because acknowledging the danger would also require acknowledging many other things that would make their lives less possible.

I scanned the sky for a sign, too, but there was none, only the white furrows of the sea whipped by the wind. When Friedman turned back, the lenses of his glasses had darkened in the sunlight, and I could no longer see his eyes.

"For twenty-five years, I taught literature at the university. But no one has time for literature anymore," he said. "Anyway, in Israel, writers were always luftmenschen—impractical and useless, at least according to the founding ideals, which, however far we've strayed from them, still reverberate. In the shtetl, they knew the value of a Bashevis Singer. However hard times were, they made sure he had paper and ink. But here, he was diagnosed as part of the disease. They confiscated his pen and sent him to pull radishes up in the fields. And if he should somehow manage to write a few pages in his off hours and publish them, they made sure he would be punished by taxing him at the highest possible rate, a practice that continues to this day. The idea that we would support the production of literature through programs and grants, as they do in Europe and America, would be unthinkable here."

"Nearly every young Israeli artist I know is looking for a way to leave," I said. "But for writers there's no way out of the language you're born into. It's an impossible situation. But then, Israel seems to specialize in those."

"Fortunately, we don't have a monopoly," Friedman said, guiding me up the steps of the small park next to the Hilton. "Anyway, not all of us agree," he said.

"None of you agree. But I don't know which disagreement you're referring to now."

Friedman looked at me sharply, and I thought I saw a flash of skepticism in his face, though it was hard to say, being unable to see his eyes. I'd meant to make a joke, but instead I must have struck him as an amateur. Before I could arm myself against it, the desire to please or perhaps just not to disappoint rushed in, and I cast around for something to say that would convince him that his instincts about me had been right; that he'd had good reason to single me out and invest hope in me.

"We were speaking about writing," Friedman said before I had a chance to redeem myself. "Some of us here never forgot its value. That the reason we continue to live on this contested scrap of land today is because of the story we began to write about ourselves in this place nearly three millennia ago. In the ninth century BC, Israel was nothing—a backwater nation, compared to the neighboring empires of Egypt or Mesopotamia. And that's what we would have remained, forgotten with the Philistines and the Sea Peoples, except that we began to write. The earliest Hebrew writing we've found dates to the tenth century BC, the time of King David. Just simple inscriptions on buildings mostly. Record keeping, nothing more. But within a few hundred years something extraordinary happened. From the eighth century, suddenly there is evidence of writing all over the Northern Kingdom of Israel—advanced, complex texts. The Jews had begun composing the stories that would be collected in the Torah. We like to think of ourselves as the inventors of monotheism, which spread like wildfire and influenced thousands of years of history. But we didn't invent the idea of a single God; we only wrote a story of our struggle to remain true to Him and in doing so we invented ourselves. We gave ourselves a past and inscribed ourselves into the future."

As we crossed a pedestrian overpass, the wind picked up, sending sand flying through the air. I knew I was meant to be impressed by his speech, but I couldn't help feeling he'd given it a hundred times before in the university lecture hall. And I was getting tired of beating around the bush. I still had no idea who Friedman really was or what he wanted of me, if he wanted anything at all.

The bridge led us into the dank, shadowy area beneath a concrete overhang, part of the complex of buildings around Atarim Square, whose threatening Brutalism made even the Hilton look inviting. What had once been a semi-covered arcade of shops had long ago been abandoned, leaving the building to erode more fully toward the hell its architect had once only toyed with; the whole place was haunted by a sense of the post-apocalyptic. The stench of urine was overwhelming, and the stained concrete blocks rose around us like a prison worse than any Piranesi ever imagined. The question I'd been unable to ask since I sat down at the restaurant rose up again, and I knew that if I didn't say it now, before we exited into the sunlight, I would lose my courage.

"Effie told me you used to work for the Mossad."

"Did he?" Friedman said. The tapping of his cane echoed in the cavernous space, along with the click of the dog's nails behind us. But Friedman's level voice gave away nothing, and I felt a flush of heat rise up my neck, part embarrassment and part annoyance.

"I was under the impression—"

But what could I say? That I'd been led to believe, had let myself believe, that I'd been selected for something special by him, Eliezer Friedman, a retired professor of literature with time on his hands? In a moment he would ask me if I would agree to come speak to his wife's book club.

"The Hilton is in the other direction. I should be heading back."

"I'm taking you someplace I think you'll find interesting."

"Where?"

"You'll see."

We walked along the tree-lined footpath that runs down the median of Ben Gurion Street. To those that passed we must have looked like nothing so much as a grandfather and granddaughter out for a stroll together. As if to play up his role, Friedman offered to buy me a fresh juice.

"They have everything," he said, waving toward the stand strung with heavy net bags of overripe fruit. "Guava, mango, passion fruit. Though I recommend a combination of pineapple, melon, and mint."

"Thank you, really, but I'm fine."

Friedman shrugged. "Suit yourself."

He asked me whether I knew the country much, beyond Tel Aviv and Jerusalem. Had I been north to the Sea of Galilee or spent time in the desert? The landscape had astounded him as a child when he'd first arrived here. Reaching into one of his pockets, he produced a potsherd and handed it to me. To walk into the setting of the Bible stories, to find what had been inscribed in his imagination corroborated by stone, olive tree, sky. The fragment of terra-cotta in my hands was three thousand years old, he said. He'd picked it up not long ago in Khirbet Qeiyafa, above the valley of Elah, where David slew Goliath; the ground there was littered with them. Some archaeologists argued that it was the biblical city of Shaaraim, that the ruins of King David's palace might be found there. A quiet place, with wildflowers growing up through the stones and rainwater in ancient bathtubs reflecting the silent clouds passing above. About this they would go on arguing, Friedman said. But the fallen walls and the broken pots, the light and the wind in the leaves—it was enough. The rest would never be more than technical. No physical evidence of a kingdom had ever been found by archaeologists. But if David's palace was the dream of the writer of Samuel, just as the brilliant insight into political power was his, what did it matter in the grand scheme of things? David, who might have been only the tribal leader of a hill clan, had brought his people to a high culture that has since given shape to nearly three thousand years of history. Before him, Hebrew literature didn't exist. But because of David, two hundred years after his death, Friedman said, the writers of Genesis and Samuel established the sublime limits of literature almost at its beginning. It's there in the story they wrote about him: a man who begins as a shepherd, becomes a warrior and a ruthless warlord, and dies a poet.

"Writers work alone," Friedman said. "They pursue their own instincts, and one can't interfere with that. But when they are guided naturally toward certain themes—when their instincts and our goals converge in a common interest—one can give them opportunities."

"What goals do you mean, exactly? To cast Jewish experience in a certain light? To put a spin on it in order to influence how we're seen? Sounds to me more like PR than literature."

"You're looking at it too narrowly. What we're talking about is much larger than perception. It's the idea of self-invention. Event, time, experience: these are the things that happen to us. One can look at the history of mankind as a progression from extreme passivity—daily life as an immediate response to drought, cold, hunger, physical urges, without a sense of past or future—to a greater and greater exercise of will and control over our lives and our destiny. In that paradigm, the development of writing represented a huge leap. When the Jews began to compose the central texts on which their identity would be founded, they were enacting that will, consciously defining themselves—*inventing* themselves—as no one had before."

"Sure, put like that, it seems extremely radical. But you could also just say the earliest Jewish writers were at the frontier of that natural evolution. Humanity had begun to think and write on a more elevated plane, giving people greater sophistication and subtlety in how they defined themselves. To suggest a level of self-awareness that would allow for self-invention, as you say, is assuming a lot about the intentions of those earliest writers."

"There's no need to assume. The evidence is everywhere in the texts, which are not just the work of one or two individuals, but a series of composers and redactors who were supremely conscious of every choice they were making. The first two chapters of Genesis, taken together, are about exactly that—a meditation on creation as a set of choices, and a reflection on the consequences that result. The very first thing we're given in the very first Jewish book is two *contradictory* accounts of God's creation of the world. Why? Perhaps because, in echoing God's gestures, the redactors came to understand something about the price of creation—something they wished to communicate to us that, if we were to grasp it, would verge on blasphemous, and therefore could only be hinted at obliquely: How many worlds did God consider before He chose to create this world? How many scales that contained neither light nor dark but something else entirely?

When God created light, he also created the absence of light. That much is spelled out for us. But only in the uncomfortable silence between those two incompatible beginnings is it possible to grasp that at that instant He created a third thing, too. For lack of a better word, let us call it regret."

"Or an early theory of the multiverse."

But Friedman seemed not to hear me. We stood at the corner, waiting for the light to change. Overhead, the Mediterranean sky was stupendously blue, utterly cloudless. Friedman stepped out in front of an idling taxi and began to march across the street.

"Read closely enough, it's impossible to deny that whoever composed and edited those first texts understood what was at stake," he said. "Understood that to begin was to move from infinity to a room with walls. That to choose one Abraham, one Moses, one David, was also to reject all the others that might have been. "

We turned onto a quiet residential street, lined with the same squat concrete apartment houses that are everywhere in Tel Aviv, their ugliness softened by the lush vegetation that grows around them, and the bright purple bougainvillea that climbs up their walls. Halfway down the block Friedman stopped.

According to the sign, we were on Spinoza Street. I assumed that was the reason Friedman had brought me there, since it was the Jewish philosopher who first claimed that the Pentateuch wasn't given by God and scribed by Moses but was rather the product of human authorship. But what would Friedman's point be? At the heart of the Dutch lens-grinder's assertions, at least where Judaism was concerned, was the idea that the God of Israel was Himself a human invention, and as such Jews should no longer be bound by the Law ascribed to Him. If there was ever a man who strained against the notion of Jewish binding, it was Baruch Spinoza.

Friedman said nothing about the name of the street, though. Instead he gestured to a gray four-floor apartment building whose facade, inset with rows of hollow concrete blocks in the shape of hourglasses, was the only thing that made it stand out from the other stucco buildings on the block.

"I know from your books that Kafka is of interest to you."

I had to suppress a laugh. It was becoming increasingly hard to keep up with Friedman. All morning I'd been trailing a few steps behind him, but now I'd lost him completely.

"He seems to make an appearance in all of your books. Once you even wrote an obituary for him, as I recall. So the story of the fate of his papers after his death is no doubt familiar to you?"

"You're referring to the note he left for Max Brod, asking him to burn all the manuscripts Kafka had left behind, which Brod—"

"In 1939," Friedman cut in impatiently, "five minutes before the Nazis crossed the Czech border, Brod caught the last train out of Prague, carrying a suitcase stuffed with Kafka's papers, saving his life and rescuing from almost certain destruction all the remaining unpublished work of the greatest writer of the twentieth century. Brod came to Tel Aviv and lived out the rest of his life here, where he published more of Kafka's work. But when he died in 1968, a portion of the material in the suitcase had still never been released."

I wondered how many times Friedman had recited this story, too. The dog herself seemed to have heard it before, because after pausing in a wide stance to see where things were going, she now traced a few pathetic circles in the grass, lowered herself with a groan, and conked down her head in such a way that she could keep a lazy upside-down eye on Friedman.

"I know all that, yes. I've read my fill of Kafka porn."

"And so you also know that everything left in that suitcase is moldering in the most heinous conditions less than three meters from where you're standing now?"

"What do you mean?"

With the tip of his cane, Friedman pointed to the window of the ground-floor apartment. It was protected by a cage of curved iron bars in whose hold three or four mangy cats were nestled in a pile. Two more cats were lazing on the front steps of the building, and the stench of feline urine hung in the air.

"Unfinished novels, stories, letters, drawings, notes—God knows what, sitting under the neglectful but pathologically obsessive watch of the now elderly daughter of Brod's lover, Esther Hoffe, whose hands they came into through various questionable channels of inheritance. The daughter, Eva Hoffe, claims to have stored some of the papers in safe-deposit boxes in Tel Aviv and Zurich to protect against potential theft. But the truth is that she is too fanatically possessive and paranoid to let any of it out of her sight. Behind those bars in Eva's apartment, along with twenty or thirty more cats, are hundreds of pages written by Franz Kafka that almost no one has ever seen."

"But surely Kafka's manuscripts can't be hidden from the world on the claim that they're private property?"

"The National Library of Israel filed a lawsuit challenging Esther Hoffe's will after she died, asserting that Brod had intended for the papers to be donated to them, and that they belong to the state. The trial has been going on for years. Each time a judgment is handed down, Eva appeals."

"How do you know that most of it's here, and not locked up in the bank, as Eva claims?"

"I've seen the papers."

"I thought you said—"

"I've only told you the beginning."

Friedman's cell phone rang, and he looked thrown off guard for the first time all day. He fumbled in his pockets, patting down the vest while the phone kept going off with the loud, alarming tone of an old-fashioned telephone ring. When he still couldn't find it, he handed me the cane and started lifting one flap after another, until at last, just as the phone gave up, he found it in his inside pocket. He glanced at the screen.

"I didn't realize it was so late," he said, turning back to me. In the silence that followed, he seemed to be studying me, and I wondered if he had found something in my face to trust. He called the dog, and the beast came to and began the long process of rising.

"Among the papers sitting in that apartment is a play that Kafka wrote near the end of his life. He nearly finished it, but just before the end he abandoned it. The moment I read it, I understood that it had to be realized. It took a long time, but at last it's happening. Shooting is scheduled to begin in six months."

"You're turning it into a *film*?"

"Kafka loved the movies. Did you know that about him?"

"That doesn't mean he would have approved!"

"Kafka approved of nothing. Little could have been more foreign to Kafka than approval. The afterlife of his work would have sickened him. And yet no one who has ever read him believes that his wishes should have been carried out."

"Why should Kafka's intentions be irrelevant," I asked, "while you glorify the intentions of the writers and redactors of the Bible who were—what was it you said before—'supremely conscious' of the choices they were making?"

"Where is the glory? We don't even know who they were, and most of their intentions were lost or overridden by the needs of everyone who came afterward. Beneath the countless revisions, there's a Genesis written by a singular person who had all of the genius and none of the moral intention. Whose greatest invention was a character called Yud-Hay-Vav-Hay, and whose book might have been called *The Education of God*, had it not been absorbed by another destiny. But in the end, it isn't up to the writer to decide how his or her work will be used."

"And the pathologically obsessive, paranoid Hoffe daughter has agreed to this? What about the National Library of Israel? In the middle of a trial, you got the rights to a piece of highly disputed material, a play by Kafka, which is going to be made into a film?"

Friedman looked past me at the house. It was clear he wasn't going to be solving any mysteries that afternoon; he was too busy sowing them.

"Changes need to be made to the script, of course. And there remains the problem of an ending."

Now I really did laugh. "I'm sorry," I said, "it's all a bit much."

"Take your time," Friedman said.

"For what?"

"To decide."

"What am I deciding?"

"Whether my proposal is of interest to you."

"I don't know what you're proposing!"

But before I could ask anything more, he gave me a grandfatherly pat on the back.

"I'll be in touch soon. Don't hesitate to contact me in the meantime."

Unzipping a bulging pocket of his vest, he removed his wallet and extracted a card. ELIEZER FRIEDMAN, it read. PROFESSOR EMERITUS, DEPARTMENT OF LITERATURE, TEL AVIV UNIVERSITY.

Out of the corner of my eye I saw the curtains of the ground-floor apartment move slightly, as if with the wind. Only the window was closed. I might have missed it had the cats lying on the bars not suddenly stiffened with alertness, feeling whoever was moving within. Their keeper.

I WALKED SLOWLY back toward the Hilton, trying to sort through everything Friedman had said. The sun had drawn everyone outdoors again, and the beach was now full of people in bathing suits, though it was too cold to swim. As I watched them, something came back to me from one of Kafka's letters, written at a vacation camp on the Baltic during the last year of his life. Next door was a summer camp for German Jewish children, and all day and night Kafka could watch them from his window playing under the trees and on the beach. The air was filled with their singing. *I am not happy when I'm among them*, he wrote, *but on the threshold of happiness.*

They were all out: the possessed *matkot* players, the only-barely-Jewish Russians, the lazy couples with young babies, the girls who, caught off guard by the sun, figured that their bras could pass as bikinis. Just as the inhabitants of Tel Aviv refuse to believe in the need for central heating, so they also seem to insist on going around underdressed, in T-shirts and flip-flops, always unprepared for the rain or surprised by the cold, and at the first sign of sun they rush outside to resume their usual positions. In this way, the whole city seems to have agreed collectively to deny the existence of winter. To deny, in other words, an aspect of their reality, because it conflicts with what they believe about who they are—a people of sun, of salt air and sultriness. A people who are, in that moment of sunbathing, of forgetfulness by the sea, as related to missiles as a man is related to the flight of a bird. And yet isn't it true of all of us? That there are things we feel to be at the heart of our nature that are not borne out by the evidence around us, and so, to protect our delicate sense of integrity, we elect, however unconsciously, to see the world other than the way it really is? And sometimes it leads to transcendence, and sometimes it leads to the unconscionable.

How else to explain myself, then? Explain why I went along with Friedman, refusing to heed all the obvious warnings. One often hears people say that it's easy to misunderstand. But I disagree. People don't like to admit it, but it's what passes as understanding that seems to come too easily to our kind. All day long people busy themselves with understanding every manner of thing under the sun—themselves, other people, the causes of cancer, the symphonies of Mahler, ancient catastrophes. But I was going in another direction now. Swimming against the forceful current of understanding, the other way. Later there would be other, larger failures to understand—so many that one can only see a deliberateness in it: a stubbornness that lay at the bottom like the granite floor of a lake, so that the more clear and transparent things became, the more my refusal showed through. I didn't want to see things as they were. I had grown tired of that.

Every Life Is Strange

H OW IT HAPPENED, for example, that one afternoon, a few months after his mother died, Epstein stood up to get a drink from the kitchen, and as he rose, his head suddenly filled with light. Filled as a glass is filled, from the bottom to the brim. The idea that it was an ancient light came to him later, when he was trying to remember how it had been—trying to remember the sensation of the level rising in his head, and the fragile quality of the light, come from far off, old, and which, in its long endurance seemed to carry a sense of patience. Of inexhaustibility. It had lasted only a few seconds, and then the light had drained away. At another time he would have chalked it up to aberrant sensation, and it would not have struck him much, the way hearing one's name called from time to time when no one is there to call it does not strike one overly. But now that he lived alone, and his parents were dead, and day by day it was becoming harder to ignore the slow drain of interest in the things that had once captivated him, he had become aware of a sense of waiting. Of the heightened sense of awareness of one who is waiting for something to arrive.

IN THOSE FIRST mornings at the Hilton, Epstein had woken to the Mediterranean and stood rapt on the terrace, watching the waves. In a long, feathery contrail dissolving in the blue sky, he saw the line of his life. Long ago, at Maya's bat mitzvah party, they'd had a palm reader. Never mind the unkosher presence of the occult: it was what she had wanted. ("What do you love most, Mayashka?" he'd once asked her as a little child. "Magic and mystery," she'd replied without pause.) To indulge her, Epstein had turned his hand over to the frail and turbaned fortune-teller, who looked like she hadn't eaten for weeks. "Get this woman some cake!" he'd shouted, and three waiters, angling for a tip, had sprung into action, bringing three pieces of heavily frosted white cake, which had the promise of a wedding baked into it. But the three slices had only sat at the pointy elbow of the fortune-teller, who was clever enough to know that eating would have lessened her aura and bungled the illusion of clairvoyance. She stroked Epstein's palm with her own dry, cool one, as if brushing off the dust, then began to trace the lines with a scarlet fingernail. Growing bored, Epstein scanned the dance floor, where the limbo bar had been lowered to the point that only one scrawny seventh-grader, an acrobatic prepubescent, could still bend backward and slide her way triumphantly beneath. Then he felt the fortune-teller's hand tighten around his, and when he turned back, he saw the look of alarm on her face. It was pure theater, Epstein knew. But he had a taste for drama, and was curious to see a display of her skill. "What did you find?" he'd asked gamely. The fortune-teller gazed at him with black eyes outlined in kohl. Then she quickly folded his palm and pushed it away. "Come to see me another time," she pleaded in a hoarse whisper. She'd slid her business card with a Bayside address into his other hand, but Epstein had only laughed and gone off to yell at the caterer, who had let the Vietnamese chicken skewers run low. The following week, when he found the card again in his pocket, he'd dropped it into the trash. Six months later, Lianne told him that the fortune-teller had died of cancer, but even then Epstein had not regretted his failure to visit her, and felt only a rustle of curiosity.

Now the contrail was slowly evaporating, widening out toward something indistinct. No, he had not believed in the predictions of fortune-tellers, even those touched by a nearness to death. The truth was that he had believed in very little that he couldn't see, and more than that, he'd had something against belief. Not just because of its grand potential for error. To be wrong—even to be wrong one's whole life!—was one thing, but what Epstein could not abide, what filled him with such distaste, was the idea of being taken advantage of. Belief, with its passive trust, required putting oneself in other hands, and as such it made one susceptible to the worst sort of insidiousness. Epstein saw it everywhere. Not just in the large strokes of religion—in the constant stream of news stories about children molested by their priests and rabbis, or teenagers blowing themselves up for the promise of seventy virgins, or performing beheadings in the name of Allah. There were also the countless varieties of small beliefs that provided opportunity for the wool to be pulled over one's eyes, for the great woolly hat of belief to obscure what would be clear to the naked eye. Every advertisement preyed on the human inclination toward belief, a tilt like Pisa's that had proved uncorrectable, no matter that what was promised failed and failed to be delivered. Good people robbed of their money and their right to peace, sometimes even their dignity and freedom, because of a structural flaw! Or so it had seemed to Epstein, who avoided believing in anything that he could not touch or feel or measure with his own instruments.

95

He would walk on solid ground, or would not walk at all. He would not venture out on the thin ice of belief. But of late he had found his legs moving under him, against his instincts. This was what was so strange. The feeling of movement against his will. Against his better judgment! His great deliberateness! Against all that he had shored up in sixty-eight years of collecting knowledge; call it, even, wisdom. And he could not say what it was he was walking toward.

Out there, a boat made its way across the white-capped water on its way toward Cyprus or Tripoli. Epstein felt an expansion in his chest. Why not take a swim? he thought, and the idea seemed so good to him, so marvelous, that he went inside right away and called down to the concierge to see if a swimsuit could be purchased in the lobby. Yes, they could have one ready for him. What was his size?

There was still an hour and a half before the car was coming to pick him up for a tour of the Weizmann Institute, which had suggested an endowment for research in his parents' names. Just last month professors Segal and Elinav had discovered that artificial sweeteners could actually raise blood sugar levels instead of reducing them, information that would help millions of diabetics, not to mention the plain overweight! And what would the Edith and Sol Epstein line of research go into? In honor of their lives, what should be investigated? What do you have, Epstein wished to ask, that could ever be big enough?

Making his way down the carpeted hallway in hotel robe and slippers, he tried to remember the last time he had swum in the sea. When Maya was still young? He recalled an afternoon in Spain when they had gone out on a boat. He dived off the bow—he never immersed himself in anything slowly—and swam around to the ladder to receive his younger daughter, whose tiny head of black curls poked out from the bulky life vest. The third time around, he had better understood the patterns of love and fatherhood, the way nearly immeasurable fractions of time and experience accumulate toward a closeness, a sweetness. Maya had let out a shriek as soon as her legs touched the water. But rather than relinquish her to Lianne's outstretched arms, Epstein had spoken softly to the child. "A great big bathtub," he'd said, "the bathtub of all life," and called up what he knew of tides and dolphins, of tiny clown fish in a world of coral, until bit by bit she had calmed down and loosened her grip on Epstein—loosened it out of trust, so that on another level her hold became tighter. Later, she didn't push her father away as her brother and sister had. Wincing, Epstein remembered how he had once tried to coax Jonah into the sea for twenty minutes before giving in to rage: at the boy's intolerable cowardice, at his lack of strength and will. For not being made of the same materials as Epstein was.

In the new yellow bathing suit, Epstein stood on the shore. The waistband was too large, and he had to tie the drawstring tightly so that it didn't slip down. Sunlight caught in the silver hairs of his chest. The black flag was up, but the lifeguard, lifting a lazy finger, gestured to a red flag a few meters away, where one was allowed to swim with caution. Epstein strode toward the water.

Behind him was the city where he had been born. However far his life had unspooled from it, he had come from here, this sun and breeze were his native conditions. His parents had come from nowhere. Where they came from had ceased to exist and so could not be returned to. But he himself came from someplace:

less than ten minutes' walk away was the corner of Zamenhof and Shlomo ha-Melekh Streets, where he had arrived in the world in such a hurry that his mother didn't have enough time to get to the hospital. A woman had come down from her balcony, pulled him out, and wrapped him in a dishcloth. She had no children herself, but had grown up on a farm in Romania, where she had seen the births of cows and dogs. Afterward his mother went to visit her once a week, and would sit drinking coffee and smoking in her tiny kitchen, while the woman, Mrs. Chernovich, bumped Epstein up and down on her knee. She had a magical effect on him. In her lap, the irascible Epstein became instantly calm. When they moved to America his mother had lost touch with her. But in 1967, when Epstein returned to Tel Aviv for the first time just after the war, he'd gone straight to the corner where he had emerged into the world, walked across the street, and rang the buzzer. Mrs. Chernovich looked down over the railing of the balcony, where she had been watching the world go by all those years. The moment he entered her tiny kitchen and sat down at her table, he'd felt the strange sensation that he thought other people must call peace. "You should have asked to buy the table," an eight-year-old Maya had famously said when she was told the story.

The cold surprised him, but he kept moving steadily until he was up to his waist. Seen from an impossible perspective, there were his legs, greenish and beaded with air bubbles, standing on the great incline that led to the bottom of the sea. What was down there after all, Mayashka? The plunder of the Greeks and the Philistines, and the Greeks and Philistines, too.

The wind was up, and the waves skipped over the breakwater. It was no longer the season for swimming, and the only people out were a small party of Russians. One of them, with pendulous breasts, spreading thighs, and a long, swinging silver cross, plopped a fat, dripping baby down on the chair: *I just found her in the sea!* Epstein knew plenty about negotiating the waves, having grown up alongside the Atlantic. Holding his breath, he dived under and began to swim through the turbulence. The water seemed to buzz with life, with something almost electrical, or maybe it was only he, Epstein, who was conducting his energies across a new vastness. Weightless, he turned a somersault.

When his head broke through the surface again, there was a tall wave moving toward him. He went under and let himself be tossed about. He swam farther out, the long, strong strokes of his youth. It was different to think in the sea than it was to think on land. He wanted to get out past the breaking waves to where he could think as one only can when rocked by the sea. One is always in the hold of the world, but one doesn't physically feel its hold, doesn't account for its effect. Cannot draw comfort from the hold of the world, which registers only as a neutral emptiness. But the sea one feels. And so surrounded, so steadily held, so gently rocked—so differently organized—one's thoughts come in another form. Freed into the abstract. Touched by fluidity. And so, floating on his back in the great bathtub of all life, the abstracted Epstein did not notice the tremendous moving wall until it was upon him.

It was one of the Russians, a bear of a man, who dragged him, sputtering, onto the shore. He had not been under for long, but had swallowed a lot of water. Retching, it came out of him, and he gasped for breath with his face in the sand. Hair plastered to one side, bathing suit hanging low on his hips, Epstein heaved with shock.

THAT NIGHT, WHILE Epstein was eating dinner in a restaurant on Rothschild chosen by his cousin, his cell phone rang. The old one had not been recovered. The Palestinian party had checked out of the New York hotel at dawn; by the time Epstein's assistant arrived, they were already aloft above Nova Scotia. In the Arctic altitudes, a stranger had nestled deep inside Epstein's cashmere coat, perhaps scrolling through his photos. But there was nothing to be done for the moment, and so the lost phone had been replaced by a new one. He still wasn't used to the ringtone, and when he finally realized it was coming from him and fished the phone out of his pocket, the caller was unidentified because his address book had not yet been transferred. It went on ringing while Epstein stalled, at a loss for what to do. Should he answer? He who always answered, who had answered once in the middle of Handel's *Messiah*, conducted by Levine! The blind woman with a crooked haircut who never missed a concert and listened to the music in raptures had nearly set her German shepherd on him. At intermission she had laid into Epstein. He told her to go to hell—a blind woman, to go to hell! But why should they not be treated equally?—and when, the next time, he saw the dog eating some chocolate it had found in the aisle, he had done nothing to stop it, though later that night he had woken in a cold sweat, imagining the woman in the emergency room of the vet, eyes rolled back to their whitish blue, waiting to have the beast's stomach pumped. Yes, he had always answered, even if only to say that he could not answer now, would have to answer later. His whole life had tilted toward his great readiness to answer, even before he knew what was being asked. At last, Epstein stabbed the screen to accept the call.

"Jules! It's Menachem Klausner here."

"Rabbi," said Epstein, "what a surprise." Moti raised his eyebrows across the table, but continued shoveling pasta *cacio e pepe* into his mouth. "How did you find me?"

They had been on the same plane to Israel. Going through security at JFK, Epstein heard his name being called. Looking around, he'd seen no one and so finished lacing up his oxfords, grabbed his rollaway, and hurried on to the business lounge to make some final calls. Two hours into the flight, already drowsing in the fully reclined position, he was roused by a persistent *tap-tap-tap* on his shoulder. No, he did not want any warm nuts. When he lifted his eye mask, though, he was met not by the painted face of the stewardess but by a bearded man leaning over him, close enough that Epstein could see the enlarged pores of his nose. Epstein squinted up at Klausner through a veil of sleep and considered lowering the mask again. But the rabbi squeezed his arm with a firm grip, his blues eyes alight. "I *thought* it was you! It's *bashert*—that you should be coming to Israel, and we should be on the same flight. May I?" he'd asked, and before Epstein was able to reply, the oversize rabbi was stepping over his legs and dropping into the empty seat by the window.

"What are you doing for Shabbat?" Klausner asked now, on the other end of the line.

"Shabbat?" Epstein echoed. In Israel, the day of rest that was ushered in late Friday afternoon and stretched until Saturday evening had always represented an annoyance to Epstein, since everything closed, and the city went into lockdown in pursuit of some ancient, lost peace. Even the most secular Tel Avivians loved to talk about the special atmosphere that settled over the city on Friday afternoons, when the streets emptied and the world drifted toward a quietness, lifted out of the river of time, so that it might be laid back down in it deliberately, ritually, all over again. But as far as Epstein was concerned, a state-enforced hiatus from productivity was merely an imposition.

"Why not come with me up to Safed?" Klausner suggested. "I'll pick you up and bring you myself. Door-to-door service, nothing could be easier. I have to come to Tel Aviv for a meeting on Friday morning anyway. Where are you staying?"

"The Hilton. But I don't have my schedule in front of me."

"I'll hold on."

"I'm at a restaurant. Can you call me back in the morning?"

"Let's say you'll come, and if there's a problem, you'll call me. If I don't hear from you, I'll be in the lobby on Friday at one. It's only two hours' drive, but that will give us plenty of time to get there before Shabbat comes in."

But Epstein was only half listening, feeling instead the urge to tell the rabbi that he had nearly drowned that day. That he had been pulled back from drowning in the nick of time. His stomach was still uneasy; he couldn't eat. He'd tried to tell Moti about it, if only to explain his lack of appetite, but though his cousin had raised his voice in alarm and waved his hands, presently he'd gone back to studying the wine list.

THE FOLLOWING DAY was busy with phone calls to Schloss, who was executing further changes to his will now that Epstein had less to bequeath, and another meeting about what his benefaction might achieve, this one with the Israeli Philharmonic. Zubin Mehta met with him personally. The maestro, wearing an Italian coat and silk scarf, strolled with him around Bronfman's concert hall. He may have been a smaller fish, but his $2 million could nevertheless endow the Edith and Solomon Epstein Chair for the first violinist. His parents had loved music. His father had played the violin until the age of thirteen, when the money for lessons ran out. At home, they'd played records at night, Epstein told the conductor, and he would listen from his bed through the open door. When he was six his mother had taken him to hear—but suddenly, to his embarrassment, he could not remember the name of the great pianist who had stepped onto the stage and approached the piano as an undertaker approaches a coffin.

Mehta's assistant glossed over the moment of forgetfulness, and took everything else down on a yellow legal pad. Afterward they sat drinking coffee in the blazing white light of Habima Square. Still trying to remember the name, Epstein recalled instead something that had happened to him around the time he was taken to see the pianist. He had been lying in his bed with his eyes closed after a nap on a very hot afternoon when a vision of a spider came to him. He saw vividly the orange hourglass on its abdomen and the tan legs with dark striations at the joints. And then, very slowly, he opened his eyes, and there the spider was on the wall in front of him, exactly as he had seen it in his mind. Only when his mother came into the room and began to scream did he learn that it was a brown widow. Epstein would have liked for the assistant to take this down on her pad, too, for it seemed to him of great significance.

But the maestro was talking, his attention leaping restlessly from his buzzing phone to the purple flowers growing in braids up the side of the wall to the mud pit of Israeli politics (he was no prophet, Mehta reported, but things didn't look good). Then he switched to an upcoming concert in Bombay where he would conduct Wagner, as he could not in Tel Aviv. He'd had five children by four women, Epstein had heard; the maestro found no need to finish one story before starting another.

When they got up to shake hands, Epstein touched his coat. He'd had one just like that, he told Mehta, who only smiled vaguely, his mind already on other things. Later Epstein discovered that the orchestra had not a single Palestinian musician, and knowing the earful he would get from his daughters if he made his donation there, he turned his attention to the Israel Museum.

In all of this, he had forgotten about Klausner's invitation and did not remember it until Friday at noon, when he tried to make a dinner reservation and was reminded by the concierge that the restaurant he wanted would be closed. An hour later, at 1:00 p.m. sharp, the front desk rang his room to say that the rabbi was waiting downstairs. Epstein weighed the matter. He could still cancel. Did he really want to spend the next two hours stuck in a car with Klausner and then at his mercy all evening? On the plane, when he'd first raised the idea of a visit, Klausner had insisted that he stay at the Gilgul guesthouse. It wasn't four stars, he'd said, but they would give him the nicest room. But Epstein had no intention of staying overnight. He could call a driver to come for him the moment he began to tire of the rabbi's hospitality. He'd been to Safed thirty years ago but could only recall some roadside stands selling silver jewelry, and the countless stone steps hairy with lichen. A beautiful place, Klausner had said of the town in the mountains of the Upper Galilee that had drawn mystics for five hundred years. A place of bracing air and incomparable light. Perhaps Epstein was even interested in learning with them at Gilgul? "And what would you have me learn?" Epstein asked with an arched brow. To which Klausner quoted a Hasidic tale about a student who goes to visit his teacher, a great rabbi, and when he is asked on his return what he learned, he answers that he learned how the great rabbi ties his shoes. Gesturing down at Klausner's black loafers, worn at the heel, Epstein quoted the words of his father: "And *this* is how you make a living?"

He had always prided himself on his ability to read people, to see what was behind the surface. But he could not yet put his finger on Klausner. A grand facilitator, he had transported the still-searching to his magic mountain by the hundreds, all the way from JFK and LAX; it was nothing for him to sweep Epstein up from Tel Aviv. And yet there was something in the rabbi's gaze—not its attentiveness, for the world had always been attentive to Epstein, but rather its depth, the suggestion of capaciousness within—which seemed to hold the promise of understanding. The events of the day before—the lost coat, the mugging, the hearse with the ebony casket shining long and dark in the hold, which that evening had come back to Epstein with a chill as he entered the dark town car waiting for him in its place—had left Epstein feeling out of sorts. Perhaps it was just an overreceptivity born of emotion, but he found himself wishing to confide in Klausner. In broad strokes, he told him about the last year, beginning with the deaths of his parents, and how he had brought his long, mostly stable marriage to an end, to the shock of his family and friends, and retired from his law firm, and finally he told him about the irresistible desire for lightening that had swelled under all of this and led him to give so much away.

The rabbi ran his long, thin fingers through his beard, and at last pronounced a word Epstein did understand. *Tzimtzum*, Klausner had repeated, and explained the term that was central in Kabbalah. How does the infinite—the *Ein Sof*, the being without end, as God is called—create something finite *within* what is already infinite? And furthermore, how can we explain the paradox of God's simultaneous presence and absence in the world? It was a sixteenth-century mystic, Isaac Luria, who articulated the answer in Safed five hundred years before: When it arose in God's will to create the world, He first withdrew Himself, and in the void that was left, He created the world. *Tzimtzum* was the word Luria gave to this divine contraction, Klausner explained, which was the necessary precursor of creation. This primordial event was seen as ongoing, constantly echoed not just in the Torah but in our own lives.

"For example?"

"For example," said Klausner, twisting around in his seat, which lacked the leg room of the pulpit, "God created Eve out of Adam's rib. Why? Because first an empty space needed to be made in Adam to make room for the experience of another. Did you know that the meaning of Chava—Eve, in Hebrew—is 'experience'?"

It was a rhetorical question, and Epstein, who was used to employing them himself, didn't bother to answer.

"To create man, God had to remove Himself, and one could say that the defining feature of humanity is that lack. It's a lack that haunts us because, being God's creation, we contain a memory of the infinite, which fills us with longing. But the same lack is also what allows for free will. The act of breaking God's command not to eat from the Tree of Knowledge can be interpreted as a rejection of obedience in favor of free choice and the pursuit of autonomous knowledge. But of course it's God who suggests the idea of eating from the Tree of Knowledge in the first place. God who plants the idea in Eve. And so it can also be read as God's way of leading Adam and Eve to confront the vacated space within themselves—the space where God seems to be absent. In this way it is Eve, whose creation required a physical void in Adam, who also leads Adam to the discovery of the metaphysical void within him which he will forever mourn, even as he floods it with his freedom and will."

It was in the story of Moses, too, Klausner went on. The one chosen to speak for his people must first have speech removed from him. He put a hot coal in his mouth as a child and burned his tongue and so was unable to speak, and it was this absence of speech that created the possibility of his being filled with God's speech.

"This is why the rabbis tell us that a broken heart is more full than one that is content: because a broken heart has a vacancy, and the vacancy has the potential to be filled with the infinite."

"What are you saying to me?" Epstein asked with a dry laugh. "That I've made myself susceptible?"

The plane began to shudder as it drifted into a pocket of turbulence, and Klausner's attention was diverted to a frantic search for the straps of his seat belt. He had already confided his fear of flying to Epstein, who had watched him gulp down two pills chased with a glass of pineapple juice he'd finagled from the stewardess, even after she'd instructed him to return to his seat in Economy. Now he cupped his palms around his face and peered out at the dark sky again, as if the cause for instability could be spied there.

The danger passed, the stewardess came to shoo Klausner away with a white cloth for the tray table: dinner was being served, and he really had to go back to his seat. With his time almost up, Klausner quickly got down to business. As much as he would have liked to dedicate himself entirely to Gilgul, he told Epstein, much of his time these days was taken up by the organizing committee of a reunion for the descendants of King David, to be held next month in Jerusalem. It had never been done before. A thousand people were expected to attend! He'd meant to raise the subject at the Plaza, he said, but Epstein had left before he'd had the chance. Would he consider attending? It would be an honor if he'd agree. And might he consider joining the advisory board? It would only mean lending his name and a donation.

Ah, Epstein thought, so that was it. But if his thoughts were jaded, his heart was not, for at the mention of Jerusalem— Jerusalem, which somehow never appeared exhausted by its ancientness, by all its collected pain and heaps of paradox, its store of human mistake, but rather seemed to derive its majesty from it—he recalled the view of its ancient hills and felt his blood-thinned heart expand.

He told Klausner that he would think about it, though he did not really plan on thinking about it. He had a sudden urge to show the rabbi pictures of his children, in case he had given an inaccurate impression of himself with his tale of letting go, of giving away. His vibrant children and grandchildren, who were proof of his attachment to the world. One had to search to find the resemblance. Jonah, darker than his sisters, needed only a few hours of exposure to the sun to become swarthy. To become a Moroccan carpet seller, Epstein used to say. But their mother always said that he had the hair of a Greek god. Maya had the same dark hair, but all the melanin had been given out by the time she was conceived, and her skin was pale and burned easily.

Lucie looked neither Moroccan nor Greek, nor even Jewish—she had about her a northern look, touched by the grace of snow and clarified by the cold. And yet there was something in the animation of their faces that was shared.

But the moment Epstein took out his phone to show the rabbi, he remembered that it was empty: all the thousands of photographs had gone with the Palestinian. Epstein thought again of the man in his coat, who by now must have arrived home to Ramallah or Nablus and hung it in the closet, to the surprise of his wife.

Having nothing to show, Epstein asked how Klausner had come to be invited to the meeting with Abbas at the Plaza, to which the rabbi answered that he was an old friend of Joseph Telushkin's. But Epstein did not know any Telushkin. "Not a descendant," Klausner said, but with a gleam in his eye, as if he were all too aware of the image he was playing to—the Jew who aspires to cliché, who, in his pious fight against extinction is willing to become a copy of a copy of a copy. Epstein had seen them all his life, the ones whose dark suits only highlight the fact that after so many mimeographs the ink has faded and blurred. But that was not the case with Klausner.

NOW THE RABBI was waiting for him in the lobby of the Hilton. Through the plate-glass window of his hotel room, Epstein could see the hill of Jaffa in whose belly thousands of years lay collapsed and dreaming, returned to the womb. A sense of languor came over him, and, not being used to it, uneasy with its implications, he forced himself to stand. He swept the shekels from the night table into his pocket and took some large bills from the safe in the closet, tucking them into his wallet. Whether strolling the green lawns of the Weizmann Institute and touring the house with the stern eyes of Israel's first president following him from out of the oil portraits, or riding out to Ben-Gurion University, where he saw huge carrion birds feeding in the desert, or even sitting across the table from his cousin, Moti, the subtext of all the conversations he'd had over the last days was money. Epstein had had enough. He would make a small gift to Klausner's kabbalah operation and be done with it. He wished to talk to the rabbi of other things.

Rounding the corner of the bank of elevators in the lobby, he spotted Klausner from behind. He was wearing the same grubby suit as before; Epstein recognized a loose thread still dangling from the hem of the jacket, which the rabbi had not yet bothered to cut, and the back was marked by what looked like a dusty footprint. A navy wool scarf hung around his neck. Klausner sprang to life when he spotted Epstein, grasping his shoulders and squeezing them warmly. He lacked the physical awkwardness of the Orthodox, who often seemed to want to get as far away from their bodies as possible, and contracted themselves to a point inside their craniums. Epstein wondered if Klausner had not been born into religion but rather had come to it later. Whether beneath the ill-fitting suit there was a body that had once played basketball, wrestled, rolled naked with a girl in the grass, a body that had been granted sway in its near constant pursuit of freedom and pleasure. Imagining this commonality, Epstein felt the warmth of friendship tingle in his chest.

He followed the rabbi through the revolving door and across the drive to where a beat-up car stood at an angle to the curb, looking more abandoned than willfully parked. Klausner opened the passenger door and rifled around, removing empty plastic bottles and some cardboard tied with twine, which he tossed into the trunk. Observing from behind, Epstein asked whether Klausner also ran a recycling facility. "In a manner of speaking," the rabbi replied with a grin, and slung himself in behind the steering wheel. Even with the seat far back, his knees were still bent at an unnatural angle.

Epstein arranged himself in the passenger seat. From the dashboard, disconnected wires bristled angrily where the stereo had been wrenched out. The engine came to life with a kick, and the rabbi swerved past a parked Mercedes and down the hotel's steep driveway. "Sorry about this. The Bentley is in the shop," said Klausner, swatting the lever for the turn signal and peering at Epstein out of the corner of his eye to see how the joke went over. But Epstein, who had once owned a Bentley, only smiled mildly.

TWO HOURS LATER, after they'd left the coastal road and climbed in elevation, a thin rain began to fall. The car had no windshield wipers—whoever had stripped it of the stereo had perhaps seen value there, too. But Klausner, whom Epstein by now understood to be indefatigable, expertly reached outside with a dirty rag and rubbed the glass clear without so much as slowing down. This was repeated every few minutes without a break in his exegesis on the life and teachings of Luria. He would take Epstein to the house in Safed where Luria had lived, Klausner promised, to the courtyard where his students had once gathered to follow their teacher into the fields, dancing and singing psalms to welcome in the Shabbat queen.

Looking out the window, Epstein smiled to himself. He would go along with it. He would not interfere. He was someplace he couldn't have predicted he'd be only a week earlier—in a car with a mystical rabbi on the way to Safed. The thought that he'd arrived here without having given any instructions pleased him. He had spent his whole life laboring to determine the outcome. But the eve of the sixth day had come for him, too, hadn't it? The ancient land spilled out all around. Every life is strange, he thought. When he rolled down his window, the air smelled of pine. His mind felt light. The sun was already low. They had been delayed by traffic on the highway, and the Shabbat queen was breathing down their necks. But Epstein, looking out at the slumbering hills, was struck by the feeling of having all the time in the world.

They entered Safed and drove through the narrow streets, where the stores were already shuttered. Twice they had to stop and reverse to let tour buses pass, their high windows filled with the weary but satisfied faces of those who have just drunk from the world's authenticity. Beyond the town center, the tourists and artists thinned out, and then they met only Hasids on the road, who flattened themselves against the stone houses as the car squeezed past, clutching their plastic bags to their bodies. What was it with religious Jews and their plastic bags? Epstein wondered. Why did these people who had been wandering for thousands of years not invest in more reliable luggage? They didn't even believe in briefcases and came to court with their legal documents in bags from the kosher bakery—he'd seen it a hundred times. Now they shook their hands in annoyance at Klausner, not for nearly cutting off their noses as he passed but for driving so close to the arrival of Shabbat. But four minutes before the closing bell, the rabbi made a sharp turn into a driveway on the edge of town and rolled to a stop in front of a building whose mottled stones were the color of teeth, though perhaps of a person too ancient to use them.

Klausner hopped out, singing to himself in a rich tenor. Epstein stood in the fresh, cool air and saw down through the valley where Jesus had performed his miracles. A rooster crowed in the distance, and as if in answer there came the distant reply of a dog. Had it not been for the satellite dish planted on the terra-cotta roof, it might have been possible to believe that the rabbi had brought him back to a time when the world was not yet consequence.

"Welcome to Gilgul," Klausner called, already hurrying up the path. "Come in, they'll be waiting for us."

Epstein remained where he was, taking in the view.

But now his phone was going off again, the ring so loud it might have been heard all the way down in Nazareth. It was his assistant calling from New York. Good news, she said: she thought she might have a lead on his coat.

Packing for Canaan

I SPENT THE REST of the night after I met Friedman stuck in the juncture between sleep and waking. Whenever I closed my eyes and drifted into a thin, disturbed sleep, my mind filled with the rows and columns of the hotel's windows, lighting up and whirring like a slot machine or giant abacus. I couldn't glean what these anxious and repetitive calculations meant. Only that they had significance for me, and what my life would come to. The events of the day stretched and warped in my mind, and at some point I became convinced that Kafka himself was sitting in the chair by the window, half turned toward the terrace. I was certain of his presence, as certain as I was, the next moment, of the absurdity of what just a moment ago I'd believed. There was the face I'd studied so many times in the photograph taken during the last year of his life: forty years old, eyes burning in either illness or the excitement of escape, cheekbones bulging from the gaunt face, pointed ears pulled sharply up and away from the skull as if by some outside force. Torqued by the strain, no longer merely human—weren't they always evidence, those ears, of an incomprehensible transformation already under way?

The door was cracked open, and through it came the gentle, slow rocking of the sea. From time to time Kafka delicately lifted a foot and rubbed his slender, hairless ankle against the long curtains. His preoccupation filled the room, heavy and foreboding, and somewhere in my subconscious the suicidal fantasy Kafka had often rehearsed in his diary of jumping out the window and smashing himself on the pavement below must have twined together with the man who had leaped to his death from the hotel terrace.

But Kafka, my Kafka, made no movement toward the terrace door, and so instead I became convinced that he was deliberating whether or not to marry one or another of the succession of women in his life. Reading his letters and diaries, one has the sense that this was the main subject he applied himself to, second only to his writing. Vaguely, I considered telling him that he had wasted far too much energy on it all. That his hysteria was useless, that he was right to believe he wasn't made for marriage, and that what he saw as his failure and weakness could also be seen as a sign of health. A health, I might have added, that I'd begun to suspect I might also possess, insofar as health is that part of one that recognizes what is making one unwell.

In a year I, too, would be forty, and the thought came to me that if my beginning was conceived at the Hilton, it would follow that my end would be, too. That this was what my research was meant to look into. In the fog of semiconsciousness, it didn't frighten me. It seemed not merely a logical thought but one touched by profound logic, and for the moment before I finally fell asleep it filled me with strange hope.

IN THE MORNING, sun streaked through the windows, and I was woken by a brusque knock on the door. I staggered out of bed. It was a woman from housekeeping come to restore order, all the way from Eritrea or Sudan. Her cart was piled high with pristine towels and little packages of scalloped soap. She peered past me into the room at the twisted bedsheets and scattered pillows, gauging the size of the job. She must have seen all kinds of things. A woman who had wrestled with sleep all night was nothing to her. But she realized that she had woken me, and she began to turn away. It occurred to me then that if anyone knew something about the man who had jumped or fallen, it would be her.

I called her back; I was checking out shortly, I explained, she might as well get started now. Get started on erasing my presence, as it were, so that the next person who arrived could enjoy the illusion that the room was meant especially for him, and not have to think about the parade of people who'd slept in his bed already.

I followed her into the bathroom, where she began to tidy up around the sink. Sensing me hovering, she caught my eyes in the mirror.

"More towels?"

"I have enough, thanks. But I wanted to ask you something else."

She straightened up, drying her hands on her apron.

"Do you know anything about a guest who fell from the terrace a few months ago?"

A look of confusion, or perhaps suspicion, clouded her face.

I tried again: "A man who fell from there—" I gestured toward the windows, the sky, the sea. "A man who died?" When this elicited no reaction, I quickly drew my finger across my throat like the Polish brute in *Shoah* who demonstrated for Claude

Lanzmann how, from the side of the train tracks, he would give the Jews a sign that they were careening toward their murder. Why I did this, I don't know.

"No English." She bent to scoop a used towel off the floor and squeezed past me. She took fresh towels from her cart, dropped them on the unmade bed, and told me she would come back later. The door clicked shut behind her.

Alone again, a depressed feeling washed over me. For months I'd clung to the idea that this ugly hotel held out some sort of promise for me. Unable to make anything out of it, I'd allowed it to keep its grip on me, and instead of giving up and moving on, I'd packed my bags and gone right toward it, actually *checked in to it*, and now here I was pressing this poor woman to make good on the possibility that someone had tossed himself to his death so that I might discover that there was a story here after all.

I PACKED MY suitcase, eager to leave the hotel and be on my way to my sister's apartment on Brenner Street, where I normally stayed whenever I came to Tel Aviv. She spent only part of the year there and at the moment was back in California. I'd spent days writing in her empty apartment in the past, so it was not impossible to believe that, no longer at the Hilton, but not so very far from it, I might finally sit down and begin my novel about the Hilton, or in some way modeled on the structure of the Hilton, which I'd had in mind to write for half a year but of which I had not written even a single chapter.

The news on TV reported that there had been no further rockets. So unnewsworthy a night had it been that between footage from Gaza and a speech from the defense minister, who was largely indistinguishable from the culture minister, there was time for a report about a whale sighting in waters north of Tel Aviv—a gray whale, whose likes had not been seen in the Mediterranean for some two hundred and fifty years, having been hunted to extinction in our hemisphere. But now a solitary member of its race had appeared here, and swum from Herzliya to Jaffa before disappearing again into the deep. A man from the Marine Mammal Research and Assistance Center was interviewed and explained that the whale was emaciated, almost certainly lost. They believed he'd become confused when he arrived at the Northwest Passage and found the ice melted, that without familiar landmarks, he'd accidentally turned south instead of north and ended up in Israeli waters. Sitting down on the hotel bed, I watched the shaky video footage of the spray from his spout and then, after a long pause, the huge, scarred tail rising.

I went out onto the balcony to take in the view a last time. Or to scan the waves for a sign of the whale. Or just to measure again how close Gaza really was. In a small boat with an outboard motor, it wouldn't have taken long to go the forty-four miles to where the Palestinians looked out at the same horizon, at the same approximation of infinite space, and were unable to go anywhere.

DOWN IN THE LOBBY there was a line at reception. A large group was checking in—aunts, uncles, and cousins all come from America to celebrate the arrival into manhood of one of their own, now perched on a bulging piece of Louis Vuitton luggage, busily trying to shake loose into his mouth the last pieces from a box of Nerds. I waited my turn, watching the security guard at the door digging down into an enormous white purse that contained in its soft, leathery depths an unknown pocket of the universe. I, too, wanted to look. The tanned woman with painted nails waiting patiently for her bag to be returned believed it was being searched for a gun or a bomb, but the thorough devotion of the guard suggested that he was looking for something of far greater significance.

The general manager emerged from the back office. A look of recognition lit up his face when he spotted me, and he sailed over to where I stood. Clasping my hand between his, he asked after my grandfather, whom he'd known for twenty years. My grandfather was dead, I told him; he'd died the year before. The general manager couldn't believe this and seemed on the verge of suggesting that I'd made it up, as I had made up all of the other things I'd claimed had happened in my books. But he stopped short of that, and, after expressing his regret, asked whether I'd enjoyed the fruit basket he'd sent up to my room. I said I had, because there was no sense in telling him that I had not received any fruit basket, with all of the drama that might kick up. I explained that I wished to check out. More surprise and concern—hadn't I just arrived? I was brought to the front of the line, bypassing the bar mitzvah party, and the general manager slipped behind the desk to attend to me himself, handling everything with speed and elegance. When my account was settled, he escorted me to the door and instructed the porter to hail me a taxi. He seemed in a hurry to see me off. Presumably it was because he had many other things to tend to, but it occurred to me that he might know I'd heard about the man who had fallen to his death. Effie, or even Matti, my journalist friend, might have called the hotel on my behalf, and news of their inquiries would have been passed on to the general manager. Or perhaps the alarmed housekeeper had alerted her superior an hour ago. While I considered this, my suitcase was dispatched to the trunk of the waiting taxi, and before I could formulate the appropriate question, the general manager had loaded me into the backseat and, with an air of bright professionalism, smiled, slammed the door, and rapped the flank of the taxi with his knuckles to send it on its way.

WE'D ONLY GONE five minutes down the road when the driver swerved toward the curb and brought the taxi to a halt. A bus honked, and through the rear window I saw it come screeching on its brakes toward us, stopping within inches of the rear bumper. The taxi driver got out, cursed the driver of the bus, and disappeared behind the open hood of his car. I followed him around to the front and asked what was going on, but he ignored me and continued to engross himself in the overheated innards of the engine. Pedestrians on the street gathered to watch. America is a place with no time on its hands, but in the Middle East there is time, and so the world gets more looked at there, and as it's looked at, opinions are formed about what is seen, and naturally opinions are different, so that an abundance of time, in a certain equation, leads to argument. Now an argument broke out about whether the taxi driver should have stopped where he did, blocking the bus stop. A man in a tank top stained with sweat joined the driver under the hood, and they, too, began to argue about what was happening there. To my husband, the world was always what it appeared to be, and to me the world was never what it appeared to be, but in Israel no one can ever agree on the way the world appears, and despite the violence of the never-ending argument, this basic admittance of discord had always been a relief to me.

I repeated my question, and at last the driver lifted his sweaty face, took in everything he ever wanted to know about me, sauntered around to the back, popped the trunk, dumped my suitcase onto the street, and went back to his tinkering. I dragged the suitcase behind me onto the sidewalk, and the small crowd parted, just barely, to let me pass. Stationing myself a few yards farther up the street, I scanned the oncoming traffic for another taxi. But it was rush hour, and they were all full. Finally I saw a *sherut*—a communal taxi van that follows a set route, stopping along the way when people shout out to the driver—and waved it down. But just as it began to slow for me, a car pulled up and the window was lowered.

It was Friedman behind the wheel, still wearing his safari vest.

"Nu?" he said, in the old Yiddish way of taking another's pulse. "What happened?" He reached across the passenger seat and opened the door, then lowered the volume of the symphony on the radio.

Did I get in? Narrative may be unable to sustain formlessness, but life also has little chance, given that it is processed by the mind whose function it is to produce coherence at any cost. To produce, in other words, a credible story.

"You're going to tell me that was a coincidence?" I demanded as Friedman merged back into the traffic. "My taxi broke down, and you just happened to be passing by?"

But the truth was that I was relieved to see him.

"I went to drop this off for you at the Hilton."

Without taking his eyes off the road he reached behind my

seat, scooped up a large, grubby brown paper bag, and deposited it in my lap.

"They told me you'd just checked out, and I remembered that you'd said you were planning to move to your sister's apartment on Brenner Street. I was on my way there when I spotted you on the side of the road."

I couldn't remember mentioning my sister's place, but then my memory was foggy from lack of sleep. Yesterday afternoon I'd forgotten an appointment I'd made to have coffee with my Hebrew translator, and after visiting an old friend, the choreographer Ohad Naharin, I'd left my bag behind at his apartment. And yet I was also ready to believe that Friedman knew everything there was to know about me; that he'd read my file. Maybe I even wanted to believe it, too, since it would let me off the hook.

I unrolled the paper bag, and a smell of mildew wafted up. Jumbled at the bottom was a pile of brittle Kafka paperbacks, the spines cracked from use.

"To help you think," Friedman said, but did not elaborate.

I crumpled the bag closed. We were stopped at a light, and a young couple crossed in front of the car, their arms slung around each other's waists. The boy was beautiful, as only a person raised in sunlight can be. His shirt was open at the neck to reveal his throat. I turned back to Friedman, who was busy fiddling with the rearview mirror. He looked too old to be driving. His right hand had a tremor—there was no question about it. Was it not possible that, like my father's cousin Effie, he too had entered into the twilight years where reality, of less and less use, begins to dissolve at the edges?

The light changed, and he turned left onto Allenby. Within a few minutes we'd arrived at my sister's small, quiet street. I pointed to number 16, fronted by a parking lot that the building overhung, and something of a garden that managed to be at once bare and wild. We both got out, Friedman with the help of his cane, which had been resting across the backseat, hairy with dog fur. His calloused feet were shod in leather sandals today, the toenails cracked. I worked my suitcase out of the trunk for the second time.

"You always pack so heavily?"

I protested that I was the lightest packer in my family; that my parents and siblings didn't go on so much as an overnight without three suitcases each.

"And this makes them happy?"

"Happy has nothing to do with it. For them, it's a question of being prepared."

"Prepared for unhappiness. For happiness one doesn't need to prepare."

He turned and gazed up at my sister's first-floor windows, shuttered by metal blinds. Lady Gaga floated toward us from the kindergarten across the street.

"You can write there?"

I paused, pretending to consider my answer; pretending, as it were, that there was a chance that I might write there, while knowing full well that there wasn't.

"If you want the truth," I admitted, "my work hasn't been going well. I hit a wall with it."

"All the more reason to try something else for a while."

"What? Finding an end to what Kafka couldn't finish, or chose to abandon, like most of what he wrote? Works that made their way into the world regardless, without any ending, to no less effect? Even if I could get past the intimidation, the sense of transgression would be intolerable. My own work makes me anxious enough as it is."

Through the large leaves of a jungle tree, the sun fell dappled on Friedman's face, and a little smile tugged at the corners of his dry lips, the inward smile that the wise give themselves in the face of other people's foolishness.

"You think your writing belongs to you?" he asked softly.

"Who else?"

"To the Jews."

I broke into laughter. But Friedman had already turned away and begun to comb through his bulging pockets one by one. The hands, their papery backs blotchy with sunspots, patted and pressed, worked open the Velcro closures. It was an ordeal that could go on all day: he was as thickly packed as a suicide bomber.

Amid the laughter, the famous line from Kafka's diary came back to me: *What do I have in common with the Jews? I have hardly anything in common with myself.* It was often quoted in the tireless argument about just how Jewish Kafka's work really was. Then there was what he'd written in his diary about wishing to stuff all of the Jews (including himself) into a drawer until they'd suffocated, opening and closing the drawer from time to time to check on the progress.

Friedman didn't respond and went on searching his pockets, which I now imagined to be filled with scraps of paper, assignments to be delivered to other writers to keep the great machine of Jewish literature rolling forward. But nothing was found or discovered, and either he forgot what he was looking for or lost interest. Jewish literature would have to wait, as all Jewish things wait for a perfection that in our hearts we don't really want to come.

"Anyway, you said it yourself," I reminded him, "no one cares about books anymore. One day the Jews woke up and realized that they needed another Jewish writer like they needed a hole in the head. Now we're back to belonging to ourselves."

A disapproving look made the already deep furrows in Friedman's forehead deeper. "Your work is good. But this false naïveté is a problem. It gives the impression of immaturity. You don't come off well in interviews."

A wave of fatigue came over me. I took up the handle of my suitcase.

"Tell me, what is it you want from me, Mr. Friedman?"

He lifted the bag of Kafka from the low wall where he'd set it down, and held it out. There was a small tear at the bottom, and it looked as if the whole thing were about to rip open. I reached for it instinctively to stop the books from spilling all over the sidewalk.

"I'm flattered that you approached me, really I am. But I'm not the writer for you. I have a hard enough time with my own books. My life is already complicated. I'm not looking to contribute to Jewish history." I tugged the suitcase toward the front path of my sister's building. But Friedman wasn't finished.

"History? Who said anything about history? The Jews never learned from history. One day we'll look back and see Jewish history as a blip, an aberration, and what will matter then is what has always mattered: Jewish memory. And there, in the realm of memory, which will always be irreconcilable with history, Jewish literature still holds out hope of having some influence."

Opening the car door, he tossed in the metal cane, slid into the driver's seat, and started up the engine.

"I'll come for you at ten tomorrow morning," he called through the lowered window. "You like the Dead Sea? Pack an overnight bag. The desert gets cold after sunset."

Then he raised an open palm and drove off, the tires crunching over broken glass.

LYING IN MY sister's familiar bedroom, I fell asleep at last. When I woke again, it was into a homesickness that felt physical, as its symptoms had been physical for seventeenth-century mercenary soldiers who'd fallen ill from being so far from home, the first to be diagnosed with the disease of nostalgia. Though never so acute, the longing for something I felt divided from, which was neither a time nor a place but something formless and unnamed, had been with me since I was a child. Though now I want to say that the division I felt was, in a sense, within me: the division of being both here and not here, but rather *there*.

I'd spent my early twenties thinking and writing about this ache. I'd tried, in my way, to treat it in the first novel I wrote, but in the end the only true cure I ever found for it had also been physical: first intimacy with the bodies of men who'd loved me, and later with my children. Their bodies had always anchored me. When I hugged them and felt their weight against me, I knew that I was here and not there, a reminder renewed each day when they climbed into my bed in the morning. And to know that I was here was also in a sense the same as wanting to be here, because their bodies created such a powerful reaction in mine, an attachment that didn't need to question itself, because what could make more sense, or be more natural? At night my husband would turn his back to me and go to sleep on his side of the bed, and I would turn my back to him and go to sleep on mine, and because we could find no way across to the other, because we had confused lack of desire to cross with fear of crossing with inability to cross, we each went to sleep reaching for another place that was not here. And only in the morning, when one of our children slid into our bed, still warm from sleep, were we repaired to the place where we were and reminded of our strong attachment to it.

Facedown in my sister's bed, I tried to reason with the anxiety seeping into me. I knew it not only from the many work trips I'd taken away from home, but also from when I dropped my children at school on mornings when they found it hard to say good-bye, when I would have to peel their hands off me and wipe the tears from their cheeks and then turn my back and go out the door as the teachers were always instructing us to do. The longer the good-bye stretched, the harder it became for the child, so they said, and what was required in such moments, if one wished to make it easier, was to detach with a swift pat and go quickly on one's way. Around us there were always children who seemed to have no trouble with this daily procedure. They didn't experience parting with their parent as a rupture or cause for distress. But neither of my children had an easy time of it. When my older son was three and began to attend preschool for a few hours in the mornings, he was so constantly distraught at separating that by late October the school psychologist called my husband and me in for a meeting, attended by his teachers and the head of the school. Behind the psychologist, colored paper leaves taped to the window fluttered in the updraft from the radiator. When he cries, the psychologist informed us, it's not the normal crying of a child. So what is it? I asked. To us—and here she looked gravely around at her colleagues to gather their support—it seems existential.

I'd argued with her. Argued for my son's happiness and well-being, and against a despair that surpassed the circumstantial. You should see him at home, I told her. A child brimming with joy! Full of humor, full of life! To support my claim, I drew from a deep well of anecdotes. But later, after the meeting was adjourned, the psychologist's comment continued to get under my skin.

The difficulty of parting had become easier with time. My son grew to love school, and there were long periods when he had no trouble at all with good-byes. But the fear of separating never fully left him, and even now it still happened that from time to time he was thrown into a panic at the entrance to school. While he pleaded with me not to make him go, I could remain calm and talk him down. But after half an hour of this—once he had exhausted himself, finally submitted to the fact that there was no choice, and went wiping his eyes through the doors, and I'd gone the opposite way without looking back—sadness would engulf me. It could take me hours before I was able to concentrate on my work, and when it neared the time to pick him up, I would leave far earlier than I needed to and hurry the whole way. And though it would be easy to say that I just felt for my son, it seems to me that if I'd examined myself more closely all those years, I'd have had to admit to the likelihood that it was in fact my anxiety and loneliness that came first, and my sons'—the oldest's, and then the younger one's—that echoed it, because in some corner of themselves they understood that it was only in their presence, attached to them, that I could feel truly here, and that it was because of them that I stayed.

I CALLED HOME on Skype. My husband answered, and then the boys' faces bobbled into view. Nothing had died since I'd been gone, they told me; none of the remaining ants in the ant farm, or the mealworms, or the guinea pigs, or our dog, who was old and blind, though they themselves seemed to have grown or otherwise changed in my brief absence. And mustn't they have? Every day, they were replacing the atoms they were born with with those they absorbed from their surroundings. Childhood is a process of slowly recomposing oneself out of the borrowed materials of the world. At an ordinary moment that passes without notice, a child loses the last atom given to him by his mother. He has exchanged himself completely, and then he is all and only the world. Which is to say: alone in himself.

My younger son told me about the story he'd written the day before, concerning a volcano with a square stuck in its stomach. He had a problem, my son explained (the volcano, not the square, for the square, at least, was dead). Some soldiers had come to him and instructed him to go to the Storm of Dawn. Had I ever heard of the Storm of Dawn? Well, in the center of the Storm of Dawn is a tiny dot that is the Storm of Doom, and that, my son informed me, is the hottest place in the world.

Behind him, I saw the familiar view of the blue kitchen cabinets, the window, the old stove, and remembered the feeling of evenings after the boys had fallen asleep, or mornings when I got back from dropping them off at school, when I'd tried to detect, again, the presence of the other life.

I began to tell them about the gray whale who'd lost his way and ended up off the shore of Tel Aviv, but only a sentence in, they began to make little noises of distress, and I realized that it had been a mistake. Ho-ho! I exclaimed, not yet sure quite how I would rescue them from this little snafu, this puddle of sadness that God forbid they should drown in because they'd never been given the chance to learn to swim. We had made such a huge production out of their happiness, my husband and I, had gone to such lengths to fortify their lives against sadness, that they had learned to fear it the way their grandparents had feared the Nazis, and not having enough food to eat. Despite the par-for-the-Jewish-course nightmares I had a few times a year about trying to hide my children under the floorboards or carry them in my arms on a death march, far more often I found myself contemplating how much personal growth they could achieve in a few weeks of running for their lives through a Polish forest.

But wasn't it possible, I hurriedly pointed out to them now, that the scientists had gotten it all wrong? That instead of a mistake, maybe the whale had come here willingly, isolating himself at great cost and risking his life to cling to what was most original in him? That the whale was on a great adventure?

Saved again, my sons soon became restless. At last, my husband reappeared on the screen. Twice his pixelated face froze in expressions that had no viable translation. But even whole, there was something unusual about his appearance. In the last months he too had begun to appear different. When you look at something for long enough, there is a point at which familiarity passes into strangeness. Maybe it was just the result of my tiredness, of the brain economizing its work by turning off the flood of associations and stored perspectives it uses every second to fill in the blanks and make sense of what the eyes transmit. Or maybe it was the early onset of the Alzheimer's I was sure would be my fate, as it had been my grandmother's. Whatever the case, more and more I found myself looking at my husband with the same inquisitiveness with which I looked at other passengers on the train, but even more so, and with added surprise, since for nearly a decade his face had been to me the epitome of the familiar, until one day it crossed out of that realm and into the *unheimlich*.

He'd been following the news and wanted to know what it was like in Tel Aviv, and which direction things seemed to be going. It was calm now, I said. Maybe there would be no Israeli airstrike, though as I said the words, I didn't really believe them. Didn't I want to come home? he asked. Wasn't I afraid? Not for myself, I told him, and repeated what I had heard others say: that one was more likely to be hit by a car than a rocket.

Then he asked how things were going with me, and what I had been up to since I'd been away. This simple question, so rarely asked, now struck me as vast. I could no more answer it than I could tell him what I had been up to, and how things had gone for me, during the decade we'd been married. All that time we had been exchanging words, but at some point the words seem to have been stripped of their power and purpose, and now, like a ship without sails, they no longer seemed to take us anywhere: the words exchanged did not bring us closer, neither to each other nor to any understanding. The words we wanted to use, we weren't allowed to use—the rigidity that comes of fear prevented them—and the words we could use were, to me, irrelevant. Still, I tried: I told him about the clearing weather, the swim I'd taken in the Hilton pool, and seeing Ohad, Hana, and our friend Matti. I told him about the atmosphere in the shelter, and the loud booms that sometimes shook the walls. But I didn't tell him about Eliezer Friedman.

ONE CORNER OF my sister's apartment was open to the dark, leathery foliage of a tree under whose leaves the air was kept dim and humid, spider-filled, and in this small outdoor room she had placed a once-expensive leather chair that had lived for a quarter century in our grandparents' apartment. When it rained in the winter, the metal shutter could be closed, but otherwise the chair, which my grandparents had been religious in their care of, rarely sitting in and protecting from the Middle Eastern sun with a sheet, was left open to the elements. This rebellious or just free-spirited act of my sister's was thrilling to me. I sat in the chair often to defuse the urge to cover it.

Opening to the first page of Kafka's *Parables and Paradoxes*, I began to read:

Many complain that the words of the wise are always merely parables and of no use in daily life, which is the only life we have. When the sage says: "Go over," he does not mean that we should cross to some actual place, which we could do anyhow if the labor were worth it; he means some fabulous yonder, something unknown to us, something too that he cannot designate more precisely, and therefore cannot help us here in the very least.

I felt a little upswell of frustration. When I thought about Kafka at a distance from his books, I almost always forgot this feeling. I would think of the iconic scenes of his life, which I'd read about enough times that I recalled them in my mind like the scenes of a film: the physical exercise before the open window, the feverish midnight writing at his desk, the painful days passed on the white, disinfected sheets of one sanatorium after another.

But frustration was more than a subject for Kafka, it was a whole dimension of existence, and the moment one begins to read him, one is delivered there again. There is never any resolution to the first aggravating, then enervating scenarios that arise in his writing; there is only the great, unending occupation of them, the nearly tantric endurance of frustration that achieves nothing except to prime the soul for absurdity. Even the sages are wrung for it: they tell us to go someplace, but we have no way of moving toward this place, and moreover they know no more about it than we do—there is no proof that it even exists. No matter that the sages are only ever finite and yet endeavor to direct us to the infinite. In Kafka's calculation, which cannot exactly be refuted, they're useless. They draw our attention to the fabulous beyond, but cannot bring us there.

I flipped ahead and reread what has always been, for me, one of the most unforgettable passages that Kafka wrote, a section from *The Trial*, which he chose to extract and publish alone. A man comes to the doorkeeper who stands on guard before the Law and asks for admittance. He is refused, but not outright— the doorkeeper tells him that he might be admitted later. The man can't advance but neither can he turn away, and so he sits down on the stool the doorkeeper offers, to wait before the open door to the Law. He's not allowed to go through; indeed, it seems the door remains open only to taunt him with the idea of passage. He spends a lifetime waiting, a lifetime on the threshold of the Law, and every attempt he makes to get in is always denied. The man grows old, his eyes become dim, his hearing faint; at last his life is drawing to a close, and "all that he has experienced during the whole time of his sojourn condenses in his mind into one question." He summons his last bit of strength to whisper it to the doorkeeper: Everyone strives to attain the Law, so why in all these years has no one tried to go through but me? To which the doorkeeper, shouting to make himself heard to the dying man, bellows, "No one but you could gain admittance through this door, since it was intended only for you. I am now going to shut it."

In the kindergarten across the street, Lady Gaga had been turned off, and the children began to sing. The tune was familiar, as were the words, though I couldn't understand all of them. I grew up with Hebrew in my ears—among other things, it was the language my parents argued in—but never enough to learn to really speak it. And yet, the sound of it felt intimate to me, like a mother tongue I'd forgotten, and over the years I'd taken up studying it numerous times. Kafka had also studied Hebrew during his last years in preparation for the move to Palestine that he dreamed of making. But of course in the end he never made aliyah—in Hebrew, the phrase literally means "to go up," and perhaps some part of him knew that he would never "go up," just as one cannot "go over" to the beyond, and can only remain stationed before the open door. After seeing a film about Jewish pioneers in Palestine, Kafka wrote in his diary about Moses:

> The essence of the path through the desert . . . He has had Canaan in his nostrils his whole life long; that he should not see this land until just before his death is difficult to believe . . . Not because life was too short does Moses fail to reach Canaan, but rather because it was a human life.

No one ever inhabited the threshold more thoroughly than Kafka. On the threshold of happiness; of the beyond; of Canaan;

of the door open only for us. On the threshold of escape, of transformation. Of an enormous and final understanding. No one made so much art of it. And yet if Kafka is never sinister or nihilistic, it's because to even reach the threshold requires a susceptibility to hope and vivid yearning. There *is* a door. There's a way up or over. It's just that one almost certainly won't manage to reach it, or recognize it, or pass through it in this life.

THAT EVENING I went to a dance class held in an old yellow school whose window frames were painted sky blue. I love to dance, but by the time I came to understand that I ought to have tried to become a dancer instead of a writer, it was too late. More and more it seems to me that dancing is where my true happiness lies, and that when I write, what I am really trying to do is dance, and because it is impossible, because dancing is free of language, I am never satisfied with writing. To write is, in a sense, to seek to understand, and so it is always something that happens after the fact, is always a process of sifting through the past, and the results of this, if one is lucky, are permanent marks on a page. But to dance is to make oneself available (for pleasure, for an explosion, for stillness); it only ever takes place in the present—the moment after it happens, dance has already vanished. Dance constantly disappears, Ohad often says. The abstract connections it provokes in its audience, of emotion with form, and the excitement from one's world of feelings and imagination—all of this derives from its vanishing. We have no idea how people danced at the time Genesis was written; how it looked, for example, when David danced before God with all his might. And even if we did, its only way of coming to life again would be in the body of a dancer who is alive now, here to make it immediate for us for a moment before it vanishes again. But writing, whose goal it is to achieve a timeless meaning, has to tell itself a lie about time; in essence, it has to believe in some form of immutability, which is why we judge the greatest works of literature to be those that have withstood the test of hundreds, even thousands, of years. And this lie that we tell ourselves when we write makes me more and more uneasy.

So I love to dance, but nowhere do I love to dance more than in this class in the yellow school, in those old rooms from whose large windows one can see the red flowers of trees that give me endless pleasure, but of which I've never taken the trouble to learn the name, and where upstairs Ohad rehearses with his company in a room with a view of the sea. The teacher told us that we should try to feel small collapses inside us as we moved, collapses that were invisible on the outside, but which were happening inside of us all the same. And then after a few minutes, she told us that we should feel a continuous collapse, soft but ongoing, as if snow were falling inside us.

WHEN THE CLASS ENDED, I walked to the beach. I sat in the sand and thought about how what was behind me had once been a desert. One day a stubborn man came and traced lines in the sand, and sixty-six stubborn families stood on a dune and drew seashells for sixty-six plots, and then went off to build stubborn houses and plant stubborn trees, and from that original act of stubbornness an entire stubborn city grew up, faster and larger than anyone could have imagined, and now there are four hundred thousand people living in Tel Aviv with the same stubborn idea. The sea breeze is just as stubborn. It wears away the facades of the buildings, it rusts and corrodes, nothing is allowed to stay new here, but people don't mind because it gives them a chance to stubbornly refuse to fix anything. And when some know-nothing comes from Europe or America and uses his foreign money to make the white white again, and the porous whole, no one says anything because they know it's just a matter of time, and when soon enough the place looks decrepit they're happy again, they breathe more easily when they pass, not out of schadenfreude, not because they don't want the best for him, whoever he is who only comes once a year, but because what people really long for, even more than love or happiness, is coherence. Within themselves, first of all, and then in the life of which they are a small part.

The tide had brought in plastic refuse ground down to confetti by the sea. The colored bits littered the sand and swirled on the surface of the waves. Narrative may be unable to sustain formlessness, but life also has little chance—is that what I wrote? What I should have written is "human life." Because nature creates form but it also destroys it, and it's the balance between the two that suffuses nature with such peace. But if the strength of the human mind is its ability to create form out of the formless, and map meaning onto the world through the structures of language, its weakness lies in its reluctance or refusal to demolish it. We are attached to form and fear the formless: are taught to fear it from our earliest beginning.

Sometimes, reading to my children at night, the perverse thought would come to me that in rehashing for them the same fairy tales, Bible stories, and myths that people have been telling for hundreds or thousands of years, I was not giving them a gift but rather taking something from them—robbing them of the infinite possibilities of how sense should be made of the world by so early, and so deeply, inscribing their minds with the ancient channels of event and consequence. Night after night, I was instructing them in convention. However beautiful and moving it could be, it was always that. Here are the various forms life can take, I was telling them. And yet I still remembered the time when my older son's mind did not produce known forms or follow familiar patterns, when his urgent, strange questions about the world revealed it anew to us. We saw his perspective as a form of brilliance and yet went on educating him in the conventional forms, even while they chafed us. Out of love. So that he would find his way in the world he has no choice but to live in. And bit by bit his thoughts surprised us less, and his questions came mostly to concern themselves with the meaning of the words in the books he now read to himself. On those nights, reading aloud to my children the story of Noah again, or Jonah, or Odysseus, it seemed to me that those beautiful tales that stilled them and made their eyes shine were also a form of binding.

I walked home up one of the little streets that led away from the sea, and by the time I got back to Brenner it was late and my legs ached, but I still couldn't sleep.

Feel ready to snap, the dance teacher had said. *But don't snap yet.*

At two or three in the morning the sirens went off, and I went downstairs and stood with an old lady and her daughter in the concrete stairwell. The wailing stopped, and in the silence we bowed our heads. When the thunderous explosion sounded, the old woman looked up and smiled at me, a smile so out of place that it could have only come from senility. On the way back to bed, I removed a few items of clothes from my suitcase and stuffed them into a plastic bag I found under the sink. For the sake of unpreparedness, I could say. Or because it was the hour when I seemed to pack for the trips I had no plans to take. Or because it would save me from having to wake up and face trying to begin the novel that by now I knew I would almost certainly never begin, though there was still a sliver of a chance that I might. Opening my computer, I checked the news, but nothing had yet been reported. I typed an e-mail to my husband. I might need some time, I said. I might need to be away for longer than I'd thought. Beyond that, I gave no explanation for what would become my silence.

Is and Isn't

E PSTEIN ENTERED THE HOUSE. Entered it with a song in his head. Entered the way a man enters into his own solitude, without hope of filling it. A man like Klausner must have his minions, and so he was not surprised to encounter three or four of them bustling about, preparing for the arrival of both Shabbat and Klausner. They were dressed in jeans and sweatshirts, and had it not been for the skullcaps, they could have been the sloppy residents of any college dorm in America. All but one, a young black man whose patchy sideburns were making slow inroads toward the rest of his scraggly beard, but who had already donned the pious uniform of dark jacket and white shirt. From the corner, hunched over a guitar, he sized Epstein up without pausing the graceful movement of his fingers across the strings. By what route had he arrived here? Epstein wondered, trying to place the melody. He pictured the boy's mother with graying temples by the window of her Bronx apartment, the Christmas tree rigged up. Later, gathered around a table set for ten, introductions were made, and the soulful guitar player was presented as Peretz Chaim. Epstein couldn't contain himself: "But what's your real name?" he asked. To which the young man, whose manners were fine, solemnly replied that Peretz Chaim was his real name, as real as Jules Epstein.

Klausner, having sent a last-chance-before-Shabbat e-mail at an outdated computer behind the front desk, and double-checked that all the lights had been left on, hurried Epstein back outside again, through the narrow streets to the old synagogue where he wanted to take him—to soak up the atmosphere, he said, rubbing two fingers together in a sign that to Epstein signaled money rather than rich air. To breathe in the spirituality. As they turned down a passage of stone steps, a large cemetery came into view below in the valley. It was planted with cypresses whose tapering forms seemed shaped by conditions separate from sun, wind, and rain.

Down below, the great sages of centuries past lay under tombs painted blue. Epstein had seen the paint everywhere in town, on paving stones and doors, in the grouting between the rough stones of the houses. It was tradition, Klausner explained, to ward off the evil eye. "A bit pagan"—he shrugged—"but what's the harm?"

They arrived at an arched door in the wall and, crossing a courtyard of broad paving stones, entered into a high-ceilinged, whitewashed room crowded with men in dark coats, fringes dangling. There seemed to be no order to the restless movement in the room, to the chanting here and swaying there, beards bristling with the tension of communication with the Almighty, while others kibitzed off-duty and helped themselves from a table laid with bottles of orange soda and cake. Klausner handed him a white satin skullcap from a table. Epstein examined the inside. Who knew how many heads it had been on? He was about to tuck it away in his pocket, but the man behind the table, beadle of the skullcaps, was watching him with fiercely narrowed eyes, and so with a wink Epstein set it on his head.

Now, as if under the command of a distant electromagnetism, the whole group joined together in song. Epstein, who had the urge to add his voice—not to sing so much as to yell out some disjointed, Tourette's-like phrase into the volume—opened his mouth, but closed it again when he was shunted aside by the traffic still coming in from behind. When the song died back into scattered chanting, Klausner was drawn into conversation by a man even larger than he, with a beard as coarse and red as Esau's.

Finding himself separated, Epstein let himself be pulled by the crowd in the opposite direction, past the shelves of gilded books and baskets of silk flowers. Caught in an eddy of black coats, he saw a huge, dark wooden chair with eagle's talons at the bottom of its legs, attached to what looked like a cradle—oh, God, was that where they performed the circumcisions? The barbarism! Then he noticed an opening in the wall, and to get away from the chair, stepped down into a small, grotto-like room where some oily candles flickered. When his eyes adjusted to the dark, he saw that he wasn't alone: a rheumy-eyed man was perched on a low stool. The musty air was heavy, tinged with the man's body odor. A little brass plaque on the wall, which Epstein tried to make out in the gleam from the candles, commemorated this as the place where the famous Luria had come to pray five hundred years ago.

The shrunken man was groping his leg, offering him something. A wave of claustrophobia came over him. The breathable air seemed to be running out. A psalm, did he want to say a psalm? Was that what the man was asking? To ask for a blessing from the sage? In the old man's lap was a package of cookies, and when Epstein refused the book of psalms, the man waved the package blindly, pushing it toward him. No, no, he didn't want a cookie, either, and when the man continued to pull on his pants leg, Epstein reached down, tore off the arthritic claw, and fled.

Half an hour later, back at Gilgul, drops of sweat were forming again on Klausner's brow. For the second time in a week, Epstein found himself seated at a table of Jews under the sway of the rabbi's exertions. But unlike the audience of American Jewish leaders gathered vaguely, expensively, to rehearse their old positions, the students around this simple wooden table seemed alert and alive, open to miracles. Glancing avidly about, Epstein waited for the show to begin. In these elevations, under his own mystical roof, Klausner was even more in his element than he had been at the Plaza. And tonight Epstein was his guest of honor, and so it was especially for his sake that the rabbi's sermon was designed—if *design* was the word, for the sentences seemed to roll from his mouth spontaneously. Rocking on the balls of his feet, he opened grandly:

"Tonight, we have in our company a man come down from King David!"

All heads turned to look. Epstein, who had come down from Edie and Sol, did not bother to correct him, the way one does not bother to correct a magician whom one has seen pull an extra card from his sleeve.

From the King of Israel, Klausner leaped to the Messiah, who it was said would come from the descendants of David. And from the Messiah, he leaped to the end of time. And from the end of time, he leaped to time's beginning, to the withdrawal of God to make space for the finite world, for time can only exist in the absence of the eternal. And from the withdrawal of God's divine light, the rabbi, blue eyes sparking with local candlelight, leaped to the empty space, whose spot of darkness held the potential for the world. And from the empty space that held the potential for the world, he leaped to the creation of the world, with its days and measures.

Like so, the tall, limber rabbi born in Cleveland, transplanted to the ancient land of the Bible, leaped like Jackie Joyner from the infinite to the finite. Epstein followed loosely. His thoughts were diffuse tonight, his focus fleeting. The words rolled through him, under the notes of an aria by Vivaldi whose steady heartbeat had been lodged in his head since he woke that morning at the Hilton.

"But the finite remembers the infinite," Klausner said, holding up a long finger. "It still contains the will of infinity!"

The will of infinity, Epstein repeated to himself, weighing the phrase in his mind as one weighs a hammer to see if it is enough to drive the nail. But the words came apart on him and raised only dust.

"And so everything in this world longs to return there. To *repair* itself to infinity. This process of repair, this most beautiful of processes which we call *tikkun*, is the operating system of this world. *Tikkun olam*, the transformation of the world, which cannot happen without *tikkun ha'nefesh*, our own internal transformation. The moment we enter into Jewish thought, Jewish questioning, we enter into this process. Because what is a question but a voided space? A space that seeks to be filled again with its portion of infinity?"

Epstein glanced at his small, pale neighbor, whose pierced eyebrow was knitted in concentration. She was young—younger even than Maya—and solemn as an icon. She gave off the air of having survived a disaster. Would she know what to do with her portion of infinity when she finally got it? Studying the tattoos on her knuckles, Epstein wasn't sure. He looked gloomily at his watch: still an hour and a half before the taxi was supposed to come for him. He thought of calling Maya, or checking in with Schloss, or reaching the director of development of the Israel Museum in the fragrant garden of her Jerusalem home, apologizing for disturbing her Friday-night meal, and announcing that he had decided to give her the $2 million to commission a monumental sculpture in his parents' names. Something rusted, immovable, dwarfing, called, simply, *Edie and Sol*.

His father first, and then, suddenly, his mother. His father had been dying for years, had been dying for as long as Epstein could remember, but his mother had been scheduled to live forever, for how else would she have the last word? Epstein had buried his father, had arranged everything—the relatives, however distant, wanted a copy of his eulogy, so moving had it been. But there was nothing he could give them, he had spoken extemporaneously. Jonah and his cousins shouldered the pine casket. "Stand on the boards!" the gravedigger had shouted. "On the *boards*!" He'd laid two thin wooden planks lengthwise across the grave, on which they were to perch to lower the coffin on ropes. But they were struggling under the weight, slipping in the loose soil in their dress shoes, and could not see where they were putting their feet. That night, after everyone had left the shiva, Epstein wept alone, thinking of how his father had looked down at his naked, bruised legs in the hospital bed, and asked, "How did I get so banged up?"

But he could still operate the heavy machinery of grief, and steered his mind away from the places that would cause the most destruction. He had arranged for the religious relatives to fly in from Cleveland and California, had arranged for someone to say the daily kaddish, had already paid the mason for the headstone a year in advance, but in all of this arranging he had failed to arrange his mother, who had always made her own arrangements, who did not want his help, who had never wanted anyone's help, who had been offended at its mere offer, and who one morning, not even three months after his father died, riding down alone in the Sunny Isles elevator, had had a massive heart attack and died. Passed away in the back of the ambulance, in the presence of no one but the paramedic.

Then Epstein had had to do it all over again. He went through the motions, as if in a fog. People spoke to him, but he barely heard, and wandered off in the middle of their condolences; all was excused, he was in shock. Three weeks later, he flew back to Miami alone. His sister Joanie wanted no part in dealing with their parents' things. As with everything, she left it to her accomplished brother. Sorting through their belongings, he knew himself to be searching for something, a form of evidence for what he had always known but had never been told, because to utter even a word about his father's past had been against the laws of their world. Even now, as he looked with trembling hands through his father's drawers, he could not speak to himself about the wife and small son his father had lost in the war. He couldn't say how he knew. The origins of his knowledge—no, it was not knowledge, it was innate sense—were inaccessible to him. But for as long as his memory went back, he had been in possession of this sense. It had informed everything. Without touching it, his consciousness had nevertheless grown around this vacuum of his father's original son.

In the end, he'd turned up nothing except for a shoebox of old photographs of his mother that he'd never seen, belly round with him, hair whipped by wind, face browned by the Middle Eastern sun, the lines of her features deep and strong. Already operating according to her own system. She was not disorganized but did things her own way. Her internal order was hidden to others, and this gave the impression that she was impenetrable. Even after a lifetime with her, standing knee-high in boxes in her closet or going through her papers, Epstein could not crack the code. Conchita was no help either. He made his own instant coffee while she moped in the bedroom and called Lima on the house phone. In the cupboard, behind the boxes of unopened tea, Epstein had noticed a tin from Ladurée—a gift from him, bought on one of his trips to Paris. Opening it, he discovered what appeared to be a few serrated gray beads at the bottom, but when he poured them into his palm, he saw with surprise that they were baby teeth. His own teeth, which his mother, whom he'd never known to possess a grain of sentimentality, had kept for sixty years. He was deeply touched, tears sprang to his eyes; he had the desire to show them to someone, and was about to call Conchita into the room. But his phone rang just then, and he'd slipped them distractedly into his pocket and only remembered them too late, after he had sent the pants to the dry cleaner's. Wincing, he thought now of the tiny teeth washing down through the drainpipes with the wastewater.

THE RABBI DREW his sermon to a close, and the blessing was made over the challah. Klausner tore hunks from the braided loaves, stabbed them into a dish of salt, stuffed one into his mouth, and tossed the rest around the table. It was a form of crudeness Epstein had been known to praise: the crudeness of passion that refuses to dull itself with manners. What good had etiquette ever done anyone? So began the little speech he liked to give to Lianne on the long rides back from visiting her parents, the dense old growth of Connecticut unfurling outside the windows. A wrong turn had been taken in the human evolution, the result of the slow drain of necessity from life. Once survival was ensured, time had opened for frivolity and daft embellishment, and this led to the absurd contortions of propriety. So much useless energy spent meeting the standards of social manners, which in the end accomplish nothing but constriction and misunderstanding. Lianne's family and their priggish formalities were the inspiration for his lecture, but once he'd gotten started, there was no stopping him until they'd pulled into the parking garage in Manhattan: humanity could have gone another way, leaving its inner self exposed!

Lianne, being unable to turn the tide of evolution, silently removed an issue of the *New Yorker* from her bag and began to leaf through its pages. It had always been that way with her. Epstein could never get through. Perhaps it was desire that had kept him there for so long: he had tried and tried to throw himself against that wall, too, to break through to her secret inner court. After a while, he lost his energy for the argument. His world was making him weary. Those were the months leading up to his announcement to Lianne that he could no longer remain married. When they were dining at the Four Seasons for her niece's sixteenth birthday, a white-coated waiter had lifted his dropped napkin from the floor and returned it to his lap, and as he did, Epstein had felt an urge to jump to his feet and cry something out. But what? He'd imagined the diners turning to him in bewildered silence, the faces of the waitstaff tightening, the rippling curtains falling finally still, and so instead excused himself, and on the way to the men's room instructed the maître d' to bring his niece the spun sugar dessert with a sparkler for a candle.

Now, at the thought of Lianne's face, finely lined, touched by faint surprise as it was whenever she opened her eyes in the morning, Epstein felt a stab of pain. It had always annoyed him, this expression of her bewilderment. He woke to the day, into argument, having rehearsed his position all night in his sleep, but she slept and forgot, and woke perplexed. Why was she not more like him? He remembered how, on the night he'd told her that he could no longer carry on in their marriage, Lianne had said that he wasn't himself. That he was still reeling from his parents' deaths, and that it wasn't the time to do anything rash. But by the way her eye twitched, he'd understood that she knew something not even he yet fully grasped. That she was the opposite of bewildered, and had come to her own conclusions. Something had needed to break, and he felt it then, the fragile bones snapping one by one under his fingers. He hadn't guessed it would be like that. He had imagined it as a huge, nearly impossible labor, but it took almost nothing. So light, so delicate a thing was a marriage. Had he known, would he have been more careful all these years? Or would he have broken it long ago?

THE STEAMING DISHES were brought out from the Gilgul kitchen. In a burned pan, a whole chicken lay plucked and yellow, bubbling in its own fat. Epstein half wondered whether

Klausner would tear off the thighs and toss them around the table, too. But one of the girls, a lesbian by the look of it, applied herself to it with a carving knife. A plate was passed down the table to Epstein, piled high with meat and potatoes. He'd barely eaten since his near drowning. His stomach couldn't take it. On account of what? Swallowing a bit of sea? From beyond the grave, his mother laid into him. What was wrong with him? The smoke from an eternal cigarette swirled around her. He used to have a stomach of steel! He took down a swallow of sour wine and set into the greasy chicken. Bracing himself, he stuffed it down. It was just a question of mental exertion over the body. Long ago, when Jonah and Lucie were still young, he'd received a diagnosis of malignant melanoma. A small mole on his chest had begun to change color with the leaves one autumn. But when the doctor scratched it off and sent it to the lab, the news came back that it was his death that had been growing there, unfurling its colors. There was a 10 percent survival rate, the doctor reported grimly. In the meantime, there was nothing to be done. Leaving the office and walking down Central Park West in the invigorating sunlight, a trembling Epstein had made a decision: he would live. He told no one of the diagnosis, not even Lianne. And he never went back to see the doctor again. The years passed and passed, and the little white scar on his chest faded and became imperceptible. His death became imperceptible. Once, passing the forgotten address, his eye had caught on the doctor's name on the brass placard, and a chill had gone through him. He pulled his scarf around his neck and laughed it away. Mind over matter! Yes, he had cured himself of a lisp, cured himself of weaknesses, of failures, of exhaustions, of all manner of inability, and as if that were not enough, he had gone and cured himself of cancer.

A stomach of steel and an iron will. Where there was a wall, he had gone through. Surely he could get his dinner down, despite the nausea he felt chewing it.

And so it went, so that it was not until much later—for the eating went on a long time, and then there was still the singing led by Klausner, who brought the group to finale with a loud, rhythmic thumping with his giant palm on the table, rattling the plates and silverware—that a full Epstein, unable to bear the churning in his gut any longer, rose and, groping down the dark hallway in search of a bathroom, came upon her.

THE DOOR HAD been left ajar, and through it warm light tumbled out across the hall. Approaching, he heard the gentle ripple of water. He did not think of turning away. It was not his nature to turn away, he had always been too curious, had taken the world as something given him to see all of. But when he peered through the opening, what he saw sent a surge of feeling through him. He gripped his stomach and held his breath, but the young woman sitting in the bath with her chin resting on her knees must have sensed his presence, because slowly, almost leisurely, without lifting her head, she turned her face. Her black hair, cut above the nape, fell back from her ear, and her eyes came calmly to rest on him. Her gaze was so direct and startling that he felt it as a rupture. Along seams that had been waiting to come apart, but it hardly mattered. Shocked, he stepped back, and as he did, he lost his footing. Falling through the dark, he flung out his hands. His palms slapped the wall, and at the sound she jumped up with a splash.

Only then did he realize that she hadn't seen him at all. Couldn't have in the dark. But for a moment he had seen all of her, the water streaming in rivulets down her body. Then the door slammed shut.

He felt his gut convulse and fled back down the hall. Coming to the front door, he shoved it open and hurled himself outside. The temperature had dropped, and in the tremendous sky the cold stars had hardened and shone. He tore through the bristled growth, wild and knee-high. A dank vegetative smell rose, released by the broken weeds underfoot. Doubling over, he began to vomit. It came out of him and came out of him, and when he thought it was over, more came. Heaving, purged of his great effort, he saw the cloud of his own breath vanishing up.

He wiped his mouth and straightened, his legs still weak. He should really call a doctor tomorrow. Something wasn't right. He looked back at the house picked over by moonlight. What was he doing here? He wasn't himself tonight. Had not been himself, it seemed, for some time. He had taken a rest from being himself. Was that it? A rest from being Epstein? And was it not possible that, resting from his lifelong logic, his epic reason, he had seen an apparition?

He couldn't bring himself to go back inside. Pushing through the nettles, he made his way he didn't know where. Around the side of the house, where blocks of stone and roof tiles had been left in disorderly piles, and a shovel stuck up out of the stony earth. Nothing was ever finished here: the world built over and over again on the same ground, with the same broken materials. Epstein stumbled, and the loose earth poured into his shoe. Leaning against the house, he pulled off the Italian loafer and shook out the dirt. He still wasn't ready to be buried. The wall retained the heat from the sun. Shivering, Epstein tried to absorb it, until a thought pierced him: What if she was not an apparition at all, but Klausner's flesh-and-blood lover? Was it possible that Klausner could carry on like that about the spiritual realms and the revelation of the divine light, waving his mystical wand, when all the while he was just as controlled by the laws of this world as anyone? Or could it be that she was his *wife*? Had the rabbi mentioned a wife? Was it possible that she, a world unto herself, sat listening to Klausner in a long drab skirt and punishing stockings, her head covered with a lifeless helmet of hair?

Coming around to the back of the house, Epstein saw light shining from a window. What more? He should go back to Tel Aviv, back to his hotel where he could fall asleep in the king-size bed, which was the only form of kingship he wanted, and wake up to his old understanding. The taxi was already on its way to him. He would go as he'd come: backward through the streets of Safed now settled in the dark, down the now-dark mountainside, through the dark valley, along the dark and shining sea, everything the reverse of what it had been, for that is what it is to live in a finite world, wasn't it? A life of opposites? Of doing and undoing, of here and not here, of is and isn't. All his life he had turned what wasn't into what was, hadn't he? He had pressed what did not and could not exist into bright existence. How often, standing atop the mountain of his life, had he felt that? In the glowing rooms of his home, while the cocktail waiters darted among the guests who had gathered to toast his birthday. Watching his beautiful daughters, whose every move was touched by their confidence and intelligence. Waking under sixteenth-century ceiling beams and a white eiderdown in a room with a view of the snow-capped Alps. Hearing his grandson play the small cello Epstein had bought him, the sheen on the rich brown wood the sheen of a good life. A full life. A life tirelessly wrestled from nonexistence into existence. There were moments when the elevator doors would open to the home where he and Lianne had raised their children like the curtains to a stage, and the world there was so fully wrought that he couldn't quite believe it. Couldn't believe what his belief in himself, and his huge desire, and his ceaseless effort had achieved.

He was exhausted. He half wished to pick up his phone and find someone to yell at. But yell what? What was it that, so late, still needed correction?

He was about to reach the window when he heard a rustling in the weeds. The light had blinded him. And yet he sensed that whatever was moving in the dark was more human than animal. "Who's there?" he called. All that came back was the sound of the faraway dog who, having not gotten back what he'd wanted, was still barking. But Epstein could feel a presence close by, and, not yet ready to give himself wholly over to the inexplicable, he called again: "Hey! Who's out here?"

"It's me." The deep-throated reply came from close behind him.

Epstein spun around.

"Who?"

"Peretz Chaim."

"Peretz—" Epstein exhaled, and felt his knees nearly give way. "You almost gave me a heart attack. What are you doing here?"

"I was going to ask the same of you."

"Don't be a smart aleck. I came out to take a piss. The rabbi's speech was heady. I needed some fresh air."

"And the air is fresher back here?"

Epstein, not entirely himself, was not yet unhimself, and rose reflexively to the challenge.

"What does your mother call you, Peretz?"

"She doesn't."

"But once upon a time she must have called you something."

"She called me Eddie."

"Eddie. Eddie, I can imagine going through the world as. I had an uncle Eddie. I would have stuck with Eddie, if I were you."

But Peretz Chaim was also quick, emboldened, perhaps, by the wine from dinner.

"Would have stayed stuck, you mean?"

Epstein now recalled how his own grandfather, whom he'd never known, had apparently changed names four times so that the evil eye wouldn't find him. But the world was larger then. It was easier not to be found.

"And how did you get here, Peretz Chaim?"

But the moment offered the young man an escape, because just then the light in the window behind them went out, and they were plunged into darkness.

"Bedtime," whispered Peretz Chaim.

A wave of exhaustion came over Epstein. He would lie down right there on the ground at the foot of her window and close his eyes. In the morning everything would look different.

"The rabbi's waiting," Peretz Chaim finally said. "He sent me to find you."

Epstein sensed the disapproval in his words. And yet weren't the two of them on the same side? Having both come late, unexpectedly, but of their own accord? Now, absurdly, he saw himself with a scraggly beard, donning the dark jacket, becoming a copy of a copy, so that he might brush against what was anciently original.

He could smell the kid's sweat. Reaching out, he laid his hand on his broad shoulder. "Tell me, Peretz, I have to know—who is she?"

But the young man sputtered a laugh, and abruptly turned and was lost to the darkness. His allegiances lay elsewhere. It was clear he didn't think much of Epstein.

THE TAXI THAT had come for him all the way from Tel Aviv was turned away—the 700-shekel fare handed to the driver through the open window, with another hundred on top. The driver, trying to decide if he should be annoyed, finally shrugged—what was it to him?—counted the money, and threw the taxi into reverse. Epstein waited until the sound of the engine died out and the night filled up again with its silent, immeasurable distances. It was a mistake, he knew. He should have gone back in the car, should have escaped while he could to the familiar dimensions of his world. Tomorrow he could have been drinking orange juice in the sun on the terrace. He should have gone, but he couldn't.

Back inside, Epstein followed the sound of voices to the kitchen. The one who'd wielded the carving knife was now making coffee with hot water from an urn, jabbering on proudly to whomever would listen about how Maimonides would turn in his grave if he could hear the rabbi. From the way she spoke, one might assume she had known the eleventh-century doctor personally. According to Maimonides, she said, God's existence is absolute. He has no attributes, there has never been a new element in Him. She carried on until the somber Peretz Chaim, whose name, Epstein had been told, meant "explosion into life," spoke up to say that, all the same, Maimonides still insisted on miracles. He was a medieval, Peretz was saying: he accepted both reason and revelation. But the girl didn't give up, and had Peretz Chaim been true to his name, it might have come to blows. But the gentle guitar player who had yet to explode, but still might explode one day, gave up the fight, and at last the conversation moved on to the cheese maker a group of them were going to visit the following day, whose Orthodox husband grew marijuana behind the house.

Epstein found the rabbi in his study, turned down his invitation to join him for a glass of brandy, and asked to be shown to his room. The rabbi was delighted. He would give Epstein a tour tomorrow, would show him how he had restored the walls and arches, had brought the place back from a century of neglect! He would show him the classroom, the small library with its collection of books donated by the Solokov family—did he know the Solokovs, from East Seventy-Ninth Street? Their son, who'd had no interest in Judaism, no interest in anything at all, had arrived in a state of lassitude and left to study philosophy, and then herbal medicine, and now, after backpacking across India, he had combined the strands of his enlightenment and opened Neshama Yoga in Williamsburg, out of whose storefront he also sold tinctures. From the depth of their thanks, the Solokovs had donated three thousand books. Epstein said nothing. And the money for shelving, too, Klausner added.

Looking around the room, Epstein saw that it was as simple as promised: bed, window, chair, and a small wardrobe, empty but for the smell of other centuries. A lamp cast warm shadows across the wall. In the corner stood a triangular sink, and beside it a hard, stiff towel hung from a peg on the wall; who could say how many pilgrims had already dried themselves with it?

Hovering behind him, Klausner had moved on to the subject of the Descendants of David reunion. With a small endowment, they might be able to get Robert Alter as the keynote speaker. It wasn't his first choice, but Alter had mainstream appeal, and was already scheduled to be in town that week.

And what would the rabbi's first choice have been? asked Epstein, who could once make conversation in his sleep.

David himself, Klausner said, turning sharply, and in the now-familiar gleam in Klausner's eyes Epstein thought he caught something else, something he might have mistaken for a glimmer of madness if he hadn't been all too aware of his own haziness and fatigue.

"So you think I go all the way back to him?" Epstein asked softly.

"I know."

At last, unable to stand any longer, the pilgrim Epstein hung his jacket and sank down onto the bed, swinging his legs up. For an absurd moment, he thought the rabbi might bend to tuck him in. But Klausner, having gotten the point at last, bade Epstein good night, promising to rouse him early. Just before he pulled the door closed, Epstein called out to him.

"Menachem?"

Klausner poked his face back around, flushed with enthusiasm. "Yes?"

"What were you before this?"

"What? Before Gilgul?"

"Something tells me you weren't always religious."

"I'm still not religious," Klausner said with a grin. But, remembering himself, his face became serious again. "Yes, there's a story there."

"With all due respect, I'd like to hear about that more than the restored arches."

"Whatever you want to know."

"And something else," Eptein said, remembering. "Why did you call the place Gilgul? It sticks in the throat a little, if you ask me."

"Livnot U'Lehibanot—to build and be built—was already taken by the place down the street, along with an endowment from the Jewish Federation of Palm Beach."

"And what do they do there?"

"*Hitbodedut.* Hasidic meditation. At the end of every retreat, they send the students alone into the woods. To contemplate. To sing and shout. Experience elevation. Occasionally it happens that someone goes astray, and the emergency rescue unit has to be brought in." But Gilgul was better than it sounded, Klausner said, and explained that the word meant "cycle" or "wheel," but in kabbalah it referred to the transmigration of the soul. To higher spiritual realms, if one is prepared. Though sometimes, naturally, to more punishing ones.

SWITCHING OFF THE bedside lamp, Jules Epstein's soul stirred under the stiff sheets and he was returned again to the intractable dark that he had stared into on countless nights when he couldn't sleep, when the arguments continued in his head, the great assemblage of the evidence of his rightness. And did the unyielding dark look different to him now, in the cease-fire that had arisen in him during these last months?

The word came to him unbidden, full of meaning. For it was only in the arena of this cease-fire—in its eerie silence, its suspension of a former directive—that he had become fully aware of what he must now think of as a war. An epic war, whose many battles he could no longer name or recall, except that he had mostly won them at a cost he did not care to explore. He had attacked and defended. Slept with his weapon under the pillow and woke into argument. His day had not officially begun, Lucie once said of him, until he had taken issue with something or someone. But he had felt it as a form of health. Of vitality. Of creativeness, even, however destructive the consequences. All of the meshugas! Embroiled, horns locked, in a permanent state of conflict—it had only ever energized him, never depleted him. "Leave me in peace!" he had sometimes roared in arguments with his parents or Lianne, but in truth peace had not appealed to him, for in the end it had meant being left alone with himself. His father used to take the belt to him. To lash him repeatedly for the smallest errors, driving him into the corner as he pulled the black leather from the loops, and laying into his bared skin. And yet it was the specter of his father lying inert in bed with the curtains drawn at ten in the morning that stirred his own rage. The fear he felt as a child tiptoeing past his father's bedroom door later turned to fury: Why didn't he rally forces and rouse himself? Why didn't he stand and come out swinging? Epstein couldn't bear being around it, and so he began to spend all of his time out of the house, where the bright energies hummed busily. When his father wasn't laid out with depression, he was another form of impossible—stubborn and fixed in his ways, easily set off. Between Sol and Edie, who went perpendicular to everything and parallel to nothing, who couldn't let be and had something to say about everything, Epstein developed in a solution of extremes. Either you were lying listless or you came out armed and loaded. Out in the fresh air and sunlight, he threw himself into the fray.

Threw the first punch. Discovered that he could be ruthless. *Saul has slain his thousands, and David his ten thousands!* So large did he grow, so taken with his power, that one night he came home, and when the father, standing in the kitchen in his stained robe, started in on the son, the son turned, swung, and delivered a clenched fist to the father's face. Punched him, and then sobbed like a child as he held a slab of ice to the fallen father's grotesquely swelling eye.

Epstein touched his own eye reflexively, got out of bed, and went barefoot to the window. What had he known of relations of grace?

He could have still gone back to Tel Aviv had he wanted. Could have called the taxi back, walked down the still-dark hallway to the waiting car, texting Klausner with the excuse of a forgotten meeting. He could have finalized the details of a donation in memory of his parents to the Weizmann Institute or the Israel Museum, finalized the hotel bill, finalized Moti, who would have come to the lobby with sweat stains under the arms to see him off and receive the usual envelope of cash, could have packed up and gone back to the airport, left the city where he'd been born, and to which he had returned countless times to regain what he could never put his finger on, flown six hundred miles an hour in the opposite direction from Judah Halevi's heart, and watched the Eastern Seaboard emerge out of the dark and fathomless. And after the pilot, fighting high winds, had brought the plane down askew to the scattered applause of those who found themselves still, surprisingly, alive, he could have sailed through Global Entry, hurtled in a taxi along the Grand Central, empty at four thirty in the morning, glimpsed the Manhattan skyline, and felt the rush of emotion that comes with returning after having been far away, at a place where one's arrival had felt very nearly final. He could have gone home had he wanted to. But he hadn't. And now other things would have to happen.

He felt the ballast gone. Everything and everyone that held him to the pattern of himself was gone now. He leaned his forehead against the glass and looked out at the immense realm of the sky, hemmed below by the jagged line of primordial masses. He felt aroused, not only by the view but by his own receptivity. Something had been dislodged, and in the cavity the nerves conducted raw feeling without purpose. He probed tenderly and discovered, as one discovers with all absences, that the emptiness was far larger than what had once filled its place.

Kaddish for Kafka

IN THE MORNING everything was calm again, the sky still and cloudless. I'd slept hardly at all, and as always during nights of insomnia, I'd had the feeling that the shore of reason, with its familiar hills and landmarks, was drifting farther and farther away from me, and was touched by the fear that I was in some way willing myself away from it, and had chosen sleeplessness as my method. I sat drinking bitter coffee on my sister's terrace. The brightness irritated my eyes, but from there I could look out for Friedman, who in my exhaustion I half hoped wouldn't show up. Sitting in my grandmother's chair, I thought of how she used to take me to the Dead Sea as a girl. She would pack us a lunch, and we would take the bus from the Central Station out to the desert, and in a couple of hours the two of us would be floating belly-up in the salty, electric blue remainder of an extinct sea, with the ancient mountains of Moab behind us. Floating in a concentration of history reduced by the slow evaporation of time, my grandmother in her white bathing cap decorated with rubber flowers. I imagined Friedman floating there, too, in his darkened glasses, controlling the transmission of national literature while his white hair rippled out on either side like underwater life.

At ten sharp he rattled up in his white Mazda, another symphony pouring through the windows. I lifted myself out of the old chair and tucked *Parables and Paradoxes* into the plastic bag that held my change of clothes. Hazily, I grabbed my bathing suit and stuffed that in, too. I glanced at the computer left open on the table from my middle-of-the-night e-mail home, then closed the door behind me, locking both upper and lower locks as my sister had instructed me to do whenever leaving the apartment for any length of time. The stairwell was cool and dark going down, and the sudden switch from the brightness made me dizzy, as if the roof over my thoughts had been suddenly raised, letting in a cold rush of space. Just beyond exhaustion there must be something else, just as beyond hunger they say there is an exalted clarity and lightness. But I'd always preferred to read about altered states rather than risk them personally. My mind was too permeable as it was; what few drug trips I'd taken had dipped all too briefly into euphoria before plunging me into panic. I sat down on the steps and put my head between my knees.

A WARM WIND came in through the open windows of the car as we drove. Friedman had brought me some chocolate rugelach from the bakery, and, feeling better, I ate these, one after another, while his dog rested her head on my shoulder, breathing in my ear. When I'd had dinner with Matti a couple nights earlier and told him about the other Friedman I'd met, who might or might not be former Mossad, Matti had laughed and said that if all the people in Israel who hinted that they worked for the Mossad actually did, then it would be the largest employer in the country. Think of all the banal domestic secrets whose cover-up the Mossad has unknowingly sponsored, he said. The truth is that by then I didn't really believe I would be called on to write the end of Kafka's "play." The idea now seemed so ludicrous that it wasn't necessary to consider seriously. The dog and the cookies, the crumpled bag of disintegrating paperbacks, the cats, the Mossad, and Friedman, who may only have been looking for a way to entertain himself in his retirement—it all struck me as almost playful. I had also retired, for the time being, from my former purpose. The purpose of writing a novel, I mean, though it is never really a novel that one dreams of writing, but something far more encompassing for which one uses the word *novel* to mask delusions of grandeur or a hope that lacks clarity. I could no longer write a novel, just as I could no longer bring myself to make plans, because the trouble in my work and my life came down to the same thing: I had become distrustful of all the possible shapes that I might give things. Or I'd lost faith in my instinct to give things shape at all.

I was along for the ride, I told myself as Friedman shifted gears. To get away from the sirens for a while, and because I liked the Judean Desert as much as I liked anyplace: its smell and its light, its millions of years, several thousand of which had been written into me via sources known and unknown, inscribed on a level so deep that it couldn't be differentiated from memory. If I didn't ask exactly where we were going or why, it was because I didn't want to know. What I wanted was to lay my head back and close my eyes, to put myself in someone else's hands for a while so that I might rest and not think.

Rest, but also, I'd have ventured had I not been so dead tired, so that I might be swept toward someplace that I hadn't meant to go. It was a long time since I'd allowed that to happen. It seemed to me now that I'd been making plans for myself for as long as

I could remember. Truly, I excelled in both the planning and execution: step by step, my plans came to fruition with such exactness that if I had looked more closely I would have seen that what drove my rigor was a kind of fear. When I was young, I thought that I would live my life as freely as the writers and artists I took as my heroes. But in the end I wasn't brave enough to resist the current pulling me toward convention. I hadn't gotten far enough along in the deep, bitter, bright education of the self to know what I could and couldn't withstand—to know my capacities for constriction, for disorder, for passion, for instability, for pleasure and pain—before I settled on a narrative for my own life and committed myself to living it. Writing about other lives can, for a while, obscure the fact that the plans one has made for one's own have insulated one from the unknown rather than drawn one closer to it. In my heart, I'd always known this. But if at night my body would twitch as I tried to sleep, as it did the night I agreed to marry my future husband next to a shining black lake, I would try to ignore it, as one tries to ignore the unexplained screw left over after assembling the bed one has to lie in. And not only because I didn't have the courage to admit the things I sensed about myself, or the man I'd agreed to join my life to. I ignored it because I also longed for the beauty and solidity of the form, the one on which all of nature (and a few thousand years of Jews) bestows the greatest praise: the mother and the father and the child. And so I turned away from the accounting that would have required me to foresee what would happen to all of us once the form had been assembled, once the atoms had all aligned in us. Instead, fearful of the kind of violent emotion I'd known in childhood from my family, I harnessed myself to a man who seemed to have a preternatural knack for constancy no matter what happened within or without. And then I harnessed myself to the habit and schedule of a highly organized, disciplined, healthy life as if everything depended on it, as if my children's well-being and happiness required this harnessing of not only all my hours and days but my thoughts, too, my whole spirit. While the other unformed and nameless life grew dimmer and dimmer, less and less accessible, until I succeeded in closing the door on it completely.

WE DROVE UP King George Street, passing the entrance to a park where I'd often taken my children to play and climb on a giant rope apparatus from whose apex they claimed they could see the sea. We had to make one quick stop before we could be on our way, Friedman told me. I thought maybe he'd forgotten something at home, and began to wonder about his life. I pictured his apartment filled with old books, and imagined a wife, large-busted, practical, with the shorn head of gray hair so common in a type of Israeli woman over sixty. Kibbutznik hair, a friend of mine calls it, though to me it always channeled the concentration camp, or would if the severity were not so often accompanied by huge earrings and a grandchild. A Yehudit or Ruth from Haifa. The father a doctor from Germany, the mother a pianist who gave lessons, both survivors, from whose darkness this Yehudit or Ruth had to free herself, though in the end she became a psychologist and spent her adult years trying to make sense of other people's traumas. The kind of woman whose kitchen people liked to come and sit in when she wasn't busy at work, who took a walk with the same two friends every morning for forty years. Already I loved her, this Yehudit or Ruth; already I was ready to take my place at her kitchen table covered in a plastic floral cloth and tell her everything. But it wasn't Friedman's apartment we were headed toward, it was the street named after the Dutch lens-grinder.

Friedman put the car into park in front of the building he'd brought me to two days earlier, where Kafka and the cats lived together in a state of unholiness, awaiting a verdict from the courts. I thought he was going to give me another lecture, but this time he got out and told me to wait. He would only be a few minutes, he promised, and before I could protest he slammed the door and started across the street with his cane.

The dog whined, watching until Friedman had disappeared into the building, then began to howl as if at some terrible injustice. She paced the cracked leather seat, gouged with a long history of such agitated waiting. I tried to soothe her, but not knowing her name or the words she would understand, couldn't help. When she seemed as if she were about to choke on her own rapid breath, I climbed over the gearshift and into the back with her. She walked across me a few times before finally settling down with her catastrophe, front paws splayed on my lap. I pulled gently at the baggy skin on her neck, just as I did to the dog I'd lived with for almost as long as I'd lived with my husband.

Ten, then fifteen, minutes passed. I thought about a story that a friend had told me many years ago, about a trip he'd taken to Prague when he was young. One night he'd gotten completely sloshed, and become convinced that he needed to go out and kiss the Altneuschul, directly across the street from where he was staying. The next morning he woke up unharmed, still embracing the shul, watched over, he imagined, by the remains of the golem supposedly buried in the attic. That afternoon he decided to go to the Straschnitz Jewish Cemetery to visit Kafka. The writer was buried next to his father, my friend told me, which was more or less the worst insult he could imagine. My friend decided he was going to say kaddish for Kafka. When he finished, he turned to go, and standing there behind him was the exact same headstone. He stood there, bewildered. A few minutes later, some kids sauntered over and explained that they'd just finished a replica of Kafka's headstone for a movie that was being shot, and had left it there while they went to lunch. I'd said kaddish to the replica, my friend told me. He helped them load it into their truck. The rubbing they'd done of the real headstone was sitting there, and he asked them if he could have it.

I wondered what Friedman could be doing inside. The dog's hot breath steadied and became rhythmic. I pictured the crowded rooms behind the window bars, humid with houseplants slowly dropping their yellow leaves over the disarray of Kafka's fading manuscripts, whose pages must have stunk of cat pheromones. Frustrated at being kept from seeing all of this for myself, I finally nudged the dog off my lap and got out of the car. The cats were absent today—gathered inside, maybe, to roll on Prague ink—but their smell still hung in the air, and the little dirty bowls set out on the ground suggested they would be back soon enough. I found Eva Hoffe's name on the top buzzer, but, peeking into the lobby at her door, and imagining the stringy-haired spinster's magnified eye blinking at me through the peephole, I backtracked and ducked under the broad fig leaves, swatting a sticky cobweb out of my face.

The night after my first meeting with Friedman, I'd read online about the trial over Kafka's archives. Everything he'd told me was corroborated there: the case, which was still being deliberated, came down to the question of whether Kafka's manuscripts—in a sense, Kafka himself—was a national asset or private property. So far no verdict had been given, but in the meantime the court had granted the National Library's request that the papers in Eva Hoffe's possession be inventoried. Eva, who often referred to the archive as an extension of her own limbs, had likened this to rape. After two appeals were overturned, keys to safe-deposit boxes in Tel Aviv were finally pried from her, but they didn't match the locks. On the day the boxes were finally to be opened by the lawyers, Eva was witnessed chasing them into the bank, shouting that the papers belonged to her. But however crazy she at times appeared to be, however bizarre the stories of her behavior, however difficult it might have been for the State of Israel to accept that a Jewish writer who meant so much to so many could be anything other than national property, her claim was not without legal strength. The results of the inventory had not been made public, but *Haaretz* had confirmed that she was sitting on a large amount of original Kafka material. And either it was everyone's and no one's, or Israel's, or only hers.

Approaching the row of ground-floor windows, I saw that behind the grid of heavy white bars enclosing them was a second layer of wire mesh, the sort used to cage small animals. It was too dark within to make anything out. Around the side of the building the conditions were even more extreme: the bay of windows, meant to allow for a kind of open sunroom, was grotesquely imprisoned by the rusted bars and filthy cage, patched or reinforced at the corners by the energetic attentiveness born of paranoia. Or was it not so much the reflection of an ill mind that had lost touch with reality, I wondered, as of the absurd reality of what against all odds was contained within: something so rare and valuable that there were those who would stop at nothing to lay their hands on it? The apartment had allegedly been broken into a couple of years earlier, though reports of the incident in the Israeli papers suggested the likelihood of an inside job.

I heard something moving. Softening my focus, so that the metal grid dissolved to the background, I saw the skinny black cat that had flattened itself between the bars and the mesh and was slinking through the narrow space between them. Had I believed in such things—and I suppose I did believe in such things—I might have taken it as an omen. A moment later I heard something being dragged down the stairs, as heavy as a body, and when I hurried back around the corner to the front, Friedman had emerged, pulling behind him a black suitcase. The stitching had come loose along the seams, and the handle was bound in duct tape. It was a suitcase more to do with a door-to-door kiddush-cup salesman than a Mossad man, or even former Mossad, or even former Mossad from the broom-closet department of Jewish literature. Not that this stopped me from believing, with a surge in the heart, that something of the lost Kafka was contained inside it.

Whatever it was, Friedman wouldn't say. Not yet, he said, glancing in the rearview mirror as we drove away. First there were things he had to tell me. We could stop in Jerusalem on the way to the desert and have lunch at a small, quiet vegetarian restaurant in the Confederation House in Yemin Moshe, overlooking the walls of the Old City. There we could talk without being bothered.

If things were not strange already, from the moment the suitcase was in our possession, things became far stranger. Now it seems to me that before the suitcase I was operating in a world of familiar laws but unusual circumstances, but afterward the familiar laws began to shiver and bend a little. More than that, it seems to me that I had been moving toward that bend for a long time without knowing it, which is to say, moving toward the suitcase, a suitcase that in some sense I'd been aware of since I was seven, having been given it in a story. But I'd had to wait all these years for it to finally open into my life.

The story was told to me by the woman who took care of my brother and me as children. She lived in our house for nearly a decade, beginning when she was twenty-two, but the word *nanny* could never be applied to her, nor even *babysitter*: she was too wild for that, too free and unconventional. She was also mystical, and though she had been raised Catholic, her beliefs drew on many sources and followed no prescription. Her room in our house was filled with crystals and her airbrush paintings of goddesses, wizards, and Disney characters, and around her throat she wore a small portrait of Jesus with a crown of thorns whose little trickles of blood induced in us both fascination and nausea. But we saw no evidence of piety or dutifulness in Anna; the many stories she told us of her childhood were always about subversion, not only of the authorities in her life but of all that lived under the regulations of normality, and which denied the magic she saw at the edges of everything. This particular story was about a job she had been hired for when she was nineteen, a few years before she came to live with us. An operation would be a better way to describe it, since all she had to do was to pick up a black suitcase in the middle of the night from one place, and drive three hours to deliver it to another. I can't remember what words Anna used to describe the nature of what was inside the suitcase, but we understood that it was illicit, and that she was putting herself in danger by undertaking the drive. The story she told us was mostly about the white-knuckled journey down a dark and winding road, during which a car, which was an exact replica of the one she was driving, began to follow her. We begged her to tell us what was in the suitcase, but she refused. My brother guessed that it was filled with money, and I guessed that it contained a magic necklace. But Anna, who in certain respects knew us better than our own parents, said we would have to wait for the answer until my brother's bar mitzvah, four years in the future.

The years passed, and sometimes my brother or I brought the suitcase up to see if Anna would finally reveal the secret contents. But she would only remind us that we had to wait until the agreed-upon point in time. And then at last my brother's bar mitzvah came—came and went, and we didn't ask. Probably we forgot, or we were old enough to suspect the answer without having to be told, and wished to avoid the awkwardness of asking. But as a result the mystery became permanent, and what Anna had given us, in the form of a story and a suitcase, outlasted the other countless things we had been given in those years and later lost or forgot.

WITH KAFKA IN the trunk, Friedman drove to the highway. It took us past palm and cypress trees, past fields above which dark flocks of starlings suddenly shifted directions in unison, then shifted sharply again. Past the new city of Modi'in, after which the landscape grew older, and beneath the grass the white skull of the world showed through. We drove past hillsides lined with broken walls from terraces long ago left to fall, but whose rows of ancient olive trees kept growing, past Arab villages and a shepherd nimbly picking his way down the hill in the wake of his sheep. A metal fence appeared on either side of the road, topped by circles of razor wire, and we passed through a checkpoint where the guards stood in riot helmets and dark uniforms thickened by bulletproof vests. After some miles, the fence was replaced by high concrete walls that ran all the way to the outskirts of Jerusalem, before giving way to forests of pine. Entering the city, we drove past Independence Park and through the streets of Rehavia, past Montefiore's renovated windmill and the renovated King David Hotel, once bombed, once no-man's-land, once, not very long ago, host to my brother's wedding.

Friedman pulled the car into a small lot next to a park, dislodged his dog from the backseat, and led me down a broad hill settled with crows. The stone Confederation House was the only structure around, surrounded by a garden of olive and palm trees, and fragrant with lavender. The restaurant was empty, and the lone waiter led us to a table by the window that looked across the narrow valley onto the walls built by Suleiman the Magnificent. The dog lowered herself with a groan onto Friedman's sandaled feet. While the waiter went to get her a bowl of water, Friedman busied himself with sorting through the wrinkled photocopies stuffed into a leather portfolio he'd brought with him from the car. Only after our order had been taken, and the waiter, who also appeared to be the cook, disappeared into the kitchen, did Friedman finally lean forward and, with a last gratuitous look around the empty restaurant, lower his voice and begin.

FOR THE NEXT two hours, I listened as he laid out his extraordinary tale. It was so far-flung that at first I was convinced that Effie the fabulist had delivered me into the hands of another of his kind, this one also potentially delusional. I made up my mind that I would wait until he had finished—it was too sensational a story not to hear to the end—but when the meal was over I would excuse myself and call Effie. He had gotten me into this, and now he could get me out. At the very least, he could give me a ride back to Tel Aviv.

And yet the more Friedman talked, the less certain I became of what to believe. I knew how highly improbable what he was telling me was. And that, if by some chance it had really happened, there was no way it would have been kept secret all this time: almost ninety years had passed since Kafka's death in a sanatorium outside Vienna. But presented with Friedman's persuasive eloquence and air of authority, and his seemingly exhaustive knowledge of Kafka, I found myself beginning to consider the distant, wholly unlikely possibility that what he was telling me might be true. And I suppose that, as with all incredulous things we open ourselves to, I wanted to believe it could be: that Kafka really might have finally crossed the threshold, slipped through a crack in the closing door, and disappeared into the future. That, thirty-five years after his funeral in Prague and his secret transport to Palestine, he could have passed away peacefully in his sleep on an October night in 1956, known only, if he was known at all, as the gardener, Anshel Peleg. That in Tel Aviv, not far from my sister's apartment, there could be a house, and behind the house a garden, and in that garden, now wild and overgrown, an orange tree that Kafka himself had planted. The last time Friedman had been there, he told me, a crow had fallen right out of the sky and landed dead at his feet just like that, without any explanation.

II

Gilgul

H IS HEBREW NAME, Anshel, was all he'd kept from his old
life. It's a Yiddish diminutive for Asher, interchangeable
with Amshel, which is also derived from *amsel*, German for
blackbird. It might easily have been discarded for a name more
commonly chosen by those emigrating to Palestine, for Chaim,
Moshe, or Yaakov, had it not held the echo of the last name he
had to give up, and which would one day become more famous
than he could ever imagine. *Kavka*, in Czech, is a jackdaw, a word
so common that Hermann Kafka chose that species of crow as
the logo for his fine goods and clothing business. That his son,
Franz, was drawn to transmogrification between human and
animal, and that at times the writer identified with the animal
side more, is obvious in works that would one day be read all
over the world. That with his glossy helmet of black hair, pulled
low over the forehead like a severe cap, and his piercing, widely
set eyes and beaklike nose, the writer looked like no animal so
much as the jackdaw is perhaps one of those accidents of fate,
Friedman asserted, which in his many stories Kafka was master
at revealing to be the projection of a conflicted inner desire. That
the surname he assumed, Peleg, was commonplace for those who
arrived during the Third Aliyah, suggests that it was chosen in
the interest of anonymity, presumably by some other authority,

who saw no reason to object to the name Anshel, or failed to see the blackbird Kafka had smuggled through inside it.

He barely survived the journey. When the ship docked in Haifa, the deckhands, who had grown fond of the pale, kind, impossibly thin man, had to carry him off on his back so that his first view of the Promised Land was of the brilliant blue, utterly cloudless sky that arched above it. A child who had been waiting to welcome a distant relative on the dock began to cry, believing it was a corpse they were unloading. So it was that the first Hebrew sentence Kafka heard spoken in Palestine was "How did he die, Father?" And the impossibly thin man, face turned heavenward, who had always been posthumous to himself, smiled for the first time in a week.

He'd been staging his own death for years, hadn't he? *Away from here, just away from here!* Remember the line? Friedman asked, his glasses casting muddy shadows over his eyes. It's what the horseback rider in one of his parables shouts when asked where he's going, but it might well have been the epitaph carved on Kafka's headstone in the Jewish cemetery in Prague. All his life, he'd dreamed of escape, yet he remained unable to bring himself to so much as move out of his parents' apartment. To be trapped and confined in a bewildering environment hostile to one's inner conditions, in which one is fated to be obtusely misunderstood and mistreated because one can't see the way out—from this, I don't need to remind you, Friedman reminded me, Kafka made the greatest literature. No one—not Joseph K. or Gregor Samsa, or the Hunger Artist or the mouse who flees as the world narrows toward its trap without realizing that all it need do is change direction—not one of them manages to escape their absurd existential conditions; all they can do is die of them.

Is it any coincidence that Kafka believed his finest passages were enactments of his own death? He once told Brod that the secret to them lay in the fact that while his fictional surrogates suffered, and felt death to be hard and unjust, he himself rejoiced in the idea of dying. Not because he wanted to end his life, Friedman said, dropping his voice as he leaned toward me across the table, but because he felt he had never really lived. The light was diffuse in Friedman's soft white hair, and for a moment he wore it like a halo. He continued: When Kafka imagined his own funeral in a letter to Brod, he described it as a body that had always been a corpse being at last consigned to the grave.

It took time, but the tuberculosis that would have killed him in Prague began to recede in Palestine. And though one might be tempted to attribute this to the care of his excellent doctors, or the frequent sojourns to the desert, where the dry air did wonders for his lungs, to do so, said Friedman, would be to ascribe to reality powers that in truth belonged to Kafka himself. He'd always maintained that his lung disease, like his insomnia and his migraines, was nothing but an overflowing of his spiritual disease. An illness born of feeling trapped and suffocated, without the air he needed to breathe or the refuge to write. At the very first hemorrhage, when the blood kept coming, he'd felt a stir of excitement. He'd never felt better, he later wrote, and that night he slept well for the first time in years. To him, this terrible illness had arrived as the fulfillment of a profound wish. And though it would almost certainly kill him, Friedman said, until then it was his reprieve: from marriage, from work, from Prague and his family. Right away, without any delay, he broke off his engagement to Felice. And as soon as he'd done that, he applied for immediate retirement from his job at the Workers

Accident Insurance Company. He was granted only temporary leave, but the eight months that followed were, Kafka often said, the happiest of his life. He spent them on his sister Ottla's farm in Zürau, in a state of near euphoria, working in the garden and fields, feeding the animals, and writing. He'd always felt that the nervous disorders of his generation came of being uprooted from the countryside of their fathers and grandfathers, estranged from themselves in the claustrophobic confines of urban society. But it was only during his convalescence in Zürau, Friedman told me, that Kafka had the chance to experience firsthand the restorative effects of being in contact with the soil. He became passionate about the Zionist agricultural schools opening all over Europe, and tried to convince Ottla and some of his friends to enroll. That same year he'd begun teaching himself Hebrew, and in Zürau he diligently worked through sixty-five lessons in his textbook, progressing far enough to be able to write to Brod in Hebrew. Woven together, Friedman said, the longing for a lost relationship to the land and for an ancient language coalesced into something more concrete, and it was during this same period that Kafka began to seriously develop his fantasy of emigrating to Palestine.

He may never have been as ardent or involved a Zionist as his closest friends, Friedman said. Max Brod, Felix Weltsch, and Hugo Bergmann, his oldest friend from school, all took active roles in the movement, first becoming involved in the Bar Kochba student group in Prague, then publishing essays, lecturing, and committing themselves to making aliyah. But Kafka's most famous line about Zionism—"I admire it, and I'm nauseated by it"—says more about his constitution than anything else, one that couldn't abide conforming to any ideology. He read the Zionist newspapers and journals compulsively, and published his stories there. He attended the Zionist conference in Vienna, and even promised to promote shares of Hapoalim, the Workers' Bank. It was through exposure to thinkers like Buber and Berdyczewski, whose lectures he heard in Prague, that Kafka came into contact with the Hasidic folk tales, Midrashic stories, and Kabbalistic mysticism that had such a profound influence on his writing. And the more fascinated and consumed he became by these texts, Friedman said, the more taken he became with that distant, lost native ground they originated from and referred back to.

And yet, Friedman said, holding up a thick finger—to truly understand why Kafka had to die in order to come here, why he was willing to sacrifice everything to do so, you have to understand a critical point. And it is this: it was never the potential *reality* of Israel that inspired his fantasies. It was its *unreality*.

Here Friedman paused, letting his watery gray eyes rest on me. Again I felt he was deliberating, that the jury was still out on me, though it seemed too late for that now that we had found ourselves sitting across from one another, with Kafka's suitcase in the trunk and his secret spilled out on the table.

Friedman asked if I remembered the first letter Kafka ever wrote to Felice. But he had written some eight hundred letters to Felice: No, I said, I didn't recall the first. Well, they'd met a few weeks earlier, Friedman went on, and as a means of reintroduction, Kafka reminded her of the promise she'd made to accompany him to Palestine. In a sense, their entire relationship began on this note of fantasy, and one might say, Friedman said, that it continued in that vein for five years, for part of Kafka must always have known that he wouldn't or couldn't marry her. Once their epistolary relationship was under way, and Felice apologized for not writing back fast enough, Kafka told her that she wasn't to blame, that the problem arose from her not knowing where or even whom to write to, because he himself couldn't be found. He who had never really lived, who only felt himself to exist in the unreality of literature, had no address in this world. Do you understand? Friedman demanded. In a sense, Palestine was the only place as unreal as literature, because once upon a time it was invented by literature, and because it was *still yet to be invented*. And so if he were to have a spiritual home, a place he might actually live, it could only be here.

The fantasy of a relationship with Felice may have begun with the fantasy of a life in Palestine, Friedman continued, but it was only the fantasy of a life in Palestine that Kafka never gave up. Over the years it just changed form. He imagined himself doing manual labor on a kibbutz, surviving on bread, water, and dates. He even wrote a manifesto for such a place, "Workers without Possessions," outlining a workday of no more than six hours, belongings limited to some books and clothes, and the complete absence of lawyers and courts, as personal relationships would be based on trust alone. Later, once Hugo Bergmann made aliyah and became the director of the Jewish National Library in Jerusalem, Kafka imagined a little bookbinder's bench for himself in the corner, where he would be left in peace among old books and the scent of glue.

But it was Kafka's last fantasy, the one he kept alive in the final year before his death in Europe, that Friedman found most beautiful, he told me, perhaps for being the most Kafkaesque. In that last year, he met and fell in love with the daughter of a Hasidic rabbi named Dora Diamant, who shared Kafka's dream of emigrating to Palestine. They would have a restaurant in Tel

Aviv, they decided, where Dora would cook, and Kafka would wait tables. He spoke about this dream more and more often, especially to his young Hebrew teacher Puah Ben-Tovim, who years later pointed out that Dora couldn't cook and Kafka would have been a terrible waiter, but also that in those years Tel Aviv was filled with restaurants run by such couples, and in that sense Kafka's surreal fantasy was more real than one might first be inclined to think. Can't you picture it? Friedman asked me with an amused smile. The wooden tables and the faded poster of Prague Castle ironically hanging on the wall, the kuchen under a glass dome on the counter? And the waiter with the black widow's peak in a short, dark jacket, who swats at a fly with a wry little smile?

Speaking in a hushed tone so as not to be overheard by Kafka's progeny drying glasses by the espresso machine, Friedman told me that some thirty years ago, one of Kafka's biographers had turned up Puah Ben-Tovim in Jerusalem, and published an interview with her in the *New York Times*. She was Dr. Puah Menczel by then, and nearly eighty years old, and to read between the lines of the article was to see the "Kafka fog machine," as Friedman called it, at work, a machine powered by Brod but which would have been impossible without Bergmann and Puah, both of whom had been instrumental in the plan to bring Kafka to Palestine in secret. Puah had been employed in Bergmann's library when she was eighteen, and the story goes that when he saw how overqualified she was for the work, he sent her to study mathematics in Prague, and even went so far as to arrange for her to live with his own parents. It's that last bit that makes one raise an eyebrow, said Friedman. Or would if one were to look askance at the official biography, which tells us that

Bergmann sent Puah to Prague not as an emissary, not to begin work on a clandestine plan already taking shape, but simply out of the kindness of his heart, and only as an afterthought decided to send her to meet Kafka, to whom she began to give private Hebrew lessons twice a week.

By the time Puah arrived in 1921, Kafka was already very ill. In the interview she gave to the clueless biographer who tracked her down sixty years later, she described the painful coughing fits that interrupted their lessons, and Kafka's huge dark eyes imploring her to continue for one more word, and one more after that. By the end, Kafka had progressed enough that they were able to read part of a novel by Brenner together. But in the *Times* article, Kafka's biographer also notes that after Puah Ben-Tovim dropped her math studies and moved to Germany, and Kafka followed her there, installing himself next door to the Jewish children's camp where she worked, she abruptly fell out of the picture and never saw him again. Among the mountains of recollections later offered in the wake of Kafka's posthumous fame, most inaccurate or of dubious authority, there is not a single word from Puah Ben-Tovim, the biographer notes. And when he finally tracks her down in Jerusalem, and she graciously invites him into her book-lined apartment, she explains her disengagement simply: Kafka was thrashing about like a drowning man, ready to cling to whoever came close enough for him to grab hold of. She had her own life to live, and she didn't have the will or the strength to be a nursemaid to a very sick man twenty years older than her, not even if she'd known then what she now knew about him. In other words, her poise was flawless, said Friedman. She managed to extricate herself, putting the biographer's curiosity permanently to rest. And now she is dead, and we can no longer ask Puah Ben-Tovim anything.

Yet had it not been for her—and most of all had it not been for Hugo Bergmann—the end would have come exactly as Kafka had imagined it. As Kafka imagined it, Friedman added, and as Brod later publicized it: the emaciated corpse lowered into the ground, the well-rehearsed death scene finally and irrevocably performed, the writer who wrote one of the most haunting and unforgettable stories of metamorphosis gone from this world without ever having, himself, transformed. That it didn't is only thanks to the small cabal spearheaded by Bergmann. Along with Puah and Max Brod, it included Salman Schocken, without whom both the transport to Palestine and the subsequent decades of Kafka's life here in Israel would have been financially impossible. I'm sure you know Schocken's name from the publishing house that subsequently published all of Kafka's work in Germany, and later in America. When Bergmann approached him in the summer of 1923, he was still just the wealthy owner of a chain of German department stores. But along with Buber, Schocken also founded the Cultural Zionist monthly *Der Jude*, which had published two of Kafka's stories. He was already also known as a patron of Jewish literature—he'd been the sole supporter of Agnon for more than a decade by then. So Bergmann wrote to him, Friedman told me, and in the fall of 1922, Brod traveled to Berlin to meet Schocken in person to discuss Kafka's situation.

Later it was Brod who got all the credit for being Kafka's savior. If anyone remembers Hugo Bergmann, it's as the first rector of the Hebrew University, and a professor of philosophy who wrote about transcendence. Unlike Brod, Bergmann never sought any acknowledgment of his part in saving Kafka. On the contrary, said Friedman, he was willing to go down as the fall guy, the selfish villain to Brod's magnanimous hero. According to the story written by Brod, it was with Bergmann's strong encouragement that Kafka made definitive plans to emigrate to Palestine in October of 1923, to travel there with Bergmann's wife and to stay with their family in Jerusalem until he was well again and found his feet. But as the time drew near, Bergmann supposedly had a change of heart. Fearing that Kafka would infect his children with tuberculosis, and that it would be too much to have such a sick person on his wife's hands, he rescinded the invitation. That no one has ever questioned the likelihood of such a sudden and callous turn in someone who for over twenty years had been one of Kafka's closest friends, Friedman suggested, can perhaps be attributed to the fact that by then the Holocaust had inured the world to stories of the countless many who refused safe harbor to even those closest to them for fear of putting themselves at risk. But the truth is that without Hugo Bergmann, Kafka would never have made it to Palestine, would have accepted his life sentence and never escaped the tyranny of his father, never have gotten out of Europe, where, had he survived his tuberculosis, he would later have been murdered along with his three sisters by the Nazis. In 1974 Bergmann was awarded the Israel Prize for "special contribution to society and the State of Israel," Friedman told me. But only a small group of people ever knew the full extent of that special contribution.

By 1924 Max Brod was the only one still left in Prague. And so he was the only one who could feasibly inherit Kafka's manuscripts after his death, and assume the role of controlling their fate beginning, supposedly, with disobeying Kafka's last request to burn everything. And because Brod was a writer, and because it was necessary to distance everyone else from the story, he also became the guardian of Kafka's legend. And because the legend didn't yet exist, and because Kafka was still almost entirely unknown, Brod became its sole author. Later, Brod would describe how in the immediate aftermath of his friend's death, he was too devastated to begin work on a biography. On top of that, he was overwhelmed by the laborious practical work of sorting through all of Kafka's papers, creating a bibliography, and preparing the manuscripts for publication. And so instead, Brod wrote what he called *eine lebendige Dichtung*—"a living literary creation"—a roman à clef in which he offered the original portrait of the suffering, sickly saint on which every Kafka portrait since has been based.

Zauberreich der Liebe, Friedman said, if you can't guess by the title—*The Magic Kingdom of Love*—is a piece of garbage that would have been carted to the literary dust heap the day after its publication had it not been for the character of Richard Garta. When the novel begins, the writer Garta has already died in Prague. So we can never meet him ourselves, can only ever know him through the memories of the novel's protagonist, Christoph Nowy, Garta's close friend and now the executor of his literary estate. Nowy recalls Garta constantly, almost obsessively, consulting with him internally and even going so far as to provide his dead friend's answers. In that sense, the novel provides not only the original portrait of Kafka but also Brod's argument for constructing an image of Kafka through his own distilled memories. Just as the readers of *Zauberreich der Liebe* can never know the saintly Garta except through the mediation of Nowy, so the world, even now, has never known Kafka except through the prism of Brod's Garta.

Friedman began to rifle through the leather portfolio he'd brought from the car until he came up with a wrinkled photocopy. "Garta," he began to read, who "of all sages and prophets that walked the earth was the quietest," who, "had he only not lacked self-confidence, would have become a guide to humanity." Friedman paused and looked at me with raised eyebrows. "It's complete schlock, no?" he said, his mouth curling into a smile. And yet, purely on the level of strategy, he continued, there's genius in it; as much genius as in the story of refusing a dying Kafka's last will to take everything he'd left behind and burn it all unread. When the world slowly woke to Brod's Kafka, he proved irresistible. And though the legend may have been Brod's own handiwork, in the decades that followed, it was expanded and embroidered upon by the hordes of Kafkologists who took up where Brod left off, gleefully churning out more Kafka mythology without ever once questioning its source. Nearly everything— *everything*—known about Kafka can be traced back to Brod! Including anything gleaned from his letters and diaries, since of course Brod collated and edited those. He introduced Kafka to the world, and thereafter managed each minute detail of his image and reputation until he himself died in 1968, leaving Kafka's estate in the hands of his lover, Esther Hoffe, and in just enough confusion and disorder to ensure that to this day his authority would never be passed on or shared out, and the Kafka golem he molded with his own hands would continue to roam the earth.

But he left us one enormous clue. "He couldn't help himself, I think," Friedman said. The temptation to divulge everything and reveal the brilliance of his own handiwork was too great, and so he hid the truth in plain sight. In *Zauberreich der Liebe*, Nowy sets off to Palestine to meet up with Garta's younger brother, who has made aliyah and lives on a kibbutz. From him, Nowy discovers that Garta was a Zionist—not just that he was sympathetic to the movement, but that his Zionist beliefs and activities were absolutely central to his life and his sense of himself. This is a complete revelation to Nowy, who hadn't had the slightest inkling of his closest friend's hidden passion. Furthermore, Garta's brother tells Nowy that Garta secretly wrote in Hebrew, and it was the "spectacular content" of these Hebrew notebooks that had convinced him to make aliyah and become a pioneer. "Ah?" Friedman said, raising his heavy eyebrows again. "Hebrew notebooks? If you were reading *Zauberreich der Liebe* for news of Kafka, might you stop to ask yourself: *What* Hebrew notebooks?"

When Brod finally got around to writing a real biography of Kafka, he described Kafka's "lonely secretiveness." How, for example, they'd been friends for some years before Kafka even revealed to him that he wrote. And yet, in a sense, Brod's overblown novel, and the whole subsequent mythology for which it serves as foundation, itself conceals a more subtle game, both revealing and obscuring the true Kafka. Not a single critic has ever picked up on the reference to those Hebrew notebooks, Friedman said, or the suggestion that Kafka may have written in Hebrew. The only known "Hebrew" notebooks of Kafka's are four small octavos used in his lessons with Puah, including the one with crumbling blue cover that sits in the archives of the National Library, where Brod deposited it. There one can find lists of German words translated into Hebrew in Kafka's familiar script, words that couldn't fit the legend more perfectly. Friedman dug around in the folder, removed another dog-eared photocopy, and pointed to each word as he translated:

Innocent

Suffering

Painful

Disgust

Terrifying

Fragile

Genius

If one didn't know better, one might take it for a parody of Brod's suffering Kafka, the one who apparently died in a sanatorium at the age of forty! "But there's another story to be told," Friedman said. "Do you understand?" he asked again, but as I did not yet fully understand, as I was drifting so oddly off course from understanding, I could only go on regarding him with what I hoped was a look of comprehension. A story of Kafka's afterlife in Hebrew, Friedman said. A story in which he escaped into that ancient and new language, just as he bodily escaped into an ancient and new land. In which he "crossed over" into Hebrew, which is the literal translation of *Ivrit*, derived from Abraham, the first Hebrew, or *Ivri*, who crossed over the river Jordan into Israel. In Hebrew, the translation of *The Metamorphosis* is *Ha Gilgul*. You know what *gilgul* means, don't you? The Yiddish title—*Der Gilgul*—is nearly the same. Which is to say, Friedman said, that for the Jews, *The Metamorphosis* has always been a story not about the change from one form to another, but about the continuity of the soul through different material realities.

Friedman fell silent at last, and turned to look out at the view. I followed his gaze to the church towers and Jaffa Gate and tried to absorb everything I'd just been told. But it wasn't just Friedman's authority and methodical presentation of the evidence that made it difficult to write him off as some excitable academic gone off the rails. If I found myself in Friedman's thrall, prepared to believe what had at first seemed beyond belief, it was because I could feel in my own body Kafka's claustrophobia and his longing for another world, and how, for him, the only possible escape was one that would be final and irreversible. And because, between the two stories of Kafka's life and death, the one Friedman had drawn struck me as having the more beautiful shape—more complex, but also more subtle, and so closer to truth. In light of it, the familiar story now seemed clumsy, overblown, and steeped in cliché.

If something didn't seem to fit, it was only Kafka's passivity about the fate of his work. Brod's editing had been notoriously intrusive. He had cut, edited, reordered, and punctuated as he saw fit. He had published books that Kafka considered unfinished. It's one thing to be turned into a saint, but how could one be expected to believe that Kafka would have stood by in silence while Brod performed his butchery?

"What makes you so sure the edits weren't Kafka's?" Friedman asked. "Or that there weren't extra-literary reasons for Brod's editorial decisions? Did you ever wonder why the novel *Amerika* wasn't published with Kafka's own title, *Der Verschollene*? Do you know what *Der Verschollene* means? *The Man Who Disappeared*. Or even *The One Who Went Missing*. Barely three years after Kafka's death in Prague, such a title was completely out of the question.

"As for publishing so-called unfinished work," Friedman continued, "can't you see the brilliance of it? Think about it: Wouldn't every writer want his stories and books and plays to be published with the claim that they remained unfinished? That he'd died, or been otherwise waylaid, before he could bring them to the state of perfection he'd envisioned for them, which lived within him, and which he would have brought to bear on the work had he only been given more time?"

The waiter came by the table to clear our plates, but though more than an hour had passed, neither of us had touched our food, and so he refilled our water glasses and returned to the kitchen.

I asked where Kafka had lived here, and Friedman told me that when he'd first arrived, he'd been put up in a house close to the Bergmanns. His health steadily improved over the summer. Secrecy was paramount, and outside of the small cabal immediately involved, the only person who knew was Kafka's sister Ottla. The moment he got off the boat in Haifa, he was no longer the writer Kafka. He was simply a thin, ailing Jew from Prague, convalescing in the warm climate of his new country. That fall, Agnon returned to Palestine after twelve years in Germany—a fire had broken out in his house there, destroying all of his manuscripts and books—but there is nothing to suggest that the two writers ever met. Schocken set Agnon up in a house in Talpiot, and a few months later moved Kafka to a house in the brand-new German Jewish garden suburb of Rehavia, where his rooms overlooked the land behind the house. In the afternoons, following the *Schlafstunde*, during which quiet had to reign in all the streets and stairwells of Rehavia, he would often go outside to sit under a tree in the plot that had been left to grow wild for centuries. He began to putter around—to weed here, and clip and prune there—and very soon he discovered that where he had been merely an average, or even less than average, gardener in Europe, in Palestine everything he touched seemed to thrive. Else Bergmann made him the gift of some seed catalogs, and he began to send away for crocuses and Algerian iris bulbs. A visitor who peeked into the garden in the afternoons might discover the thin man with the cough bent over some roses whose roots he was soaking in Epsom salts, or removing stones from the soil. In no time at all, the plot behind the house in Rehavia began to bloom.

Not long ago, Friedman told me, he'd come across the following lines in Kafka's *Diaries*: "You have the chance, if ever there was one, to begin again. Don't waste it." And a few pages later: "O beautiful hour, masterful state, garden gone wild. You turn from the house and see, rushing toward you on the garden path, the goddess of happiness." The entries were dated to his first days in Zürau, and yet I can't help but believe, Friedman said, that they were written after he moved to the rooms in Rehavia instead.

When I expressed confusion, he reached into the leather portfolio for the last time, and produced a final photocopy, which he pushed across the table. The passage in question was underlined with shaky pen. "Why did I want to quit this world?" it read.

Because "he" would not let me live in it, in his world. Though indeed I should not judge the matter so precisely, for I am now a citizen of this other world, whose relationship to the ordinary one is the relationship of wilderness to cultivated land (I have been forty years wandering from Canaan); I look back at it like a foreigner, though in this other world as well—it is the paternal heritage I carry with me—I am the most insignificant and timid of creatures and am able to keep alive thanks only to the special nature of its arrangements.

I read the extraordinary passage three times. In the upper right corner of the page was the title of the book it was taken from, *Letters to Felice*. When I looked up again, Friedman was watching me. "Do I need to remind you," he whispered, "that Schocken didn't publish these letters until 1963?" Trying to keep pace with him, I asked if he was suggesting that there were things Kafka wrote *after* 1924 that Brod had slipped in among the pages he published from his diaries and letters. The corner of Friedman's mouth lifted into a smile. "Tell me, my dear," he said, "did you really believe that Kafka wrote eight hundred letters to one woman?"

A sense of what Friedman might be asking of me began slowly to sink in: not to write the end of a real play by Kafka, but to write the real end of his life. Max Brod and his fog and schlock were long gone. Soon Eva Hoffe would be, too. In the meanwhile, the case would finally be decided by the Supreme Court, and if Eva Hoffe lost, which was almost certain, Kafka's hidden archives would be handed over, and his false death and secret transport to Palestine exposed to the world. Did Friedman want to get in front of the story to control how it would be written? To shape, through fiction, the story of Kafka's afterlife in Israel, as Brod had shaped the canonical story of his life and death in Europe?

As if he sensed my awareness, Friedman now moved swiftly toward the end of the story. The newly built neighborhood of Rehavia, he told me, soon became filled with intellectuals from Berlin and Vienna who played at the Tennisplatz, met at the coffeehouses they opened, and built art deco houses similar to the ones they'd left behind in the Rhineland. Kafka had moved there in 1925, the same year Brod published *Der Process* in Europe. If the risk of running into someone in Rehavia who'd known him from home already hung over him, by the following year, when *Das Schloss* was published in Europe, the situation had become untenable. At his own request, Kafka was transferred to a kibbutz in the north, close to the Sea of Galilee. There he was given a simple house on the edge of the lemon groves and took up work, also at his request, under the head gardener. The life of the kibbutz suited him. Though at first his reticence and penchant for solitude was frowned upon, in time he gained a reputation as a skilled gardener who put in long hours among the plants, and after he found a way to treat the diseased ancient sycamore tree, in whose deep shade the kibbutz members often congregated, his value was secured and he was left in peace to do as he pleased. He was beloved among the children for the little dolls and balsa-wood airplanes he used to make for them, and for his mischievous sense of humor. Because Kafka loved to swim, at least once a week he bathed in the Galilee, where he would swim so far out that to those on the shore he became nothing more than a tiny black dot.

For the next fifteen years, he lived in obscurity on the kibbutz. Even as the writer Kafka gained fame in the rest of the world, Friedman said, in Israel he remained unknown. The first Hebrew translation of a Kafka novel—it was *Amerika*—wasn't organized by Schocken until 1945. *The Trial* wasn't translated into Hebrew until 1951, and *The Castle* only in 1967. Schocken had good reason to hold off so long, but even once Kafka was available in Hebrew, he wasn't embraced in Israel. He was a Galut writer—one who embodied the placelessness of exile, and who'd swallowed the sentence of his overbearing father—and this put him at odds with the muscular culture of Zionism, which demanded a total break with the past, an overthrowing of the father. It was only in

1983, on the centennial of his birth, that a conference on Kafka was finally organized in Israel, but to this day, there is still no Hebrew edition of his complete works. Yet this neglect was what allowed Kafka to preserve his anonymity and his freedom.

Hermann Kafka, who'd nearly collapsed at Franz's funeral, never got over the loss of his son: his health rapidly deteriorated, he became confined to a wheelchair, and in 1931 the cruel and domineering father whose tyranny and obtuse lack of understanding Kafka blamed for the majority of his sufferings died a broken man. It's impossible to imagine that Kafka didn't suffer in a different way when he learned that the death he'd carefully staged, and the mourning he'd childishly fantasized about, had hastened his father's death. It must have made him question whether his father had been half the colossus he so feared. In March of 1939 Hitler's troops entered Prague, and in 1941 Kafka's two older sisters and their families were sent to the Lodz Ghetto. Ottla remained in Prague until August of 1942, when she was transported to Theresienstadt. Brother and sister almost certainly exchanged letters, but if anything of that correspondence still exists, it must be hidden in the trove at Spinoza Street. In October of the following year, Friedman told me, Ottla volunteered to accompany a group of children from Theresienstadt to what she believed would be safety abroad. Instead, they were taken to Auschwitz and murdered in the gas chambers. The last known letter of Ottla's was written to her husband, who wasn't a Jew and so had been able to stay behind in Prague with their two daughters. She told him that she was fine. Presumably she wrote something similar to her brother. Almost six more months passed until Kafka got the news of her death.

"I don't believe he was ever the same after that," Friedman

said. He left the kibbutz soon afterward and, beginning in 1944, took up residence in various apartments in Tel Aviv, restlessly moving around the city, hounded by the idea that he would be found out and exposed. At the end of 1953 the gardener Anshel Peleg moved for the final time. He had come to love the desert during his early sojourns there, when the doctors had prescribed its dry air for his lungs. After fifteen years in the kibbutz, and the perennial drifting around the city, he had very few belongings. Max Brod, who by then lived in Tel Aviv as well, kept all of his papers. And so it was with little more than a small suitcase and a backpack full of books that he set out for the desert in the jeep that Schocken had provided.

Forests of Israel

Epstein dreamed he was walking through an ancient forest. It was cold, so cold that his breath hung frozen in the air. The black needles of the pine trees were dusted with snow, and the air was fragrant with resin. Everything was dark—the damp ground, the great high boughs of the trees bathed in muted cloud light, the bark, the cones hanging on above—all except for the white snow and the pair of red slippers on his feet. Surrounded by the tall trees, he felt a sense of being protected, safe from anything that might wish to harm him. There was no wind. The world was still, a stillness very close to joy. He walked a long time, the snow crunching under his feet, and only when he stumbled on a root across the path did he look down and recognize the slippers. Of red felt, brought by his mother's cousin from Europe, more beautiful than functional, the soles so thin that they barely did their work of protecting his feet from the cold below. The sensation of seeing something long forgotten but intensely familiar washed over him, and in that instant it dawned on him that he hadn't grown up after all. Somehow, unknown to everyone, most of all to himself, he'd remained a child all this time.

At last he came to a clearing, and in the center of the glade he saw a stone pedestal. Bending, he brushed away the snow and the golden letters appeared under his fingers frozen with cold:

IN MEMORY OF SOL AND EDIE

THE SUN AND THE EARTH

When he woke, a shivering Epstein discovered that he had sweated through the sheets. He stumbled through the hotel room and turned off the icy blast from the air conditioner. Pulling back the heavy drapes, he saw that it was already morning. He slid open the glass door to the terrace, and a warm breeze floated in, carrying the sound of breaking waves. He felt the sun on his skin and inhaled the salty air. In damp pajamas, he leaned over the railing, squinting at the oily light that sat heavily on the surface of the water. He thought about swimming again. It would feel good after the strange intensity of the last days. He thought again of the Russian who'd pulled him out from under the waves, who had only laughed and clapped him on the back when he'd offered remuneration, and told him that if he stayed out of the water it would be payment enough. But why shouldn't he go back in again? On the contrary, it was exactly *because* he had nearly drowned that he should now march right back into the sea, before there was a chance for the fear to gather tension and solidify into an impasse. He was a strong swimmer, had always been a strong swimmer. This time he would pay more attention. And anyway, the water was calmer today, the black flags gone.

But as he reentered the cool room in search of his bathing suit, the dream of the forest came back to him, the darkness and the white snow all as vivid as before. Suddenly he gleaned something of its essence, and halted excitedly in front of the unmade bed. He sank down on the duvet, only to leap up again a moment later and begin to pace. But why hadn't he thought of it before? Back on the terrace, he dipped his body out for the whole view. Of course—but yes—it made such beautiful sense!

He dug through the damp bed sheets in search of his phone, and had a fleeting thought of the lost one. Who knew where it was now? Somewhere in Ramallah, making calls to Damascus. The rumpled bed was empty. He checked the desk, then came back and lifted the book he'd laid facedown on the night table before going to sleep, and discovered the new phone under its pages. He dialed his assistant Sharon, but after two rings remembered that it was the middle of the night in New York. After the sixth, he gave up and called his cousin instead.

"Moti, it's Jules."

"Hold on—חתיכת חרא! חרא!—Unbelievable! This son of a bitch just cut me off. What did you say? Go ahead, I'm listening."

"Who do I speak to about planting—"

"נבלה!"

"What?"

"Go on, speak to who about what?"

"Trees. Planting trees."

"*Trees?* Like for, what do you call it—"

"Trees! The way they've been doing since before there was a State. My mother used to send me out with a blue-and-white collection box." Epstein could remember how the coins would jangle in the tin box as he ran from house to house, but could not recall the name of the foundation. "Trees for the slopes of Jerusalem, I think. I don't know, for Mount Hebron. Later on, in Hebrew school, they showed us the photograph of kids wearing the *kova tembel* planting the saplings we'd raised money for in America."

"What, Keren Kayemeth LeIsrael?"

"Yes, wait—the Jewish National Fund, right? Can you get me in touch with someone there?"

"You want to plant *trees*, Yuda?" Moti asked, using the Hebrew nickname Epstein had gone by as a child.

"Not trees," Epstein said softly, "a whole forest." The goose bumps rose on his arms as he remembered the stillness gathered under the soft, dark boughs.

"We have enough trees. Now it's water that's the problem. Last I heard they were working on turning salt water into fruit. I wouldn't be surprised if they tried to convince you to dig a hole in the ground instead. The Edith and Solomon Epstein Memorial Reservoir."

Epstein pictured his parents' hole, and the winter rain falling.

"Of course they're still planting trees," he snapped. "Can you get me a number or no? If not, I'll talk to the concierge."

But Moti wouldn't think of letting Epstein go to someone else for a favor he himself could do that might later be repaid. "Give me half an hour," he told Epstein, lighting a cigarette and exhaling into the phone. When he got to Petah Tikvah he would make some phone calls. He thought he might know someone who had a connection there. And Epstein didn't doubt it: there was nothing that Moti—who had fought in three wars, married and divorced twice, and had more professions than Epstein could recall—couldn't rustle up.

"Tell them I want to build a forest. Pine trees, as far as the eye can see."

"Sure, a two-million-dollar forest, I'll tell them. But, God help me, it hurts. In case you change your mind, there's a place I can show you, all glass and Italian marble, and a Jacuzzi with a view all the way to Sicily."

But when Moti called back later that afternoon, he told Epstein that everything had been arranged. "We have a meeting with them tomorrow," he said. "One o'clock at Cantina."

"Thanks. But there's no need for you to come. It's not your kind of thing. There'll be no naked women."

"That's what worries me. What you do with your life is your own business, but you're sixty-eight, Yuda, you're not going to live forever, and here you are finally divorced, free, and you have your mind on rabbis and forests, oblivious to the fact that there are always naked women everywhere. I'm looking at one right now, wearing a yellow dress. And this is a form of joy, I tell you, that you will never find in a forest in memory of your parents, who, as far as I remember, had no interest in trees. Am I wrong, Yuda? But a woman, this is something your father, may his memory be a blessing, could have understood. Think about what I'm telling you. I'll see you tomorrow at one," he said, and before going back to the shiva call he was paying, phoned the owner of Cantina to tell him to put aside his most expensive bottle of Chardonnay.

A FEW DAYS LATER, Epstein was standing atop a mountain, flanked by the JNF's head of outreach, one of their forestry experts, and Moti, who had insisted on taking off from the real estate office where he worked to accompany his cousin. The JNF's director of development was abroad, but Epstein had refused to wait, and so the head of outreach had been sent instead, a small publicist in cheap sunglasses who'd worn the wrong shoes. She'd been driving all day, and, having brought him to three different sites, was now at the far edge of her outermost reach, and had begun to lose patience. The last place she'd brought him had been devastated by forest fires and was in desperate need of rehabilitation. His gift would be enough to replant the whole area, she'd explained. One day his children would come to walk there in the cool shade of their grandparents' forest, and his children's children, and, God willing, their children after that.

But, surveying the landscape of charred stumps, Epstein had shaken his head. "Not it," he'd murmured, and turned back toward the car.

What exactly was he looking for, then? the head of outreach had demanded, catching up to him.

"You heard him," Moti had piped up from behind, throwing himself once more into the backseat next to the forestry expert, a young woman in khaki shorts, fluent in all things arboreal, who, as far as Moti was concerned, was the only thing that had made the day bearable. "He says it's no good, so it's no good. *Yallah*."

Pushing down the strap of her sandal, the head of outreach rubbed her blistered heel in the driver's seat while Epstein only repeated that he would know the place when he saw it. And so she swallowed back her frustration and started the engine, turning up the air conditioner to the max, and blotting the sweat from her forehead with a tissue on which her orange makeup came away. Behind her, Moti began to shake a cigarette from his crumpled pack but, feeling Galit the forestry expert's disapproving look, shoved the pack back in his pocket, coughed, and checked his phone again to see if there was reception. Leaning forward, Galit told Epstein about the forestation work the foundation was doing in the wadis to stop erosion. But Epstein wasn't interested in planting in the wadis, and so after a while she too fell silent and leaned back in her seat, having told Epstein nearly everything she knew about the Mediterranean region, the Irano-Turanian and Sahara-Sindi regions, about arid and semi-arid, average yearly rainfall, seedlings per dunam, soil quality, slopes and plains, the Jordan Rift, the lithology of Mount Hebron, the advantages of Mediterranean oak, pistachio, carob, tamarisk, Aleppo pine, and Christ's thorn, names that seemed to her to rustle something in the depths of him, without ever touching on whatever it was he really wanted to know.

Twenty minutes later, they reentered a cellular zone and the head of outreach's phone buzzed with a text from the office suggesting a last location. Moti slumped down with a groan and threw back his head, either because of the texts that had just tumbled through to his own phone or because he had already considered Epstein's money in the clear, his work for the day done.

Slowly turning his head, he opened his eyes and looked at Galit.

"Sweetheart," he said quietly in Hebrew, "is there anything you like aside from trees? Because if you can arrange for this forest not to happen, I can get you a week in a hotel in Eilat with your boyfriend. My friend has a place right on the Red Sea. You'll go scuba diving, lie on the beach, and you'll see how quickly you'll forget all about this erosion business." And when Galit only rolled her eyes, Moti turned his face the other way and looked out at the desert.

AND SO AFTER driving back down through the Jordan Valley as far as Mount Hebron, at almost five in the afternoon they'd finally arrived here, on a slope of a mountain in the northern Negev. And here, where there was nothing except the sky and the stony earth turning red and gold in the sunset, Epstein was asked to imagine a forest.

The light filled his head. Filled it from the bottom to the brim, and threatened to overspill him. When the sensation had passed, and the light drained, the awe remained behind like a sediment, a fine sand as old as the world. Dizzy, he walked away from the others to stand alone on an outcropping above the sloping hillside, and saw endless rows of saplings unfurling in the beating sun.

There was a time, Galit had told him, when the whole southern and eastern Mediterranean, from Lebanon down through North Africa and Greece, had been covered with forests. But with each war they had been plundered for timber, turned into fleets that in the end had sunk to the bottom of the sea with their drowned. And bit by bit, as the trees were stripped away and the land plowed into fields, the earth dried out, and the fertile soil was blown away by hot winds, or washed away by the rain and rivers, and where once six hundred cities had flourished on the coast of North Africa, the population dwindled, and sand blew through and covered the ruins of empty cities with dunes. As early as the fourth century BC, Plato wrote about the devastation of the forests that had once covered all of Attica, leaving behind only the skeleton of the land. And so it had been here, too, Galit told him. Mount Lebanon was stripped for the temples at Tyre and Sidon, and then the First and Second Temples of Jerusalem; the destruction of the forests of Sherin, Carmel, and Bashan was the theme of the prophet Isaiah in 590 BC, and Josephus wrote about the widespread devastation of huge swaths of forests during the

Jewish Wars some five hundred years later. Jerusalem, too, had once been surrounded by forests of pine, almond, and olive, and the whole region from the Judean Hills all the way down to the coast: all of it once covered with lush, dark forest, a word, Epstein realized, after a lifetime of uttering it in ignorance, was composed of the words *for rest*.

Moti came up behind him, lit a cigarette, and exhaled with feeling. Even he was muted by the boundless expanse. They stood together in silence, like old friends who had spoken about many personal things over the course of their lives, when in reality, despite all the years they'd known each other, they had never really spoken about anything at all.

"What is it with Jews and hills?" Epstein finally said, more to himself than Moti. "They're forever going up to experience their important things there."

"Only to come hurrying down again." Moti crushed the butt of his cigarette into a rock. "Unless they have to be brought down in body bags, like from Masada, or from Beaufort, like Itzy's son. Personally, I prefer to stay to the bottom." But Epstein's back was to him, so Moti couldn't see his response, if there was any.

"Yuda," he said again after a long while, "what are we doing here? I'm asking you seriously. I've known you my whole life. You don't seem like yourself these days. You're forgetting things— the other day you couldn't remember that Chaya is called Chaya, though you've been calling her for fifty years, and then you left your wallet on the table after you paid. And you've lost weight. Have you seen a doctor?"

But Epstein didn't hear, or chose not to hear, or had no wish to answer. Minutes passed, in which they sat looking out at the distant glowing hills in silence, until finally Epstein spoke.

"I remember when I was seven or eight, soon after we moved to America. There was this kid, two or three years older, who started up with me after school. One day I came home with a bloody nose, and my father caught me in the hall and dragged the story out of me. He was livid. 'You go back there with a stick right now and crack him over the head!' My mother heard this and came rushing into the room. 'What are you saying?' she shouts at him. 'This is America. That's not how they do things here.' 'So how do they do things?' my father bellows back. 'They go to the authorities,' my mother says. 'The *authorities*?' my father said, mocking her. 'The authorities? And what do you think the authorities will do? Anyway, that's snitching, and our Yuda is no snitch.' My mother shouted that I would never be a brute like him. Then my father turns back to me, and I can see he's thinking things over. 'Listen,' he finally says to me, narrowing his eyes. 'Forget the stick. You go right up to him, and you grab him like this,' he says, and with one huge hand he takes me by the neck and pulls my face to his, 'and you tell him, *You do that again, and I'll murder you.*'"

Moti laughed, relieved to hear something of the old, familiar raconteur.

"You think she would have wanted this, your mother?" Moti asked, thrusting his chin out toward the barren hillside. "Is that why you're doing it?"

Do what you want, you're a free person, his mother used to yell at him, which was her way of saying *Do what you want if you want to kill me*. Inside the hem of his independence she'd sewed her command, so that at his greatest moments of freedom he felt her pull on him like gravity. Even going away from her, he was going toward her. All that was loyal in him and all that was seditious originated in grappling with that waxing and waning span, even if later it flung itself out toward other entities. No, she had not been a calming force, his mother. Her favorite piece of jewelry was a double strand of pearls, and on occasions when they lay around her throat, Epstein could not help but feel that her attachment to them had something to do with the irritant at their core that had gone and produced such luster. She had brought him to a state of vibrancy by means of provocation.

"She wanted a bench in a crummy park in Sunny Isles. If that."

"So why? I don't understand, Yuda, I really don't. It's none of my business, but they were frugal people, your parents. They didn't like to waste. One tree, two trees. But four hundred thousand? For what? You remember how I came to America for the first time when I was twenty-one? Your mother wouldn't let me throw out my own toenail clippings."

Epstein didn't remember any such visit. He would already have been married by then, Jonah and Lucie both born. He would have been preoccupied with his work at the firm, and a hundred forms of struggle.

"They brought me to see you and Lianne. I came to your Park Avenue apartment, and it was like something out of another world. I'd never seen people live like that. You took me out for lunch at an expensive restaurant and insisted on ordering a lobster. Because you wanted to treat me, or impress me, or because you were having a little fun with me, I couldn't tell which. And the waiter brings this huge boiling-red creature, this terrifying insect, to the table and puts it in front of me, and all I can think about are the swarms of giant red locusts that come every seven years and lie washed up on the beach. You got up and went to the bathroom, leaving me alone with it. And after a while, I couldn't stand its beady black eyes staring at me anymore, so I put my napkin over its head."

Epstein smiled. He had no recollection of it, but it didn't sound unlike him.

"That night, I went back to the house in Long Beach. Your mother put me up in your old bedroom. And, lying there in your bed, listening to your parents go at each other in the kitchen, I kept thinking about that lobster. For the first time since I'd arrived, I felt homesick. All I wanted was to go back to Israel, where we might have had plagues of locusts, but they were my locusts, and at least I understood what they meant. I was lying there listening to your parents tear each other apart, and thinking about what it must have been like to be you. And suddenly I heard something slam hard against the wall with a thud. Then silence. I was already a man by then, just out of the army, with the reflexes of a soldier, and I jumped out of bed and ran to the kitchen. I saw your mother leaning against the wall, holding her face, and I understood that some things are everywhere the same, and it was like I was back in my childhood kitchen again, with my own mother."

Epstein looked up at the sky, bloodied to the west. Had he been better acquainted with this side of Moti, hidden under the coarseness and the wise cracks, or had the thought itself not been so abstract, he might have said something about the way, out of chaos, a few singular images are sometimes thrown up that come to seem, in their unfading vividness, the summation of one's life, and all that one will take from it when one goes. And his were almost all of violence: his father's or his own.

Instead, he said, "I think of my parents now, and I think, my God, so much argument. So many battles. So much destructiveness. It's strange, but when I think about it, I realize my parents never once encouraged me to make anything. To build anything. Only to take things apart. It struck me the other day that only in arguing did I ever feel truly creative. Because it was always there that I defined myself—first against them, and then against everything and everyone else."

"So what are you saying? That's what this is about? A belated desire to stop fighting and make something? Yuda, let's sign up for a pottery class, please. It will save you a lot of money. Come to think of it, I know a painter with a studio in Jaffa. For a small sum he'll happily go to Rio for the month and leave you his place."

But Epstein didn't laugh.

"OK, it's just that I don't see it. You have three children. You were a great lawyer. You built a huge life. Isn't that creation enough? If it were me we were talking about, a total failure in nearly everything, that would be a different story."

"In everything?" Epstein asked, with genuine interest.

"It's a part of me, very strongly connected to Jewishness, to the fact that I belonged to a cursed tribe."

Epstein turned to look at his cousin, but at that moment Moti stood, hitching up his loose jeans and snapping a photo of the view on his phone, and in his slack expression Epstein saw no chance of being understood. He turned back to the desert, set ablaze by the sinking sun.

"This is it," he said softly. "Go tell her this is the place."

THE CAR WAS silent on the drive back. A screen of darkness fell over the hills, and the temperature dropped. Epstein opened the window, and the cold air tumbled into his lungs. He began to softly hum the Vivaldi. How did it go? *Cum dederit* something,

something, something *somnum*. He heard the countertenor, and saw the blind woman's German shepherd with its eyes closed, listening outside the human range.

His phone began to vibrate in his pocket, and he ignored it. But when it started up again with new urgency, he checked and saw that it was Klausner trying to get through, and that he'd already missed three calls from him. Seeing the date, he realized that it must be the reunion Klausner was calling about. He looked back out at the darkening landscape, and against his natural persuasion he felt a little shiver at the thought that the real David must have walked and fought, loved and died, somewhere out there.

When his phone rang again, he gave in and answered to get it over with.

"Jules! Where are you? Are you in Jerusalem already?"

"No."

"Where then?"

"In the desert."

"The desert? What are you doing in the desert? We're starting in an hour!"

"It's tonight, is it? I've been busy."

"Good thing I got through to you. I was starting to get worried. There's still time. I'm at the hall now supervising the preparations—hold on—the musicians just arrived."

"Listen, I'm on my way back to Tel Aviv now. It's been a very long day."

"Come for half an hour. Just to absorb the atmosphere. Eat something. Jerusalem isn't so far out of your way. I don't want you to miss this, Jules."

Epstein felt the gnarled hand of the little man in the Safed shrine reach out once more for his pants leg. But this time he had no intention of yielding.

"To think that the Messiah might be there on the guest list. But no, really, I can't."

Klausner took no offense at the joke, and unwilling to take no for an answer, said he would try him again in half an hour. Epstein bade him good-bye and turned off his phone.

"What was that all about?" Moti asked.

"My rabbi."

"Mother of God, what did I tell you?"

But Epstein really was exhausted now. The driving, the sun, and the long day of being with people had taken it out of him. What he wanted was to shower away the dust and to lie alone under the air conditioning, thinking about the forest that would one day cover the slope of the mountain, rustling and alive under the moon. Moti couldn't understand. Neither would Schloss. Nor Lianne, who had never understood him, who in the end had not really wished to look, though he had tried and tried to reveal himself to her. He no longer needed to be understood. The night outside was thickening. He lowered the window all the way so that the wind drowned out the sound of his cousin's voice, and inhaled the fragrant smell of the desert.

HE DID NOT attend the reunion, but that night, exhausted as he was, he could not sleep, and stayed up reading from the weathered book on his bedside table. Walking one afternoon down Allenby, he had seen it in a display case full of sun-faded books in English, all the colors moving toward blue. He had gone down the narrow alley and into the crowded, dusty bookshop to inquire about it. The owner was playing jazz over the stereo and tallying his accounts at a cluttered desk. The contents of the display case had not enticed anyone for ages, and it took a long time for the key to be found. But at last the case was pried open, releasing the musty smell of trapped weather and disintegrating paper. The owner reached in and removed *The Book of Psalms*, and Epstein tucked it under his arm, and went back out again into the crowded street and made his way toward the sea.

Was there a more complicated hero in the Bible than David? David who manipulated the love of Saul, of Jonathan, of Michal, of Bathsheba, of everyone who ever came close to him. A warrior, a murderer, hungry for power, willing to do whatever it took to become king. Betrayal was nothing to him. Killing was nothing. Nothing was left to stand in the way of his desires. He took what he wanted. And then, to let him rest from what he had been, the authors of David ascribed to him the most plaintive poetry ever written. Had him, at the end of his days, stumble into the discovery of what was most radical in himself. Into grace.

IN THE MORNING Epstein slept late, and was woken by the ring of the hotel phone. It was reception calling. Someone was waiting for him downstairs.

"Who?" he asked, still in the fog of sleep. He was not expecting anyone: he had no money left to give.

"Yael," the receptionist reported.

Epstein roused himself and squinted at the clock. It was only just past eight. "Yael who?" he asked. He did not know any Yael, except for his mother's cousin, who was buried in Haifa. There was a muffled pause, and then a woman's voice came on the line.

"Hello?"

"Yes?"

"It's Yael." She paused, as if waiting for his memory to be jogged. Had it gotten that bad? Epstein wondered, rubbing his eyes with a dry knuckle.

"I have something for you. My father asked me to make sure that you got it."

Still dazed, Epstein recalled how, at the first sign of light on Sunday morning, unable to stand another minute in the hard little Gilgul bed, he'd splashed his face with cold water and gone in search of a cup of tea to soothe his still uneasy stomach. On his way, he nearly smacked into Peretz Chaim, who was coming out of his room. Peretz had rolled up his sleeve, and was tightening the black band of his phylacteries around his bicep the way an addict ties a tourniquet. But it was Epstein who'd felt the longing: the hunger for the vein that goes straight to the heart. He touched his fingers to his chest, over the beating muscle that could not handle his thick blood.

"You want me to just leave it here at the desk?" she asked. "I'm kind of in a hurry."

"No! Don't," Epstein said in a rush, already standing and reaching for his pants. "Wait. I'm on my way down."

With trembling fingers, he pushed the buttons through the holes of his shirt, brushed his teeth, splashed water on his face, and paused in front of his dripping image in the glass, surprised to find that his hair had grown so long.

HE SAW HER in the lobby before she saw him, bent over her phone, her pale, high forehead wrinkled in a frown. She was wearing jeans and a leather jacket, and now that she was fully dressed he saw that his Bathsheba's nose was pierced with a tiny diamond. But as he approached, he was struck by something familiar in her profile, some likeness that he had not noticed that night two weeks earlier. When he said her name, she raised her head, and their eyes met for the second time. But if she remembered, she didn't let on.

She was working on a script about the life of David, and had attended her father's reunion in Jerusalem with the film's director. At the end of the night, as she was getting ready to drive back to Tel Aviv, the rabbi had asked her to bring this to him— and from her bag she produced a golden folder. It was imprinted with the words DAVIDIC DYNASTY, above which was a shield with the lion of the Kingdom of Judea and the Magen David. She held it out for him, but Epstein remained unmoving.

"You're making a film?" he asked in wonder. "About David?"

"Why the surprise? When I tell people, it's always the same reaction. But there's never been a good film about David, unlike Moses, even though he's the most complex, fully wrought, and fascinating character in the whole Bible."

"It isn't that. It's just that I happen to be—" But he stopped himself from telling her that for many nights now he had been reading the Psalms. That something in him, strong and flawed, might go all the way back to an ancient story. "I'm interested in David."

"You should have been there last night, then."

"Should I have?"

With an amused smile, she described how the guests had entered under the fake stone arch, guarded by two messengers decked out in royal garb, who announced each one, followed by a trill on their bugles. A harpist in trailing velvet had plucked golden strings in the foyer. You couldn't have cast it better had you tried, she said.

Glancing again at her phone, she told him that she really had to leave; she was late to meet someone.

"Where do you need to go?" Epstein asked.

"Jaffa."

"I'm going that way, too. Can I give you a lift in the taxi? I want to hear more about the film." He stopped himself from saying that he wanted to know why the rabbi's daughter, who looked upon her father's pet project with irony and appeared to have gotten as far from religion as she could, would want to make a film about David.

She put on her sunglasses and smiled faintly at something over his shoulder as she lifted her heavy bag off the floor.

"But we already know each other, don't we?"

Something to Carry

W E'D ONLY DRIVEN for ten minutes after leaving the restaurant in the Confederation House when a row of green army vehicles appeared, blocking the road. The northwest traffic had been brought to a standstill, and each car was being stopped and checked by soldiers. Friedman switched the radio dial to the news, which flooded into the interior with rattled urgency. When I asked what was going on, he said it could be anything: breach of the wall, bomb threat, a terrorist attack in the city.

The atmosphere grew more ominous by the minute as we crawled along, waiting to get to the front of the line. When we finally did, two soldiers with automatic weapons slung across their chests circled our vehicle, looking into all the windows and underneath the car with a mirror attached to a long handle. I couldn't understand either their questions or Friedman's answers, which seemed to me far longer than required to satisfy these teenagers in fatigues, following orders that must have meant little to them. The girl was tall and pigeon-toed, still fighting off acne but with the promise of yet becoming beautiful one day, and the boy was squat, hairy, and arrogant, too interested in the power the situation lent to him. Friedman, already tense, grew quickly annoyed with the questioning, and this only stoked the arrogance of the boy—one couldn't really call him a man, and maybe that was the problem, or one of the many problems. I waited for Friedman to reveal his secret connections that would bring about our immediate release and a flurry of embarrassed apologies. But when he finally fished out his wallet from one of the voluminous pockets of his vest, the card he removed from it and held out with his tremulous right hand was nothing more than a standard ID. The soldier plucked it away, studied it briefly, then turned and addressed me in Hebrew.

"I'm American."

"What's your business with him?" He gestured at Friedman with his chin, which had a cleft in it, like a thumbprint, where the otherwise dark, intractable hair refused to grow.

"Business?"

"How do you know him?"

"We met a couple of days ago."

"Met why?"

Friedman tried to interrupt in Hebrew, but the soldier silenced him with a raised palm and a few sharp words. "Why did you meet him?" he demanded again.

Various answers flitted through my mind. I thought of telling him that Friedman was some sort of distant relative that my father had sent me to be in touch with, a lie that at least had an oblique relationship to the truth.

"We don't have all day."

"He has a project he thought I might be interested in," I finally said, a reply that seemed innocuous enough until the words came out of my mouth.

The soldier raised his heavy eyebrows, knitting them together so that they formed one large hairy bar across his forehead, then went round to the back of the car and opened the trunk.

"You didn't let me finish," I called to him, trying to amend my mistake while maintaining the illusion that I couldn't care less what he thought, that his modicum of power had no currency with me. "I'm a writer, if you want to know. I write novels." But the sentence and its meaning struck me as pathetic.

"You packed this yourself?" He pointed at the suitcase from Spinoza Street.

"Myself?" I echoed, stalling. Around us, the other cars were being waved through, their passengers eyeing us with heavy-lidded curiosity. I thought it would be nice if one them recognized me now, and got out of their car to tell me they had named a miserable child after one of my characters. But as the cars went by at a distance, it was clear my fantasy had little chance of coming to fruition, which in a cosmic sense was for the best, since the moment readers become useful to writers should always be suspect, anyway.

"It's been in your possession the entire time? Anyone gave you something to carry?"

I knew I should have lied outright, but instead I said, "No, I didn't pack it. We picked it up an hour ago in Tel Aviv. But it's only papers inside. Go ahead and see for yourself." I thought to ask him whether he had read Kafka. Surely *The Metamorphosis* or *Ha Gilgul* or whatever name it went by had been assigned in his high school in Ra'anana or Givatayim. "This is all just a simple misunderstanding," I went on. "Everything will be cleared up if you'd just open—"

I felt the pressure of Friedman's hand on my arm, but it was too late. The soldier had unhooked the walkie-talkie from his belt and began to radio his superior. A garbled reply, deep-throated and filled with static, arrived as if from far away. The soldier listened, eyes fixed on the suitcase, and when it came his turn to respond, he seemed to deliver a disquisition, not only on the beat-up piece of luggage extracted from the apartment of the elderly daughter of Max Brod's lover, but on many other things—the patterns of history, the flawed nature of human relations, the irony of the incommensurate, the genius of Kafka. Twice I heard him say it, turning his back on us and gesturing expansively toward the foothills, where bits of white stone showed through the red dirt like bone: *Kafka*, and then again, *Franz Kafka*, though later I wondered whether it was the word *davka* I'd heard, which has no translation in English beyond its literal meaning, *exactly*, but which sums up the Jewish mode of something done just to be contrary.

"Can't you do something?" I hissed at Friedman, now losing my patience with everything I had been asked, or allowed myself, to go along with. "Why don't you talk to someone higher up?"

The soldier, still gesticulating over the phone, grabbed the suitcase from the trunk and hauled it to the ground, where it landed with a sickening thud. Yanking up the collapsible handle, he rolled it over to the female soldier, who tested its weight with a skeptical look, as if she suspected the dead Kafka himself to be curled up inside of it. Slowly, she began to tug it toward the row of army vehicles.

"You think I didn't try?" Friedman said, sounding resigned, even melancholy. If I'd managed to imbue him with a certain authority until then, now it was vanishing before my eyes. He seemed not only old but helpless, and the invincible plural—the

"We" he'd summoned when he spoke of pride in my work—had now dissolved into the eccentric singular. "He wanted to make a problem, so he made one. It should give one hope, no? That they don't only torment the Arabs."

The soldier came back around to my side.

"You have your passport?"

I dug around in my handbag until I found it at the bottom. He narrowed his eyes and looked from the photograph to me, and back again. It was true that it had been some years since the picture was taken.

"Remove the glasses."

Everything dissolved into a blur.

"You look better in the picture," he snapped, slipping the passport into his shirt pocket.

He ordered us to get out of the car. The dog, which until then had remained calm, broke into a fit of frantic barking as soon as Friedman reached for the door handle, causing the soldier to flinch, his hands flying reflexively to his rifle. I braced myself for the worst, imagining a bullet through the animal's skull. But a moment later he relaxed his fingers, and gingerly reached an open hand through the window and patted the dog. A faraway smile twitched on his lips.

"Wait here," he ordered me, still cradling the rifle. "Someone will come."

Only as I watched Friedman walk away, clutching his worn leather portfolio to his chest, and disappear into the back of an army truck, glancing back at me over his shoulder, did I begin to consider, with mounting panic, that what he'd taken from Eva Hoffe's apartment he might have had no right to take. I replayed the scene of him hurrying out of the lobby on Spinoza

Street, and the sweat he'd wiped from his forehead as he started up the car.

What had I gotten myself into? Why hadn't I questioned him when he came out of the fanatically protected fortress of Eva's apartment, dragging a suitcase? Who cared who he was? He could have been David Ben Gurion himself, and what difference would it have made to a woman who obsessively guarded the papers after her mother's death, who claimed to feel biologically connected to them, who'd fought tooth and nail to keep them in her possession, who would, she'd said, only allow them to be taken away over her dead body? What had led me to accept that Friedman, of all people, with his safari vest and his tinted glasses, should have been granted special privileges, should have been permitted to remove even a page, let alone an entire suitcase?

But it was too late for questions now. The pigeon-toed soldier had returned, and without a word motioned me to follow her. She walked with a stoop, one of those girls who for years will move through the low-ceilinged, narrow cave of her life until one day, if she is lucky, she'll finally emerge under an open sky. She led me to a covered jeep with benches on each side, presumably used for the transport of soldiers.

"Get in."

"In there? I don't think so. I'm not going anywhere until someone explains to me what's going on. I have a right to speak to someone," I said. "I want a phone call put in to the American embassy."

The girl clucked her tongue, and shimmied her shoulders to shift the strap of the heavy rifle.

"You'll speak, you'll speak. Calm down. There's nothing to worry about. You can call who you want. You have a phone, no?"

"I'm an internationally published writer," I said stupidly. "You can't just cart me off like this, without reasonable cause."

"I know who you are," she said, pushing a strand of hair out of her face. "My ex-boyfriend gave me one of your books. If you want to know, it wasn't my thing. No offense. But relax, OK? Feel easy. The sooner you get in the jeep, the sooner you'll be on your way. Schectman here will take care of you."

She exchanged a joke in Hebrew with the tall soldier waiting in the back of the jeep, with a face like half of the boys I went to high school with. He reached out his hand to help me up, and the gesture inspired a confused trust, or maybe I was just too tired to argue any further. Under the canvas roof, it smelled of rubber, mildew, and sweat.

As the driver started up the engine, the girl slapped her forehead. She instructed Schectman to hold on a minute, and he called out to the driver in the front. Then, while she ran back for whatever she'd forgotten, Schectman folded his hands over his knee and smiled at me.

"So," he said, "you like Israel?"

When the soldier returned, she was leading Friedman's dog by her collar. I protested, trying to explain that she wasn't mine, that she belonged to Friedman, but the soldier seemed to have no idea who Friedman was; already she'd forgotten he existed. What a cute dog, she said, petting her behind her wilted ears. She wanted to get a dog like that herself one day, when she finally got out of here.

"Go on," I said hopefully, "you can take this one."

But Schectman climbed down and lifted the old dog into his arms and placed it inside the jeep, and for a moment, while it lay cradled in his arms, I thought that we looked, the three of us, like some sort of demented crèche. Then the dog skittered down onto the floor, and as if she knew something that I didn't—as if she, too, had forgotten Friedman's existence—she licked my knees, turned around twice, and curled up at my feet. The soldier handed up my plastic bag, the one that I'd taken from my sister's apartment with a change of clothes and my bathing suit, and Schectman tucked it carefully under his seat, next to Friedman's suitcase.

The jeep's engine roared into action, and we went bumping along the graveled shoulder until the enormous wheels grabbed hold of the tarmac. But instead of turning around and heading back to Jerusalem, we continued the way Friedman had been headed, right out to where everything planned and constructed ended and it was, quite suddenly and irrevocably, desert. And as we did, the incongruous thought of Kafka's gardens came to me, gardens Friedman had told me he'd cultivated wherever he'd lived, in the kibbutz in the north, and behind the various houses he'd occupied in Tel Aviv, before he finally became famous enough, and—because he never really aged, because he never stopped looking exactly like the Kafka one inevitably falls a little in love with when one sees him on a postcard for the first time—he had to leave the city for good. I pictured his gardens filled with roses and honeysuckle, cactus and huge fragrant lilacs. As our military vehicle plowed on into the yellow hills, I saw Kafka with startling clarity, delicately leaning his little trowel against a stone wall and looking up at the sky as if to inspect it for signs of a gathering rain. And suddenly—they always come suddenly, these bright sparks of childhood—I remembered something that had happened a year after my brother found the earring in the Hilton pool. We had been staying at our grandparents' house in London while our parents were abroad in Russia, and one afternoon my brother and I were overcome with the desire for the chocolate sold in a nearby shop. I don't know why we didn't ask my grandmother for the money: we must have thought she'd refuse, or maybe we were thrilled by the idea of laying hold of the chocolate surreptitiously. In the garden in front of their semidetached house, my grandfather grew roses that remain, for me, the archetype of a rose; I can't think or say the word without summoning those delicate, fragrant English flowers. We found my grandmother's heavy metal shears in the kitchen, and squeezed the stems between the blades, high up under the flowers' sepals, until the large heads rolled. Coolly, we wrapped the stumps in aluminum foil, and decided that a lie would be necessary to convince people to buy them. We stood out on the street, and began to sing: *"Roses for sale, roses for sale, roses for children's charity!"* A woman stopped. I remember her as lovely, with tidy, dark hair beneath her woolen hat. She set down the bags she was carrying. "Are you sure it's for charity?" she asked us. Later it was her question that undid us. She had given us the chance to reconsider and come clean, but instead of taking it, we dug ourselves more deeply in. We nodded: quite sure, yes. She took out her wallet and unburdened us of our handfuls of roses— six or eight of them. My brother took the coins, and we began to walk quickly in silence. But as we made our way toward the shop, a crushing black guilt descended on us. We had done something we couldn't undo: beheaded our grandfather's roses, sold them off, lied to a stranger, all to serve our appetite. The sense of the permanence of our wrongdoing, our inability to ever correct it, was immensely heavy. I don't remember whether I turned to my brother and finally spoke, or whether it was he who turned to me, but I remember the words clearly: *Are you feeling what I'm feeling?* There was nothing more to be said. We bent down in the earth alongside the sidewalk, dug a hole, and buried the coins. That we would never breathe a word of what we had done to anyone was implicit. One day, I told my children the story. They were crazy for it, and wanted to hear it again and again. For days, they continued to bring it up. But why did you bury the money? my younger son kept asking. To be rid of it, I told him. But it's still there, he said, shaking his head. To this day, if you go to that spot and dig, the coins will still be there.

From time to time, as the wind sailed in through the back of the jeep, lifting the canvas sides and causing them to flap like a trapped bird, Schectman would catch my eyes, and then he would venture to smile at me, a gentle and knowing smile, possibly even touched with sadness, and the dog, whose name I'd never asked, would let out a groan as if it had already lived a thousand years, and already knew the end of every story.

The Last King

Epstein, new again to everything—new to the blazing white light off the waves, to the crying of the muezzin at dawn, new to the loss of appetite, to the body lightening, to a release from order, to the departing shore of the rational, new again to miracles, to poetry—took an apartment where he would never have lived in a thousand years, had he been living a thousand years, which, new again most of all to himself, he might have been. The sun didn't wake him because he was already awake, the windows all thrown open so that the waves sounded as if they were crashing right inside his room. Agitated, pacing barefoot, he discovered that the whole floor sloped toward the shower drain, as if the house had been built for a time when the sea would finally try to drown it. The agent had barely unlocked the door when Epstein announced he would take it, offering three months' rent in cash on the spot. In his polished shoes, he must have looked out of place in the broken-down apartment, which is to say, perfectly fitting the part. How many times had the agent seen him? The wealthy American, come to Israel to dip into the rich, authentic Jewish vein all those US dollars have gone to protect, so that he knows it's still alive over here and doesn't have to regret too much; come to turn himself on again in the bracing atmosphere of Middle Eastern passion. The agent had already been shrewd enough to inflate the rent, while claiming to be giving him a special deal as a friend of Yael's. But one look at Epstein's rapture as he surrendered to the horizon and he regretted not raising it higher. Still, he knew better than to trust the first flush of American enthusiasm. Knew how they came, and for a week fell in love with the urgency and the argument and the warmth, with the way everyone sits in the cafés and talks and gets into each other's lives; the way that even if on the outside Israel is obsessed with borders, on the inside it lives without boundaries. How there's no disease of loneliness here, and every taxi driver is a prophet, and every salesman at the *shouk* will tell you the story of his brother and his wife, and next thing you know the guy behind you in line is chiming in, and soon enough the crummy quality of the towels doesn't matter anymore, because the stories and the mess and the craziness—all that life!—are so much more essential. They come to Tel Aviv and find it so sexy, the sea and the strength, the nearness to violence and the hunger for life, and how, even if Israelis are living in an existential crisis all the time, and sense their country is lost, at least they live in a world where everything still matters and is worth fighting for. Most of all, they fall in love with how they feel here. This is where we come from, they think as they duck through the tunnels under the Western Wall, slink through the tunnels dug by Bar Kochba, scale Masada, stand in Levantine sunlight, hike the Judean, camp in the Negev, come to the Kinneret, where the children that could have been their own grow up wild and barefoot and related to the past mostly through acts of discontinuity: It's this that we didn't know we missed.

But the agent knew well that after a week or two they start to feel differently, these Americans. The strength starts to stink of aggression, and the directness becomes pushy, it begins to grate how Israelis don't have any manners, how they have no respect for personal space, no respect for anything, and doesn't anyone do anything in Tel Aviv aside from sit around talking and going to the beach? The city really is a shithole, isn't it, everything that isn't new is falling apart, the whole place smells of cat piss, there's a sewage problem right under the window and no one can come for a week, and actually Israelis are impossible to deal with, so stubborn and intractable, so frustratingly immune to logic, so damn rude, and it turns out most of them don't care for anything Jewish, their grandparents and parents ran as far away from it as they could, and the ones that do care, they're over the top, those settlers, totally out of their minds, and frankly the whole country is a bunch of Arab-hating racists. And so just in the nick of time, before they put down the deposit on a two-bedroom in the new glass high-rise going up over Neve Tzedek, it's back in the cab to the airport with their suitcases fragrant with za'atar and laden with silver Judaica from Hazorfim, and their Lexus keys newly hung on a *hamsa*.

And so the agent, lighting a cigarette, letting the smoke curl out his mouth and inhaling it back through his nostrils, squinted at his well-heeled client and said it was a deal if he was willing to drive to the ATM right then and there. He had his motorbike parked in front, he added, cracking open a window so that the smell of the sea could help Epstein think. But Epstein didn't need to think, and five minutes later he was clutching the agent's waist as they flew over the potholes, not caring a bit if someone somewhere might confuse him for a cliché.

That evening, the sky going orange to violet, Epstein stood shirtless before the sea and felt an exuberance, a birdlike freedom, and believed that he at last understood what all his giving up and giving away had been in service of: This sea. This lightness. This hunger. This ancientness. This flexibility to become a person drunk on the colors of Jaffa, waiting for his cell phone to illuminate with a message from the other side; from a larger existence; from Moses on Mount Sinai who had seen it all and was hurrying down now to tell him; from a woman to whom he had nothing left but himself to give; from the people he had entreated to deliver four hundred thousand trees to a barren mountainside in the desert.

His days became diffuse. The line between water and sky was lost; the line between himself and the world. He watched the waves, and felt himself to be also endless, repeating, filled with unseen life. The lines from the books on his table swam up from the pages before his eyes. At dusk, he would go out and walk, agitated, waiting, lost among the narrow streets, until, turning a corner and coming upon the sea all over again, he was unskinned.

IT WAS THE location manager who'd invited him, and who now spoke rapidly over a second espresso while they waited for Yael to show up at the café in Ajami. Epstein had been awake since four that morning, and it had been days since he'd spoken to anyone. But the location manager, who wore a terse Mohawk to get around his receding hairline, and was skinny enough to be feeding an addiction but too affable to need it, spoke so voluminously into Epstein's silence that nothing was required of him. Israeli filmmaking, he announced to Epstein, was at the pinnacle of its creativity. Until 2000, the great Israeli talent wasn't making films. When Epstein asked what the great Israeli talent was doing before 2000, the location manager appeared stumped.

Half an hour passed, and Yael still had not arrived, so the location manager ordered a third espresso from the young waitress, took out his phone, and began to show his captive audience clips and stills of his work. Epstein studied a photograph of an old house in Jerusalem, its dusky, sunken living room crowded with books and oil paintings, a small walled garden visible from the window. There was nothing unusual about the room, he thought, and yet its elements all cohered into something unquestionably warm, intelligent, and inviting. The location manager had visited fifty houses before stumbling onto this one, he said. The moment he'd walked in, he'd known it was the place. Nothing had to be moved for the set, not a stitch of furniture. Even the little dog curled on the chair was perfect. But what a job to convince the owners! He'd had to come back four times, the last time with an obsolete part the couple needed for their anciently dripping faucet, which he'd procured from a plumber whose shop he'd once shot a scene in. That was what sealed the deal: a little copper circle that had eluded them for years. But as soon as he'd won them over, the next-door neighbor stuck out her foot. The old woman did everything in her power to get in the way of the filming. All day long she sat in her window and screamed at them, and refused to keep her cat inside. On the contrary, she'd deliberately let the cat out the moment the cameras began rolling. The scenes constantly had to be interrupted by this cantankerous woman, who threatened to drive the rattled director crazy. But he, Eran, had found a way.

Had listened and listened, and slowly understood that the old woman was jealous, that like a child she felt left out, overlooked, and all he had to do was offer her a minuscule role as an extra for her to become instantly cooperative. Ten times they'd had to do the take of her being pushed down the sidewalk in a wheelchair he'd gotten from props, because every time she'd either smiled broadly into the camera or tried to squeeze in an improvised line. But in the end it had been more than worth it: from then on the old woman was quiet as could be, and guarded her cat as if it were a python that—God forbid it escaped—could devour her film whole. Yes, finding the right location was really the smaller part of his job, despite what you might think. The true essence of his work was in the management of the borders between this world and the one that the director was trying to create. Out of the present reality of houses and streets, furniture and weather, the director aimed to create another reality, and for however long the shot endured, it was up to him, Eran, to guard the borders between them. To make certain that nothing unwanted from the real world penetrated through to that other world, or in any way interrupted or threatened to dissolve its delicate conditions. And for this, one had to have a multitude of talents. But most of all one had to be skilled in dealing with people. After weeks of shooting came to an end, the location manager said, this skill had been so overused that all he wanted was to live like a hermit or misanthrope. And what do you do then? Epstein asked.

But at that moment Yael arrived, apologetic but serene, as if she had just stepped down out of a painting. If Epstein had no pressing desire to talk before, now he found again that in her presence he was nearly speechless. She had brought along

Dan, the director, who was in his forties and had the small eyes and sharp protuberant nose of an animal that spent most of its time underground, forever seized by a frenzied desire to dig its way into the light. Epstein had met him before, and taken an immediate dislike to him. He had obvious designs on Yael. The thought of her in his tribally tattooed arms made Epstein want to cry.

The location manager launched excitedly into a description of the spot he'd discovered: some caves close to where the Dead Sea scrolls had been found, but far enough away from any archaeological site that they could shoot there without permits, and with a vista so untouched as to be purely biblical. The caves were incredible because of the way they were lit, with a hole above that brought in shafts of sunlight. It was entirely possible that David himself had hidden in them. At the very least, the Essenes had probably occupied them two thousand years ago, while preparing for the War of the Sons of Light against the Sons of Darkness.

But the director and Yael, son of darkness and daughter of light, were in a low mood, and no cave, however authentic, could lift them out of it. That morning they'd received bad news: Neither Hot nor Yes had come through. On the basis of the synopsis and treatment she had written, Yael explained to Epstein, they'd gotten production grants from both the Jerusalem Film Fund and the Rubinstein Foundation. At first it had seemed like enough, but once they'd understood what sort of budget was required to really do the film right, they found themselves short of money. They'd hoped that one of the big cable companies would get behind the project, but neither had. Shooting was supposed to begin in two weeks, and if something else didn't come through quickly, everything would have to be put on hold.

How much did they need? Epstein asked reflexively.

HIS TREES WERE growing at a kibbutz in the Kinneret. A month after he'd signed his name to the $2 million donation, Epstein was taken to see them. The head of the JNF, having returned from her travels in South America, brought him personally. They dined under a grape arbor that the kibbutz rented out for weddings, and drank the wine produced by its sister kibbutz across the valley. Epstein's glass was refilled, and afterward, tipsy, he was driven out to the fields in a tractor. The air was heavy with the smell of manure, but the view was wide and fertile, with green fields, yellow grasses, and brown hills. Epstein stood, loafers sinking into the soil, and saw the rows upon rows of shivering saplings. Is that all? he'd asked. All four hundred thousand? It seemed to him that even with so many, there were still not enough. The head of the JNF double-checked with her assistant, who confirmed that a further hundred fifty thousand saplings, broadleaf rather than pine, would be brought from another kibbutz, but that what he was looking at, right here in front of him, was the heart of the Sol and Edith Epstein Forest.

HIS BOOKS LAY OPEN on the table. He was reading Isaiah and Kohelet. He was reading the *aggadot* in Bialik's *Book of Legends*. The man behind the crowded desk in the secondhand bookshop on Allenby understood the vein he was mining, and always had something waiting. But now, close to midnight in the apartment in Jaffa, Epstein left off from their pages and began once more to pace. The saplings still needed six weeks before they could be transplanted. Come March it would be spring, and then the valley would burst into flower, ranunculus and cyclamen would cover the hills, and the saplings would be ready. They would be dug up and wrapped in burlap, transported to the mountain in the northern Negev, and placed in the ground by an army of laborers. In Israel, where the warm sun almost always shone, trees grew twice as fast as in America. By summer they would already be up to Epstein's chest, and by fall they would surpass him. Galit was overseeing the project; on this Epstein had been insistent. In his impatience, he phoned her once a day. His energy for the subject of forests and trees was inexhaustible, and only she could keep pace with him. The word *humus*—which she used when referring to the rich soil that the trees held in place, and replenished when they died, suffusing it with the minerals they had mined from the depths of the earth—sent a shiver down Epstein's spine. He developed a great interest in the topic of erosion, not only in the wadis, where the rain from flash floods spilled down the barren slopes and came sluicing through in search of the shortest path to the sea, but across the world, and through time. When the owner of the bookshop on Allenby failed to procure any books on forestry, Galit arranged for certain titles to be delivered to Epstein's Jaffa apartment, and in these he read about how the great empires of Assyria, Babylon, Carthage, and Persia were all destroyed by the floods and desertification brought on by mass clearing of their forests. He read about how the felling of forests in ancient Greece was soon followed by the vanishing of its culture, and how the same destructive clearing of the virgin forests of Italy later caused the downfall of Rome. And all the while, as he read, and the sea rolled its great dark waves against his windows, his own saplings were growing, their leaves unfurling, their leaders stretching upward toward the sky.

Epstein took up his book again: *Rescue me, God, for the waters have come up to my neck.*

His phone rang.

> *And there is no place to stand*
> *I am come into deep waters,*
> *where the floods overflow me.*

IT WAS SHARON, breathless to have gotten through, since he rarely answered anymore. She had still not given up the search for his lost phone and coat. Standing on the cold Jaffa floor, it all struck Epstein as long ago: Abbas at the Plaza, the coat clerk with a limp, the mugger who ran the shining knife across his chest. But Sharon had not forgotten, and—in Epstein's absence, without instructions otherwise—had remained doggedly on the case. With excitement, she reported that she had traced the phone to Gaza.

Gaza? Epstein echoed, turning to the south and looking through the dark windows.

Using Find My iPhone, she explained, she had been able to track it over GPS. And, after many hours on the phone with a technician in Mumbai, she had disengaged Lost Mode and triggered an app installed when Epstein's phone was new that allowed one to remotely command it to take pictures. Within a matter of hours, Sharon announced with pride, tomorrow at the very latest, the photographs taken by Epstein's itinerant phone would be transmitted through to her computer.

Epstein imagined bombed buildings nestled in the lost phone's archive next to the stream of photographs Lucie had sent him of his grandchildren.

Sharon's tone now switched to one of concern. But how was he? She had not heard from him for two weeks; messages she had left had not been returned. Did he want her to book his return flight?

He assured her that he was well, and that he didn't need her to do anything at the moment. Not wishing to get into it further, he hurried off the phone, without pausing to ask her what it was she meant to do once the pictures from his phone in Gaza finally came through.

He put on a jacket and went down the dark stairwell, not bothering to turn on the lights. When he got to the landing of the floor below, a cat streaked out through an open door and wound itself around his legs. His downstairs neighbor came out, apologized, scooped up the ginger cat, and invited him in for a cup of tea. Epstein politely declined. He needed some air, he explained. Perhaps another time.

On the jetty made of boulders and concrete blocks, some Arab men were fishing in the dark. What are you trying to catch? Epstein asked in his simple Hebrew. Communists, they told him. And when he did not understand, they gestured with their thumb and forefinger to demonstrate the smallness of the fish they were after. He stood watching them throw their lines for a while. Then he touched the elbow of the youngest of them and gestured south, toward the open water. How far to Gaza? he asked. The boy grinned and reeled in his line. Why? he asked. You want to visit? But Epstein had only been trying to gauge the distance, a skill that along with others seemed to be slowly abandoning him.

HE WAS KNOWN at Sotheby's. Known by the heads of old master paintings, of master drawings, of modern art, of rugs. Known by the curator of primitive sculpture and Roman glass. Ordering his cappuccino on the tenth floor, Epstein would be intercepted by the tapestry specialist who had a piece from the Brussels workshop he really must see. At previews, he did not fall under the purview of the DO NOT TOUCH signs, and was allowed to finger what he wished; when he arrived at an auction, his paddle was always waiting. But however known he was, and however eager they might have been to offer his extraordinary *Annunciation*— which they also knew well, having sold the fifteenth-century altar panel to him ten years earlier—they could not pick the painting up themselves, for reasons of liability. Neither was there time to organize third-party transport, if he wanted it included in the upcoming auction: the catalogue was closing in two days.

Schloss was out of the question. So were all three of Epstein's children, since each would have sounded a different kind of alarm. And Sharon's concern for him was such that he couldn't risk the possibility of her calling Lianne or Maya when she discovered that he had decided to sell off the *Annunciation* to fund a film about the biblical David. Epstein settled on phoning the lobby on Fifth Avenue. The first time Haaroon wasn't on duty, only the small Sri Lankan whose name he forgot a moment after he'd been reminded of it. Had Jimmy answered, the slender, remote Japanese who rode the elevator enveloped in a distant privacy and never said a word, Epstein might have gone ahead and explained what he'd wanted. But the Sri Lankan had always exhibited too much curiosity to be trusted. When he called back a few hours later, Haaroon had arrived for his shift and answered after the first ring. He asked Epstein to hold while he procured the yellow legal pad and pen that he kept in the drawer of the lobby console.

"Yes, sir," he said, balancing the pad on his arm while clamping the phone between ear and shoulder, and set to copying down his instructions. Oh no, it would be no trouble at all, he could pack it tonight—yes, he would be exceedingly careful—nearly six hundred years old—how extraordinary, yes, truly, sir—first thing tomorrow morning to Sotheby's, Seventy-Second and York—oh, he would carry it like a newborn—yes, the Virgin, sir, hah-hah, very funny—oh really, a Madonna!—certainly, Mr. Epstein, no trouble at all.

It was five in the morning when Haaroon's shift came to an end and he hung his uniform in the basement office, took the spare key to the Epstein apartment, rode up in the elevator, and fingered the prayer rug from Isfahan in front of the door, loomed for bowing prostrate rather than wiping dirty feet. He removed his shoes and lined them up under the brass-footed bench. Letting himself in with the key, he searched in the dark for the light switch but, catching sight of the glittering view, he stopped. Overwhelmed all over again, he crossed the empty living room, large enough to have fit the houses of both his brothers in Punjab. He looked out over the park. The hawk would still be asleep in his nest now. His new mate would be getting ready to lay her eggs, and soon Haaroon would have to watch the sky for flocks of ravenous crows. Last year a fledgling had fallen out of a tree right in front of the building, and he had run to its rescue, stopping traffic, but after a stunned moment the bird had righted itself and taken flight again. The faithful doorman pressed his nose to the cold glass, but could see nothing in the still-black sky.

He found the painting in the master bedroom, just as Epstein had described it. It was smaller than he'd expected, and yet its radiance was such that he could not bring himself to touch it right away. Standing nearly upon it, he had the feeling of intruding on something intensely private. And yet he couldn't take his eyes away from the girl Mary and the angel. Only after some time did he notice that in the corner, half outside the frame, was a third figure, a man who was also looking, long fingers pressed together in devotion. The man's lurking presence bothered him. Who was he meant to be? Joseph? Useless Joseph, who had to insinuate himself there into the scene? But, no, he didn't look like Joseph at all; a man with a face like that surely could have nothing to do with the illuminated girl kneeling before the angel.

The sky was already beginning to lighten when Haaroon stepped out through the building's service entrance with the package tucked under his arm. Spring was not far off, but it was still cold enough that his breath froze under the streetlamps. There were three hours until Sotheby's would open, and so he entered the park, gazing up toward the barren treetops. The bench where he liked to spend his lunch break was taken by a homeless man in filthy boots, sprawled across the length of it under a ratty blanket the color and texture of loam. Practicing to be buried, Haaroon thought, and sank down two benches away, laying the precious parcel on his lap. From there, the great swath of sky was partially obscured by the branches of a giant tree, but he could still see enough of it to keep watch. His eyes followed the darting sparrows for a while. When he looked down, he saw with wonder how the light falling from the streetlamp through the clear wrapping still glinted on the Virgin's halo. That he, a man born in Punjab Province to a farmer, should be sitting in New York City holding a masterpiece painted in fifteenth-century Italy—he felt a sudden urge to break the little painting in two and shivered. To his brothers, such a thing would hold no value at all, and he felt a wave of sadness at a distance he could no longer cross.

As if deliberately out to disturb him, a crow came angling down, strutted across the grass, and began to shriek at him. Such aggressive and conspiratorial birds, so maliciously intelligent— they seemed to remember him from the time he had pelted some of their kind with acorns to protect one of the fledgling hawks, and now they cawed angrily whenever they came across him. Haaroon took hold of his parcel and stood, waving his free arm and shouting back at the crow: *Go back to where you come from!* The bird flapped off, its black wing feathers reflecting the blue of the sky, and the homeless man stirred under the brown surface. After a moment, a matted head of hair popped out, followed by his weathered face.

"Asshole!"

"Sorry," Haaroon muttered, and grimly took his seat again.

The homeless man eyed him from his horizontal position.

"What are you looking for, drones?"

"Not really."

"Yesterday I saw one fly *right* by that window"—the homeless man pointed a steady finger at a high floor of a building across the street—"and hover there for two minutes, looking in."

"Really?"

"Spy mission," he said, propping himself up on one elbow.

The park had begun to fill with early-morning joggers, and the homeless man watched them go by on the path.

"If you're not looking for drones, then what?"

"A hawk, actually."

"You missed him. Wind-fucker. Already caught a pigeon this morning. Ripped its head off in one bite."

"Really!"

But the homeless man had pulled the blanket back up to his nose.

Haaroon zipped up his collar and watched the wind swiftly carry the clouds. He knew that the hawk preferred to wait until the sky was fully light before flinging himself out for the hunt. Feeling himself beginning to nod off, the doorman blinked and drove his fingernails into his palm. After the night shift he normally went straight home to bed, and slowly his fatigue began to win out, his eyes drifted closed, and his chin fell forward onto his chest.

HE COULDN'T HAVE been asleep for long before he jerked awake and saw the white underside of the hawk soaring above. Heart pounding, head thrown back, he leaped to his feet with a shout. Oh, the magnificence! What beauty under heaven! The doorman could barely believe his luck. Riding a current of air, the hawk's wings were outstretched and nearly still; it was only the tilt of its body that caused it to wheel, turning a circle high above the treetops. Then it stopped in tense idle, hovering, and plummeted down in a dive.

Haaroon raced in the direction where it had gone down, pushing the lashing branches out of his way until he was through to the grassy clearing on the other side of the trees. And there, in a patch of sunlight, stood the magnificent bird, shoulders hunched and neck curved almost tenderly over the prey struggling in its talons. In a moment, it was over. The limp mouse hung from the hawk's beak, and the bird flapped, its heavy wing beats carrying it up again.

Only after he had lost sight of the hawk did Haaroon look down and realize that his own hands were empty. Once more he shouted. Heart pounding, he raced back through the trees toward the bench. But he could already see that it was empty. Not wanting to believe it, he desperately ran his fingers over the wooden seat, as if the Madonna might still be shining there invisibly.

When he turned, he saw that the bench where the homeless man had lain was now empty, too, but for the brown blanket that hung shapelessly from the seat. The doorman moaned, raised his hands to his head, and pulled on his thin hair. Turning in a desperate circle, he scanned the paths and trees. But all was still but for the sparrows.

To the Desert

I HAD NO SENSE of how much time passed after Schectman dropped me there. In the silence of the desert, at the mercy of a fever, I lost track completely. It could have been a week or ten days, or far longer. By then my family might have been searching for me quite desperately. My father would have been the most stalwart and indefatigable of the searchers. He has an extraordinary capacity to organize and accomplish under great duress, my father; has what people often call a commanding presence and an iron will. Right away he would have gotten Shimon Peres—who'd been an acquaintance of my grandfather's half a century ago, attended my parents' wedding at the Hilton, and once even told me over an expensive meal that he had read my books and liked them, though I was not inclined to believe him—on the phone. But despite all of these threadbare connections, what Shimon Peres could have done for my father is anyone's guess, since by then Peres was only a figurehead of what he knew had been lost. Yes, I decided, my father would have been the most obvious and cogent leader of the search party, whereas my mother, in her distress, would have been disorganized and largely useless. Surely my children would not yet have been told anything. As for my husband, I really had no idea how he would have responded to the news that I'd disappeared: it was very possible that he might have felt ambivalent, and perhaps even relieved at the prospect of being able to go through the rest of his life without me looking skeptically over at him.

Schectman had said that someone would come for me. His orders had been to drop me in that desert shack with the suitcase and the dog, and in due time, presumably after I'd completed my assignment, someone would be back to get me. The assignment itself was never mentioned outright. He must have assumed that I knew what I was supposed to be doing there. Carefully, with the shy, delicate pride of a groom leading his bride into their new abode, he brought me into the house and showed me the kitchen with its black stove, the narrow bed covered in a tartan wool blanket, and finally the worktable by the window, on whose sill two or three flies had given up the ghost. The house was tiny, almost comically so in proportion to the vastness pressing up against it from all sides. On the desk was a glass containing a few pens, a stack of paper held down by a smooth oval stone, and an old typewriter. But it's Hebrew, I said, awkwardly clutching the shopping bag with my change of clothing. I'd never written anything on a typewriter, and had no use for one, and so I can only surmise that my reason for pointing this out was to subtly bring to Schectman's attention the problematic nature of the situation in general. But he kept up an air of insouciance, and only looked at the typewriter appraisingly, with, at best, the interest of someone who likes to take mechanical things apart into tiny pieces.

He offered to make me coffee, and I stood leaning against the wall with my arms crossed, watching him move about the tiny kitchen. He couldn't have been more than twenty, but he handled the kettle and the stove in a way that suggested he'd been used to doing things for himself from a young age. The window was framed by the sort of white lace associated with alpine chalets, as if whoever had hung it had hoped to look past it to drifts of sparkling snow. But all that could be seen was the blanched, dry landscape stretching out in all directions, and the driver smoking a cigarette as he leaned against the jeep.

I could have refused, or yelled, or otherwise put up a fight so that they wouldn't have left me there. I couldn't have called anyone, because my phone had no reception. But I had the impression that I could have appealed to them, or at least to Schectman, who from time to time continued to regard me with his gentle, sad smile, as if he regretted having to leave me there on my own. But I didn't object or even complain; at most, I pointed out that the typewriter was useless to me. Maybe I wanted to impress him with my independence and professionalism. Or didn't want to disabuse him of the notion of untold talents, which, the moment he drove off, would be put to use for the good of the Jews. Or maybe I suspected that I'd already gone far enough that there was no turning back anymore. Whatever the case, from the moment Schectman extended his hand to help me up into the back of the jeep, I'd gone along with everything. As far as I remember, the only question I asked was about Friedman.

I was worried about him, I explained to Schectman, as we drank our coffee. I wanted to know where they had taken him, and if he was all right. But Schectman showed no sign of recognition of Friedman's name, and when I pushed him further, he admitted that he had never heard of any Friedman. He had arrived in the story midway, it seemed, without knowing anything about what had happened prior to my becoming his charge, or what would happen after. All he knew was his part, which involved getting me from a roadblock at the edge of Jerusalem to this shack in the desert, with the suitcase and the dog. But I suppose that's how they do things in the army, never giving any of the participants the whole story. In the military, the entire idea of narrative must be completely different, I thought. You learn to be satisfied with your small piece, without having any real idea of how it fits, and yet you never have to worry about the whole because somewhere someone who knows everything has thought it all out, down to the last detail. The story exists, who knows where it arrived from and where it is going, all you have to do is apply yourself to your part, which you can polish until it shines in what is otherwise darkness all around. In light of this model, it really did seem like sheer vanity to ever imagine that one could possibly know the whole thing, and, considering this, I momentarily forgot about Friedman, too. But when I caught Schectman looking at me over the top of his coffee cup, all my concern surged back with a force that took me by surprise. I would have given a lot to be told that Friedman was all right. I'd known him so briefly, but at that moment I missed him the way I'd missed my grandfather the last day I'd seen him alive in the hospital, when I'd said good-bye and he'd called after me, *Come back if you can*. And then, *Go, I'll wait. If you don't hear from me, open the door*. It seemed to me that Friedman had been trying to tell me things that I had been too slow to grasp.

I need to know what happened to him, I told Schectman again. My anxiety must have been plain, because he reached out and touched my shoulder and told me not to worry. I was overwhelmed with gratitude, and wanted to believe him. This must be how it begins with captives who develop a bond with their captors, I thought: one small, unexpected gesture of mercy begets what can only be called love. I pictured us watching soccer games on the little TV Schectman would bring for my birthday, which we would only be able to get in Arabic.

Did you know that I have children? I asked him quietly, wishing to extend the moment of intimacy. He shook his head. Two boys, I told him. The older one must be nearly half your age. And the younger? he asked, politely. For some reason, I don't why, I said: The younger one is probably standing by the window, waiting for me right now.

I watched a drop of darkness seep under Schectman's eyes. Maybe I was trying to test him, to see where his true feeling lay. But when I looked down, I saw that it was my own fingers that were shaking.

We drank the rest of our coffee in silence, and then it was time for him to go. He offered me some cigarettes, which I took, as I would have taken anything he offered me. I watched from the doorway as he climbed into the passenger seat next to the driver. I could see the jeep for a long time, getting smaller and smaller until finally it became only a cloud of dust, and when even the cloud vanished, I turned back into the house.

I washed the cups and left them to dry on the edge of the sink, and gave the dog more water. Then I went into the only other room of the house and eyed the suitcase still standing upright by the door. But it was not yet the moment for that, I decided. Instead, I turned my attention to the few old books on the shelves. They were all in Hebrew, and I tried to work out the titles. One caught my eye. It was called יערות ישראל—*Forests of Israel*—and inside were black-and-white photographs of places that didn't look like they could be in Israel at all: wild forests where one might still have a chance of being raised by wolves; thick, dark woods swept through with snow. I looked at the pictures for a long time, and because I couldn't understand the captions, I had to content myself with imagining what they said, but as I could not very well imagine what the captions of photographs of forests that couldn't possibly grow in Israel and yet had been gathered together under the title *Forests of Israel* might say, I was free to enjoy the magic of that discordance. In one photo I found a small white hare almost completely camouflaged by snow.

In the closet there were some rusted tools, a couple of shovels, what looked like a metal milk pail, a first aid kit, some rolls of twine, a wool scarf, a canvas backpack, and a pair of leather slippers worn smooth at the heels. I kicked off my shoes, put them on, and padded to the bathroom. The tap ran brown as if the desert itself were coming in through the pipes, while the kitchen faucet produced water that was merely cloudy and bitter. I drank from there.

When I'd seen everything there was to see inside, I went outside to explore. On one side of the house was a small picnic table scored by knife marks, and at the back was a covered stone well. There must have been an underground spring or aquifer, because there was a lot of scrub surrounding the house, and three or four small thorny trees. Tamarisk maybe, or acacia. Soon the rain would arrive here, too, and the desert would be carpeted in green, but here it was still dry and barren except for a few lone spots of life. I saw quite a lot of animals; their drinking source must have been nearby. There were horned ibex in the hills, and a family of small antelopes that came to chew on the scrub, and once a desert fox with amber fur, huge pointed ears, and a little thin snout came hurrying past the house and stopped to look through the open door, as if he half expected to greet someone familiar. But when he saw me, he trotted off again, not bothering to get involved. There were plenty of mice, too, which came and went as they pleased.

Only after investigating the house inside and out did I approach the worktable. Approached it casually, I should say, with no plans whatsoever of doing anything there, least of all writing. And it was only then, as I sat down in the chair and mindlessly lay my fingers on the typewriter's letters, that it dawned on me that this was Kafka's house that I'd been brought to. The house where he'd lived alone at the end of his life—lived and died for the second time, under the minimal conditions he yearned for, confined at last to only that which was unquestionably within himself. That this was where Friedman had intended to bring me all along.

VERY SOON AFTER THAT, maybe even the following day, I fell ill. It came as a wave of weakness and heaviness in the limbs, and at first I thought it was just exhaustion from lack of sleep. All afternoon I lay on the bed looking listlessly out the window at the desert ever changing in the light. Lay unmoving, as if already exhausted by whatever it was that I was going toward. When I began to shiver, and a low ache spread down from my skull and through my limbs, I thought it must be psychosomatic, a way to avoid having to try to write, or to confront what I was really doing there, or to fully consider what in my heart I already knew was to come. I no longer feared physical pain, but I did fear emotional pain—my own, but far more so the pain I might inflict on my children, which everything in me leaped to shield them from for as long as possible. Forever, if I could. But by then I had begun to sense that I could only delay their pain, and that the more I delayed it, the more their father and I continued to uphold a form we no longer believed in, the more hurt they would ultimately be. I know I should add that I feared the pain my husband would feel, too, and as much as I did, I find it difficult to write that sentence now. In the years that followed, he behaved in ways that continually shocked me despite their near constancy. We walked away from our marriage side by side, and though afterward both of our sufferings were great, I do believe I could have gone on feeling very much for him all my life, this man with whom I'd borne our children, who had poured his love into them, had he not become someone I could no longer recognize. Not just his face, which I continued to study with perplexity for a long time afterward, but his whole being. I think it must often be the case that after one parts from someone one has been with a long time, many things spring out that were suppressed or constrained by the presence of the other. In the months after the relationship ends, a person can seem to grow at a lightning rate, like in a nature documentary where weeks of footage is run at high speed to show a plant unfurling in seconds, but in reality the person has been growing all along, under the surface, and it is only in their new freedom, in their hair-raising aloneness, that the person can allow for these underground things to break through and unfurl themselves in the light. But there had been so much restraint and silence between my husband and me that when we parted and broke into our separate light and volume at last, the person that came into view was impossible to hold close. Perhaps he didn't wish to be held close, or couldn't, for which I don't blame him. And now, far enough on the other side of grief, I find I feel only surprise when I think of him. Surprise that for a time we ever believed we were walking in the same direction at all.

At what moment does one fall out of a marriage? Unlike love

and care, the promise of time can be measured, and so to marry another is to bind oneself to him for a lifetime. And now I think that I left mine by falling out of time, which was the only way for me, just as packing my suitcase in the haze of insomnia was the only way. Awake in Kafka's bed, I fell out of time's old order and into another. Outside the window there was only time, and inside, too: the light that crossed the floor was time, as was the hum of electricity from the generator, the tick of the bulb that brought a dim illumination to the room, the wind whistling around the corner of the house, all of it only time swept up from somewhere and deposited here, having given up any attachment to sequence.

A long time ago, before I was married, I read a book about ancient Greek. It was during a period when I was particularly interested in Greece, and went to the Peloponnese with a boyfriend whom I lived with for a while on the long finger of the Mani that juts impertinently into the sea, where we both tried to write, but mostly just fucked and fought savagely in a tiny cottage infested with rats. The book was filled with many fascinating things, and I remember that it went quite deeply into the ancient Greek words for time, for which there were two: *chronos*, which referred to chronological time, and *kairos*, used to signify an indeterminate period in which something of great significance happens, a time that is not quantitative but rather has a permanent nature, and contains what might be called "the supreme moment." And as I lay in Kafka's bed, it seemed that what was gathering up all around me was that kind of time, and that when I was well enough again, I would endeavor to sift through it all to locate the supreme moment around which my life until now had secretly coalesced. Finding this needle in the haystack seemed to me of urgent importance, as presumably the moment had come and gone without my having the least understanding of what it had offered. I became convinced that it must have come along during my childhood, come like a moth going toward the light, only to slam into an obtuse screen, a screen newly placed there by some nascent responsibility to what was expected of me now that I was eight or ten, whereas before I lived with all of my windows and doors wide open to the night. I remembered that from that book I'd read in the front garden of the cottage, while in the kitchen the rats were scurrying along the weighted pulleys that held up the shelves, and in the shade of the back garden the boyfriend was producing pages upon pages as if just innocently passing time while he waited for me to find yet another reason to unleash on him my fury—from that book, I'd also learnt that in the ancient art of rhetoric, the word *kairos* referred to the passing instant when an opening occurs that must be driven through with force, with all the force one can muster if one wishes to overwhelm any remaining resistance. And now I grasped that, in my ignorance, I'd failed to seize upon or even recognize this instant, which— had I possessed the necessary force—might have allowed me to break right through to that other world I'd always sensed existed beneath. In my obliviousness, I'd missed my chance, and since then I'd had to resort to trying to claw my way there with my fingernails.

Sometimes I believed it was Kafka's bed, and sometimes I didn't. Sometimes I think I almost forgot, blissfully, who Kafka even was. His suitcase stood by the door, but at times I no longer remembered who it belonged to, or what was in it, though I never lost the sense that it mattered very much, and that whatever happened to me now, I couldn't lose it. That somewhere somebody's life, perhaps my own, depended on it. Sometimes I called the dog Kafka, as the name was readily available, and because using it for the dog felt like a stroke of lucidity. She came, too, though by then she was so hungry, the poor animal, that she probably would have answered to anything. Maybe it was that hunger that brought out such a deep intelligence in her eyes. I gave the dog whatever I could find in the cupboard. I think she took this to be a greater sacrifice than it was, and it aroused her loyalty. But by the time I became ill, there was very little left in the house for either of us to eat, except for a large supply of a peanut-flavored snack called Bamba. When she heard the familiar crinkling of the bags, she would come immediately. Great clouds of dust or maybe dry skin would rise up from her when she shifted, and I got it into my head that this, too, was a form of time, of whatever time she had left.

Sometimes I addressed the dog. Long monologues, to which she would listen with ears pricked as she wolfed down pieces of snack from my pocket. Once, all out of Bamba, I turned to her and said, "Why don't you have a corned beef sandwich?" which is what my grandfather said to me from his hospital bed, right before he asked me if he was dead yet. But I knew I wasn't dead; on the contrary, there were moments that I felt, in that illness, thrillingly alive. More alive, I think, than I had felt since I was a child. Awake to the sound of many kinds of wind, and the swelling and contracting of the house, the wings of a fly caught in a web who had not yet given up, and the low, steady note of sunlight playing across the floor. I had always been a little feral in my ways, despite all of the domestic fuss I'd made to the contrary, but left alone now, stroked by fever, I gave up on washing my clothes in the sink and slept often during the day and awoke at night and didn't bother to brush my hair or sweep the floor, which was slowly being covered with the fine grit of the desert. In the closet I found an old wool coat, and I took to wearing this, even to bed. When the pain became unbearable, I would seize on some small discoloration on the wall or ceiling, or a smudge of dirt on the window, and force myself on this tiny defect with enormous intensity, boring down on it with every last shred of concentration. Either as a result of this, or of the patience that naturally develops from being alone and confined to bed, I slowly became aware of a sharpening of my vision, and after experimenting with this clarity, studying the fibers on the blanket that stood up like the hairs on an insect's leg, I discovered that I could also apply it when looking inward. For a while, it seemed to me that I needed only to brandish the razor of my acuity for the subject, whatever it was, to immediately surrender itself up to be flayed. But then a foreboding thought cast a shadow over the rest, blunt and unadorned, and it was simply this: that for most of my life I had been emulating the thoughts and actions of other people. That so much that I had done or said had been a mirror of what was done and said around me. And that if I continued in this manner, whatever glimmers of brilliant life still burned in me would soon go out. When I was very young it had been otherwise, but I could hardly recall that time, it was buried so far below. I was only certain that a period had existed in which I looked at the things of the world without needing to make them subordinate to order. I simply saw, with whatever originality I was born with, the whole of things, without needing to give them a human translation. I would never again be able to see like that, I knew that, and yet, lying there, it seemed to me that I'd failed to fulfill the promise of that vision I once had, before I began to slowly learn to look at everything the way others looked, and to copy the things they said and did, and to shape my life after theirs, as if no other range of being had ever occurred to me.

It's not impossible that it was myself that I was flaying, because at times the pain was quite spectacular. It was all through my body, to the very core; I've only once felt anything like that. But as I already said, physical pain doesn't frighten me anymore. It ceased to frighten me after my oldest son was born. The night before I went into labor, a woman came to the house to give me some baby clothes she no longer needed, and, sitting on my sofa, she told me that in the throes of childbirth, the last thing she had wanted was to be prone on her back, numb from the lower spine down. On the contrary, the only conceivable approach was to be able to get up and walk right toward the pain, to meet it with every ounce of strength she had. This sounded like such common sense to me that when my water broke the very next night and I found myself in the hospital, doubled over with pain, I refused everything, refused even the IV that they insisted on trying to jab into the back of my hand the moment I arrived, and for the next seventeen hours I went right toward the pain of bringing a nearly ten-pound baby through what had always struck me as a rather narrow passage. When I could finally speak again, having come to after the blood lost from all the tearing, and was lying flat out on the bed, trying to sweep together the shredded filaments of my mind, I told someone who called on the phone, curious to know what it had all been like, that I felt like I had met myself in a dark valley. That I had gone down and met myself in the valley of hell. And so this pain, this flaying of the self or whatever it was that was happening to me now, was not about to do me in. This pain, as if my whole being were being pared away from the bone. Or maybe I was not afraid of the pain because I believed that my illness, whatever it was, was also a form of health, the continuation of a transformation already under way.

IT MUST HAVE been during the eye of the storm of my fever that I found myself half a mile out from the house, without a clue as to how I'd gotten there. I was watching a blot in the sky that I took to be an eagle circling overhead. It cried out, and as if the cry had come from me, I suddenly felt that what was straining behind my lungs was joy. A wild exultancy of the kind that would sometimes attack me without warning in childhood. A joy so powerful that I thought it might break my chest. Then it did, it must have broken right through, because for a moment I wasn't contained inside anything anymore. I went clean through to the sky. Isn't that the meaning of ecstasy, as the Greeks gave it to us? In that garden on the Mani, in love and fury, I'd read it: *Ex stasis: to go out of oneself.* But as much as I may have admired the Greeks then, in the end I could never be that, and if you are a Jew standing in the desert going completely out of yourself, falling out of the old order, it will always be something different, won't it? *Lech lecha*, God told Abram, who had not yet become Abraham: *Go—go away from where you live, the land of your fathers the land of your birth, to the place that I will show you.* But *Lech lecha* was never really about moving from the land of his birth over the river to the unknown land of Canaan. To read it like that is to miss the point, I think, since what God was demanding was so much harder, was very nearly impossible: for Abram to go out of himself so that he might make space for what God intended him to be.

IN THE EYE of the storm—I don't know what else to call it. It must have also been then, during that bolt of energy that came from the cessation of pain, that I decided to drag the bed outside. It was difficult to get it through the door. I had to turn the bed at an angle to fit the headboard through, and naturally it jammed and I had to climb out through the window and come round the front to pull it. While I tugged maniacally, the dog howled from inside, skittering around and sniffing the other side of the bed. I think she thought that I meant to trap her inside and leave. When the headboard suddenly popped free, I fell back and the dog shot out of the house.

I dragged it some twenty feet out. With great satisfaction, I smoothed out the bedsheets and the tartan blanket and lay down under the tremendous sky. The dog finally cooled off and lowered herself onto the stony ground next to the bed. She rested her chin on the edge of the mattress, waiting to see if I had anything more to add. She must have once had a litter, maybe many, because her teats hung morosely down from her belly. I wondered where they were now, her children. I wondered if she ever considered them. Perhaps I spoke to her like that: as one creature that had borne the physical demands of bringing life into the world to another, who had the story of life-giving written into her body from conception, leaving her no choice, it seemed, but to enact it. Who felt the sheer force of its law move through her, and wondered whether there was any difference between it and love. Otherwise, I no longer remember the subject of our talks.

It was late afternoon, and the desert was turning ochre and

the temperature was perfect as I watched a few pink clouds pass overhead. I was pleased with the results of my work. So much so, that after a while I decided to drag the rest of the furniture outside, too. The reading chair covered in a piece of old canvas to hide the ripped seat, the worktable, and even the typewriter and the stack of pages and the stone paperweight, which would now serve a purpose, as without it the pages would have been scattered by the wind. At first it looked like some sort of desert tag sale, which was not at all what I'd had in mind, and so I spent a long while arranging the jumble out in the open in front of the house, adjusting the spaces between each pair of items, laying it all out toward some inexpressible perfection. When it was almost perfect but not quite, I nipped back into the house and came out with the slippers, which I placed next to the bed, and *Forests of Israel*, which I laid on the night table.

A wave of exhaustion broke over me. I could barely take another step, and sank down on the mattress. I couldn't imagine how I'd found the strength for it all. And yet, lying there out in the open, I felt close to that fullness that one sometimes senses is there beneath the surface of everything, invisible, as Kafka once wrote, far away, but not hostile, not reluctant, not deaf, and which, if we call it by the right name, might come.

I must have fallen asleep. When I opened my eyes again, it was night, and I was shivering in the cold, looking up at the raging stars. I pulled the old woolen coat more tightly around myself. Searching for the constellations, I thought of the day the boyfriend and I drove all the way down the crooked finger of the Mani to the supposed gate of the Underworld. Old lives are always coming back, but during the decade of my marriage, that particular day had returned to me more often than others, and now it came to me again. To see into the small mouth of the cave, I'd gotten down on all fours, and as I did, the boyfriend had lifted my dress and mounted me from behind. The tall blades of grass rustled gently in the wind, and so as not to scream out, I sank my teeth into his arm. When we got home, we discovered that a rat had fried itself in the electrical box, and that night, we had no choice but to have mercy on each other in the dark. And now, flat on my back under the stars, it struck me that that's what had lain behind all of my Greek fury: the abrupt moment when resistance gives way to nearly shocking love. I don't believe I have ever known real love that does not come with violence, and at that moment, lying under the desert sky, I knew that I would never again trust any love that doesn't.

I WAS TOO WEAK to drag anything but the bed back inside. I left it in the middle of the room, and discovered that from there I could see out through all three windows. The only book I had in English was *Parables and Paradoxes*, and after rereading the section on Paradise a few times, I looked out the windows and was struck by the thought that I'd misunderstood something about Kafka, having failed to acknowledge the original threshold at the source of every other in his work, the one between Paradise and this world. Kafka once said that he understood the Fall of Man better than anyone. His sense came from the belief that most people misunderstood the expulsion from the Garden of Eden to be punishment for eating from the Tree of Knowledge. But as Kafka saw it, exile from Paradise came as a result of *not* eating from the Tree of Life. Had we eaten from that other tree that also stood in the center of the garden, we would have woken to the presence of the eternal within us, to what Kafka called "the indestructible." Now people are all basically alike in their ability to recognize good and evil, he wrote; the difference comes after that knowledge, when people have to make an effort to act in accordance with it. But because we lack the capacity to act in accordance with our moral knowledge, all our efforts come to ruin, and in the end we can only destroy ourselves trying. We would like nothing more than to annul the knowledge that came to us when we ate in the Garden of Eden, but as we are unable to do so, we create rationalizations, of which the world is now full. "It's possible that the whole visible world," Kafka mused, "might be nothing more than the rationalization of a man wanting to find rest for a moment." Rest how? By pretending that knowledge can be an end in itself. Meanwhile, we go on overlooking the eternal, indestructible thing inside ourselves, just as Adam and Eve fatally overlooked the Tree of Life. Go on overlooking it, even while we can't live without the faith that it is there, always within us, its branches reaching upward and its leaves unfurling in the light. In this sense, the threshold between Paradise and this world may be illusory, and we may never have really left Paradise, Kafka suggested. In this sense, we might be there without knowing it even now.

IT BECAME CLEAR that no one was coming back for me. Maybe they'd forgotten. Or maybe whoever was in possession of the whole story had been called away or killed in the war. Kaddish for the whole story. I hadn't even tried to do my part: the suitcase sat untouched where Schectman left it. But, no, that isn't entirely true. Before I fell ill, and at times in my fever, too, I'd thought a lot about Kafka's afterlife. I imagined his gardens most of all. Maybe it was the barrenness of the desert all around that gave me a thirst for lushness, for the heavy, almost sickeningly overripe smell of crowded leaves, but I found myself repeatedly conjuring their fragrant paths, busy with insect life, their arbors, fruit trees, and vines. And always Kafka among them, at work or at rest, mixing peat or lime, fingering hard buds, untangling root balls, watching the work of the bees while still dressed in the dark suit of an undertaker. I never pictured him in clothes appropriate to outdoor work or the heat. Even after my vision of his gardens fell into keeping with what I knew could grow there, after I filled them with honeysuckle and pomegranate trees, I still couldn't see him in anything but that stiff suit. The suit, and sometimes that odd bowler hat that always looked too small for his head, as if the merest wind might knock it off. If I couldn't fully accept the idea of him shedding his old clothes, however inappropriate in his new life, I suppose it was because I couldn't fully accept that he would prefer to plant a tree, to water and fertilize and prune, than to organize the light through its leaves, to put it through the paces of three hundred years in a sentence or two, and to kill it at last in a hurricane that brought too much salt to its roots and left it as fodder for the ax. Could not, finally, accept that he would want to toil under nature's harsh and limiting conditions when his powers extended to being able to surpass them for something that, in his prose, had always been soldered to the eternal.

There was a Hebrew dictionary on the shelf, and I turned its pages, trying to imagine that after his death in Prague Kafka really had crossed over into Hebrew, and gone on writing in those ancient letters. That the results of the union between Kafka and Hebrew was what had really lain hidden all this time in the fortress of Eva Hoffe's Spinoza Street apartment, protected by a double cage and her paranoia. Was there such a thing as late Kafka? Was it possible that the unspoken subtext of the ongoing court case between the National Library of Israel and Eva Hoffe, acting as Brod's agent, was really that: the struggle to preserve the myth, versus the struggle to claim Kafka by the state that regards itself as the representative and culmination of Jewish culture, and which depends on an overcoming of the Diaspora, on the Messianic notion that only in Israel can a Jew be authentically a Jew? The knowing smile that played on Friedman's lips that day he'd dropped me at my sister's apartment came back to me again: *You think your writing belongs to you?* Only now that he was gone was I ready to argue with him, to tell him that literature could never be employed by Zionism, since Zionism is predicated on an end—of the Diaspora, of the past, of the Jewish problem— whereas literature resides in the sphere of the endless, and those who write have no hope of an end. A journalist interviewing Eva Hoffe once asked her what she thought Kafka would have made of it all had he been alive. "Kafka wouldn't have lasted two minutes in this country," she'd shot back.

The dog watched me from her place in the corner as I got up to return the Hebrew dictionary to the shelf. She had sat there all through my fever, whining only when she had to go outside to relieve herself. Otherwise she didn't leave my side. I won't soon forget the look in her dark, wet eyes: as if she understood what I myself didn't. But now she seemed to know that the fever had broken, and began to stretch and move about, and even thump her tail against the floor, as if she also sensed that time was returning to us. When I went to the kitchen to get her some water, she leaped up and trotted after me with a new spring in her step, as if in the course of my fever she had shed many years. There was nothing left to eat, the kitchen was bare. I had no interest in discovering what it felt like to starve, or to watch the dog starve. All night I'd heard her stomach bubbling with hunger.

The suitcase was still waiting by the door. The moment I laid my fingers on the handle, the dog began to pant with excitement. I pulled it across the empty room while she watched. It was far lighter than I'd expected. So light that for a moment I wondered whether the army had left the wrong suitcase, or whether Friedman had really taken anything from Spinoza Street at all.

I filled some large jars with water and put them in the musty canvas backpack I'd found in the closet. I was still wearing the coat that might have been Kafka's coat, but instead of returning it to the hanger, I buttoned it up to my chin. Then I took one last look around the room, which seemed to hold no more memory of his time here than it did of mine. I drew the thin curtains, which did little to keep out the light. Kaddish for Kafka. May his soul be bundled in the bundle of life. He might have lived there, but I never could. I had children who needed me, and whom I needed, and the time when I might have been able to live confined to what was unquestionably within myself had passed when they were born.

I opened the door, and the dog didn't hesitate. She ran out thirty or forty paces ahead, then turned to wait for me. She seemed to want to show me that she knew the way, and could be trusted to lead. The furniture was still laid out under the sky. The slippers stood waiting side by side on the dusty ground for whoever would come. Soon the rain would arrive and come down on everything. I looked back on the house, which seemed even tinier from the outside.

The dog hurried ahead, alternately sniffing the ground and turning back to be sure I was following. The suitcase bumped along behind me over the rocky ground. What at first seemed light soon became heavy, as is always the way. If I lagged too far behind, the dog circled back and trotted at my heels, and when I stopped and sat down on the ground, she whined and licked my face.

We walked for hours. The sun began to fall toward the west, sending our shadows ahead of us. The skin of my palms became raw and blistered, my arms had lost their feeling, and by then my belief in the dog's preternatural ability to guide me had been worn thin by exhaustion and fear that I would die out there, and never see my children again because I'd been foolish. It was not without disgust with myself that I abandoned the job of wheeling a suitcase that I was afraid to find out was empty across the floor of a desert that once had been the bottom of a sea. The dog looked at it pitifully for a moment, then raised her nose to the sky and sniffed the air, as if to demonstrate that she was already on to other things.

It was late by the time we reached the road. I wanted to get down on my knees and cry into the tarmac that someone had taken the trouble to lay down there. I shared out the last of the water with the dog, and we curled against each other for heat. I slept intermittently. It must have been nearly six in the morning when we heard the rising hum of an engine approaching from the other side of the hill. I jumped to my feet. The taxi came tearing around the bend, and I waved frantically at the driver, who slammed on the brakes, glided slowly toward us, and lowered his window. We were lost, I explained, and not in good shape. He turned down the Mizrahi music coming from the stereo and smiled, revealing a gold tooth. He was on his way back to Tel Aviv, he said. I told him that's where we were headed, too. He looked skeptically at the dog, whose body had become tense and rigid. She seemed prepared to spring forward and sink her teeth into his jugular, if necessary. She looked nothing at all like a shepherd, neither German nor any other, but in the end Friedman was right, that's what she was. She was an extraordinary dog; to think that I almost gave her up to the soldier. After I got out of the hospital, I tried to find her. I'd half expected her to be waiting on her haunches exactly where I left her outside the entrance to the emergency room. But she must have been long gone by the time I was released. She'd done her part, and had gone off in search of her master. Later I looked for him, too. But there was no trace of Friedman. At the offices of Tel Aviv University, they told me that they had no record of any Eliezer Friedman—no one by that name had ever been employed by the department of literature, or any other department, for that matter. I'd lost the card he'd given me. I checked the telephone listings, too, but though there were hundreds of Friedmans in Tel Aviv, there was no Eliezer there, either.

Lech Lecha

WHEN THE PHOTOS came through, they showed neither rubble nor flames. The first was a foot next to what looked to be colored plastic bags. The second was of the same foot, blurred. The third was only a streak of colors. And so on, until the sixth photo finished downloading and popped open on his screen, and Epstein found himself looking into the eyes of a child. A boy of no more than eight or nine; eleven if one took into consideration the way malnutrition can keep a child small. His impish face was smudged with dirt, and beneath the arches of his brows his dark eyes shone. His mouth was closed, and yet he seemed to be laughing. Mesmerized, it took a minute for Epstein to realize that the navy collar from which the delicate neck protruded was his own, the coat his own. He pictured the boy picking his way through the rubbish, leaping over tires, and scurrying down an alley with the tattered hem trailing like a cloak. Then the face on his screen was abruptly replaced by an incoming call from Schloss. He hit the red button, sending his lawyer through to his voice mail, which was already full.

It was four in the morning. Epstein sat on the toilet, letting the hot water from the shower drive the chill from his bones. The roll of toilet paper had to be kept outside the door, but once he'd made this small adjustment, he began to appreciate the convenient situation of the showerhead, with its ready seat below. He washed himself, soaping between his toes as his mother had taught him to do. The mirror above the sink became fogged. He stood and rubbed the glass, and his eyes appeared under his fingers. Vanishing again under the steam, he repeated the trick. Then he went to find his clothes, shivering in the cold and leaving a trail of wet footprints across the floor. Naked before the wardrobe mirror, he saw his thin, veined legs and the folds of loose skin around his belly. Stepping away, he hurried into his clothes.

He slipped his copy of the Psalms into his briefcase, patted his jacket pocket for his wallet, wrapped his neck in a scarf, and stood for a minute in the dark, trying to remember if he had forgotten anything. Then he double-locked the apartment door behind him. The taxi he'd called was already waiting downstairs. A cat ran into the beam of the headlights and yowled. Epstein got into the passenger seat, and the driver greeted him, and after a minute of silence turned up the Mizrahi music on the radio.

THE LOCATION MANAGER met him with a car at the appointed place by the side of the road, in the desert not far from Ein Gedi. Things were going terribly, he reported, running his free hand through his thinning hair. Did Epstein mind if he smoked? Epstein rolled down the window, which brought in the sulfurous smell of the Dead Sea. Because the budget was tight until they got the funds from him, they'd had to make compromises. This had turned the already moody and irascible director into a tyrant. Even he had come to despise him, the location manager told Epstein. His sole motivation had always been to please the directors he worked for. All he wanted from his effort, and the endless hours he put in, was to make the director happy. But Dan was impossible. Nothing was good enough for him. If he weren't so talented, no one would have put up with it. He blew his top over the smallest mistakes, and made a show of humiliating those responsible. When the assistant director let Bathsheba go home, thinking she was done for the day, Dan threatened to cut off his dick. When Goliath's greaves were nowhere to be found, he also went batshit. "Goliath has four lines," he screamed, "and one of them is 'Bring me my bronze greaves!' So where the fuck are his greaves?" In less than an hour, Props had found some shin guards and spray-painted them gold, but though they looked convincing enough, Dan took one look at them and threw a chair. The next day, when the tech guys had no dolly for a battle shot, Dan stormed off the set, and could only be soothed back after Yael shut herself up with him in the van for over an hour. But rather than return peaceably, he came back demanding a larger crowd of Philistines. Seeing as he had just fired the casting director, and the budget wouldn't stretch for more paid extras, Eran—though by now he wanted to kill Dan—had posted a call for volunteers on Facebook, and had his rock-star cousin share it to his three hundred thousand followers, with the vague hint that he himself might show up.

And how many came? asked Epstein.

The location manager shrugged, tossed his cigarette, and said they would see tomorrow. The battle scene had been put off until they could locate a crane.

WHEN THEY ARRIVED at the set, the sun was starting to rise. Dan and Yael were still on their way from the hotel at a nearby kibbutz, but the DP was rushing to set up, and wanted to begin as soon as possible, while the light was still magic. They were supposed to shoot three scenes of David in the wilderness on the run from Saul. First, David and his band of misfits and outlaws showing up at the house of the wealthy Calebite, Nabal, to demand provisions in return for the fact that, under their watch, no harm has come to Nabal's shepherds and three thousand sheep. After that, the scene of Nabal's death, and his wife, Abigail, being forced to marry David. At midday, when the sun would be too hard for anything else, the DP wanted to shoot inside the cave, where David secretly snips off the corner of Saul's cloak while the king relieves himself. Just before sunset, they would do one final shot from the end of the film.

David was in the truck, getting his makeup done. Thirty sheep were on their way, led by their Bedouin shepherd. Saul, who struck Epstein as too eager, was wandering around in costume, joking with the grips. Next to Epstein, Ahinoam, Saul's ex-wife, was curling a lock of hair around her finger as she mouthed her lines. She was having problems, she told him. Epstein asked her why, and she explained that her part was one of the more controversial aspects of the script. She's mentioned only twice in the whole Bible: once as the wife of Saul, mother of Jonathan, and once as the wife of David, to whom she's apparently already married when he weds Abigail, too. But nowhere does it say anything about how David must have stolen Saul's wife— which amounted to an attempted coup—and that's the reason he had to flee into the wilderness, and why Saul wants him hunted down and killed. But since the point of the book of Samuel was to establish David's kingship as an act of divine will, obviously the biblical author couldn't go too much into the whole Ahinoam debacle, Ahinoam explained, which would have exposed David as the ambitious and cunning prick that he really was. But they also couldn't totally ignore what everyone knew back then, either. So they had to stick Ahinoam's name in on the sly—oh, yeah, by the way, David also had this other wife, whoops—and then gloss over it, just as they had to do with the fact that David joined the Philistines and probably really did raid the towns of his own people in Judah, just like he told Achish. But Yael had a different vision, Ahinoam told him. Her David was a little closer to the real David, and her script also emphasized the female characters' roles, which was good for Ahinoam, otherwise she wouldn't even have a part. Still, she only had three lines in the wedding scene, so she had to squeeze a lot in. Handing over the script, she asked Epstein to prompt her.

AFTER A LONG morning they broke for lunch, with only the final scene to shoot in the early evening. But by three thirty the actor playing the elderly David still had not appeared. A call came through on the satellite phone: Zamir was ill. He'd thought it was nothing, and hadn't wanted to cancel, but now it was something. He sent his regrets from Ichilov Hospital, where he was getting some tests. The director, too exhausted to scream anymore, slowly poured the remains of his coffee onto the desert floor and walked off, talking to himself. The set was nearly empty now. The other actors had all returned to the kibbutz, and only a small group had driven in jeeps to this remote spot. Yael huddled with the production manager and producer. A head taller than both, she had to stoop to keep their voices within their circle. Under stress, in the chaos of the set, she alone remained unflappable. Without her, Dan would have been lost, and, understanding this, Epstein begrudged him her attention a little less.

The director was throwing small rocks at the tire of the van when the little circle broke. Epstein, sipping his tea, watched Yael approach him. She really was something beautiful to see. She didn't lay her hand on his shoulder, didn't baby him or tiptoe around him like the others. She just stood serenely, like a queen, waiting for the director to come back to himself. Only then did she begin to talk. After a while, they both turned and looked in Epstein's direction. He tilted his head to look up at the sky, and took another swallow of tea.

THEY HAD BEGUN at the end, and two weeks ago had shot the scene in which Solomon leans over David to hear the dying king's final words. There were no lines left for the old David: only a long shot in which he walks into the desert. As such, the loss of the actor Zamir need not have been a total disaster. The final shot was meant to be at twilight, lit by torches, everything cast in shadows. Epstein was nearly the same size and build as Zamir. They only needed to shorten the hem of the cloak a centimeter, two at most. The wardrobe person kneeled at his feet, needle between her pursed lips as she knotted the thread. But when everyone stepped back to admire her handiwork, they concluded that something wasn't right. Epstein straightened the heavy belt buckle while Yael bent her head toward Dan. He looked neither regal enough, nor fallen enough, the seamstress whispered to him, making a quick, irrelevant adjustment to his sleeve. A crown was found by the prop master. But the gold was deemed too bright, and black shoe polish was used to tarnish it.

The torches were lit. All he needed do was walk between their two rows in the opposite direction of the camera, then continue walking until the director yelled for the cut. But just as they began to roll, a wind came up and blew half of the torches out. They were relit, but a moment later went out again. There would be a storm that night, someone said. The rain, when it finally came to the desert, was always violent: the production manager checked his Android phone, and announced a flash-flood warning in the area. Bullshit, Dan said, checking his iPhone, there was nothing about flash floods. Epstein looked up at the sky again, but saw no clouds. The first star was already out. The wind was strong, and nothing the lighting technician did would keep the torches lit. The air became heavy with the smell of kerosene. They would have to do without them, the production manager argued. But Dan refused to budge. Without torchlight, the scene was useless.

The director and the production manager went on loudly arguing. Soon the producer joined in, and even the DP, whose light was quickly vanishing. The wind blew. Epstein heard the Vivaldi in his head. He thought of his trees, growing even now. The mountainside couldn't have been very far from here. Was it possible they had already begun to transport the saplings? He'd lost track of the date. Surely someone would have told him? He thought of calling Galit, but his phone was in the pocket of his jacket, which someone from Costumes had taken from him, along with his pants.

The wool cloak had begun to itch. Deep in argument, no one noticed when he wandered away from the double row of torches and found his briefcase under a chair. He took off the cloak, left it draped over the back, and began to walk up the slope toward the ridge above. From there, he would be able to see. For a while he could still hear them arguing. The wind blew his hair, and reaching up to brush it back, he realized he was still wearing the tarnished crown. He took it off and lay it down on a boulder, then turned and slipped into a wadi carved by thousands of years of water, thousands of years of wind. If the rain came, in the absence of forests, the water would cascade down the slopes and flood its ancient path, carrying everything away toward the sea. The temperature was dropping. He would have liked to have his coat now. Better the boy should have it. He was breathing heavily by the time he reached the ridge. Down below, he heard them calling his name. Jules! But their voices, echoing off the ancient rock, rolled back without him: Jews! Jews! Jews! He could see very far now, all the way to Jordan. When he looked up, the star was gone, and clouds had wiped out the moon. He could smell the storm coming from Jerusalem.

AND NOW THE Philistines appeared, cresting the hilltop, a trembling mass disturbing the light and the air. Some of them knew they were Philistines, and others knew only that they were part of something enormous, gathering itself for elemental reasons, the way the ocean gathers itself to break on the shore.

The Philistines stood waiting. Holding their breath. A helmet clanged to the ground. A red flag rippled in the wind, silk torn. A great silence sounded across the valley. But there was no sign of David.

And now a Philistine held his arm up high, and snapped a picture with his iPhone. *Where are you?* he typed, and, straightening his battle gear, the Philistine pressed SEND, releasing his message into the cloud.

Already There

THE NIGHT I spent in the emergency room felt like three. The shot of hydromorphone the nurse finally gave me quieted the pain and made me woozy. For the hours before that, I'd harnessed myself to the broad and beautiful face of an Ethiopian woman who sat with quiet patience on the other side of the open curtain, cradling her pregnant belly. But after the needle went in and the tingling spread up my spine and later down to my toes, I needed her less, and she, too, must have lost her need for me, for whatever my face did for her pain, because after a while she got up and walked away and that was the last I saw of her. By now she must have a child, and the child a name, whereas I no longer have my virus whose name they never discovered, and have given up searching for.

Eventually there was evidence in the overhead window that the night was giving way. Something was changing inside the hospital, too, or so I thought as I lay on my back on the gurney. A kind of lull had settled over everything. The night shift had come to an end, and the doctors and nurses who'd spent it ministering to so many emergencies would now wash their hands of them and return home, but not before briefing their replacements, going over the charts in a burble of medical shorthand, who was due for what when, until they had at last completed all their duties and were free to change into their street clothes and leave through the automatic doors, exiting into the morning. Who in that hospital didn't wish to be released? I'd thought of giving up the interminable wait plenty of times and escaping through those doors myself. Once I'd tried, scooting off the gurney with the IV port still plugged into the vein of my arm, but I didn't get far down the hall before the brusque nurse in triage blocked my path.

At some point my fever began to soar again, and that was what finally got the doctors' attention. Actually, it was the Arab with the mop and stethoscope who noticed my condition. From where I lay, half-concealed by a curtain, I could look out onto the cubicle occupied by the Ethiopian woman, and the hallway between her liminal space and mine where the hospital staff came and went, as well as the patients, increasingly residents, of the emergency room, who passed by in wheelchairs, gurneys, or occasionally on their own two legs. I remember that the Arab man went past, and I watched him pushing the long rectangular mop that left behind a wet, shiny trail like a slug. A few minutes later he reappeared, pushing the mop back in the other direction, and when he got to my cubicle he stopped and looked in. He had kind eyes, deep and brown, and seemed too old to be doing such work. After a moment he put the mop down and approached me. I thought he might remove the stethoscope from around his neck and use it on me, or maybe I hoped he would, because by then I was in need of an act of kindness. But instead he reached out his hand and pressed the back of it to my forehead and then my cheek, said something quietly in his language, and disappeared, leaving the mop where it was so that I understood that he would return. When he did, it was with a nurse I hadn't seen before, slender with gray roots in her blond hair. I thought I might have a better chance with her, and so I tried again to describe what had happened to me.

The nurse put a hand on my arm and turned to the computer station on a trolley, making it clear that everything she needed to know would come not from me but from that other, more reliable, source. Once she'd caught herself up, she turned and asked the orderly a question in Hebrew, to which he answered in the affirmative, taking the opportunity to pop into the cubicle and retrieve his mop with its dirty, tangled head, before retreating back to the hallway. He continued to stand there, absently twisting the handle between the hands he'd used to gauge my temperature, and whose accuracy would now be checked against the thermometer in its disposable plastic sheath that the nurse stuck under my tongue. It began to beep wildly, and the nurse snatched it out of my mouth with a perturbed look that soon shifted to surprise.

She went away and came back with some bitter syrup in a paper cup, and then vanished again, presumably to find the doctor. What I remember next is that the orderly, still standing in the hallway, now looked around him furtively, first left and then right, until, judging the coast clear, he approached again, rested the mop against the wall, and again laid his hand on my forehead, this time with the palm down so that I felt the refreshing coolness of his skin. Looking up at his face, it seemed to me that he was listening intently. As if he were straining to hear after all, not with the stethoscope that still hung inert around his neck but with the hand itself. As if the sensitive instruments of his cool fingers could read my mind. And though I know this is impossible—that the memory I invoked under his touch had not yet happened to me—it is there all the same, impervious to reason.

With the orderly's cool hand on my forehead, I recalled an afternoon the following winter when my lover arrived home and entered the bedroom carrying his bag. Get undressed, he said to me. It was a bright day, so cold outside that his fingers had frozen inside his gloves. I remember that from where I lay I could see the bare branches of the plane tree, with its spiked fruit still hanging on far past their season. I pulled my shirt over my head. Leave the curtains open, I said. For a moment he seemed to consider this. Then he proceeded to close them anyway, and removed four black ropes from his bag. They were very beautiful things, black and silken, but thick enough that a sharp knife would be needed to cut through them. The deftness with which he knotted my wrists to the bars of the headboard surprised me. What did you tell them it was for when you bought it? I asked. For tying someone up, he replied. And do you know what they asked me? I shook my head. A woman or a child? he told me, running his freezing fingers across my breasts and down my ribs, and delicately turning my necklace until he could get at the clasp. What did you say? I asked, shivering. Both, he whispered, and the gentleness with which he touched me, and understood this simple thing, filled me with peace and made me want to weep.

BY THEN, THE brief winter war was over. A single missile had fallen through the Iron Dome and killed a man on the corner of Arlozorov and Ben Ezra. The barrier had been broken, a tear in the sky, but the reality of that other world didn't come pouring through. There was only another incommensurable onslaught of violence in Gaza, and then, at last, a fragile cease-fire. After

I was released from the hospital, I spent another week in Tel Aviv, monitored by Dr. Geula Bartov, the petite and forceful GP whose care I'd been placed under while recuperating. Since the fever had come and gone intermittently, Dr. Bartov had been firm about waiting with the flight back to New York until I had been afebrile for forty-eight hours and they received the results of the battery of tests they'd done. It struck her as odd that I didn't appear more interested in getting to the bottom of what had infected me; she saw it as a symptom, and marked it down as apathy.

The pain had gone, but in its wake I was weak and exhausted, and still had very little appetite. My father had not called Peres, but he had called his cousin Effie, who'd sent the police to bang down the door of my sister's apartment, which they had left—because this was Israel, after all—hanging half off its hinges. Someone had taken this as an invitation to enter the apartment, rip the TV off the wall, and carry it away, but not before having a roll in the bed and eating the peaches I'd left in the refrigerator.

I'd told my family that I'd gone camping in the desert for research, had been without phone reception, and had gotten sick. For now, it seemed to be enough that I was all right, and they didn't press me any further, though my father did insist on sending Effie to check in on me. As a result, I found myself locked in a two-hour argument with the second intruder to sidestep the busted door, this one four feet eleven inches of totally impossible. In the end it became clear that he couldn't forcibly remove me to his Jerusalem house to convalesce under Naama's care if I didn't want to go, and so Effie settled for driving me back to the Hilton. On the way, I asked him to tell me everything he could about Friedman, but the details of their friendship seemed to grow vaguer and vaguer the more he spoke, until at last he drifted off the subject entirely, leaving me to wonder how well he had ever really known Friedman.

I was given a room on the north side of the hotel this time, overlooking the pool below and the sea to the west, which I promptly went out to greet, swiveling my waist as was necessary. The general manager called up to welcome me back, and this time the fruit basket he sent actually materialized, full of the sweet Jaffa oranges called Shamouti, from the Arabic for "lamp." Either he'd forgotten his former wariness or I'd only imagined it. When I caught sight of him the following morning on the way to breakfast, he greeted me with a smile, his golden lapel pin sparkling, and when my passport was returned by two IDF officers who left it at reception, he had it sent up in a Hilton envelope, along with a little box of chocolates.

I spent those final days in Israel lying on a chair by the pool, still weak. My mind felt hollowed out, and I didn't have the concentration even to read, so I looked out at the surf, or watched the few bold enough to swim off-season, mostly the elderly doing their slow, repetitive laps across the pool. I asked the young attendant who managed the umbrellas and towels whether Itzhak Perlman ever came anymore. But he had never heard of Itzhak Perlman, God bless him. I kept my phone by my side, hoping Friedman might still call—"out in the blue," as Effie had said that first time—but he never did. Though the fever was gone, my dreams remained vivid, and when I dozed off, Friedman often appeared in them, mixed with what was nearest. The dreams wore me out, and I would have preferred a dreamless sleep, barricaded from the workings of my mind, but by that stage I was still grateful for any kind of sleep at all. I stayed outside until late, after the attendant had stripped the chairs of their mattresses. Five o'clock in the Mediterranean, such beautiful light, it's easy to understand how empires rose and fell in it, the Greek and Assyrian, Phoenician and Carthaginian, the Roman, Byzantine, Ottoman.

It was while lying there, by the pool, that I looked up for a moment at the looming monstrosity of the Hilton, and, shielding my eyes from the sun, saw him there, on a terrace of the fifteenth or sixteenth floor. He was the only one out on the whole north side of the building, and for a moment I had the feeling that he was about to perform a trick. Twenty years ago, I'd come out of Lincoln Center and seen a small knot of people looking up at a building in which every window of the upper floors had been darkened but for one. And there, in that illuminated rectangle, a couple could be seen slowly dancing together. It might have been only serendipity that all the other windows were dark, and the couple may have been clueless that a small crowd had gathered below to watch. But there was something deliberate in their movements that filled us with the sense that they knew. I think it must have been that which drew my attention to the man standing on the terrace of his room on the fifteenth floor: a concentrated sense of intent and drama that animated his body as he leaned out over the railing. I was riveted and couldn't look away. I felt I should call the pool attendant and alert him, but what would I say?

It happened very quickly. He shifted his weight forward onto his hands, and vaulted one leg over the metal rail. A woman getting out of the pool shouted, and in a matter of seconds the man had swung the other leg over, and was perched on the railing, legs dangling over the two-hundred-foot drop. He seemed, suddenly, to be filled with enormous potential, as if the whole rest of his life had slammed forward into him. And then he leaped with arms open, like a bird.

Thirty-six hours later, the taxi that drove me from JFK through the corrosive orange dusk falling on fast food restaurants and funeral parlors, on the Baptist churches and the Hasids in Crown Heights hurrying through old snow, turned onto my street at last, and the driver waited while I made my way up the front steps with my suitcase. The lights were on inside our house. Through the front window I could see my children playing on the floor, heads bent over a game. They didn't see me. And for a while I didn't see myself either, sitting in a chair in the corner, already there.

Author's Note

The title of this book is taken from the following lines of Dante, translated by Longfellow, and quoted to me some years ago on a long drive to Jerusalem:

> *Midway upon the journey of our life*
> *I found myself within a forest dark,*
> *For the straightforward pathway had been lost.*

I hereby excuse all those named in this book, including Eliezer Friedman, from all liability. Should he ever wish to contact me, he knows where to find me.

About the Author

NICOLE KRAUSS has been hailed by the *New York Times* as 'one of America's most important novelists'. She is the author of the international bestsellers *Great House*, a finalist for the National Book Award and the Orange Prize, and *The History of Love*, which won the Saroyan Prize for International Literature and France's Prix du Meilleur Livre Étranger, and was shortlisted for the Orange Prize, the Prix Médicis and the Prix Femina. Her first novel, *Man Walks into a Room*, was a finalist for the *Los Angeles Times* Book Prize. In 2007, she was selected as one of *Granta*'s Best Young American Novelists, and in 2010 she was chosen by the *New Yorker* for their 'Twenty Under Forty' list. Her fiction has been published in the *New Yorker*, *Harper's*, *Esquire* and *Best American Short Stories*, and her books have been translated into more than thirty-five languages.

nicole-krauss.com